ALL CITY

ALL CITY

ALEX DIFRANCESCO

SEVEN STORIES PRESS

New York · Oakland · London

Seven Stories Press
140 Watts Street
New York, NY 10013
www.sevenstories.com

Library of Congress Cataloging-in-Publication Data

Names: DiFrancesco, Alex, author.
Title: All city : a novel / Alex DiFrancesco.
Description: New York : Seven Stories Press, 2019.
Identifiers: LCCN 2019010167| ISBN 9781609809393 (paperback) | ISBN 9781609809409 (ebook)
Subjects: | BISAC: FICTION / Urban Life.
Classification: LCC PS3604.I3845 A78 2019 | DDC 813/.6--dc23
LC record available at https://lccn.loc.gov/2019010167

College professors and high school and middle school teachers can order free examination copies of Seven Stories Press titles. To order, visit www.sevenstories.com, or send fax on school letterhead to 212-226-1411.

Printed in the USA.

9 8 7 6 5 4 3 2 1

*This book was informed and made more vibrant
by the work of several visual artists. To that end,
I'd like to dedicate it to:*

BANKSY,
whose NYC residency coincided with the
writing of the first draft

JEAN-MICHEL BASQUIAT,
whose ghost whispers in Green-Wood

JOHN LURIE,
on an island somewhere where
nobody will find him

ALL CITY

The wind came first, and with it brought the clouds that came between the city and the sky. The clouds were heavy and low, the color of a sinister night; more steel than sky. The steel slammed down into the skyline and turned off all its light. The wind whipped the clouds, it tore at street signs, it lofted the garbage cans, and it gave wings to anything that wasn't nailed down, and to some things that were. The bridges swayed and broke, their cables popping like gunshots, huge chunks of concrete and metal falling down and down, splashing into the water and disappearing to the bottom of the river.

The rain came down in sheets. It was a wall, impenetrable, hitting all it reached with a sting of weight and gravity. The rain came sideways and down as it swirled in gusts of the feverish wind.

The sea, turbulent in the storm, began to surge into the New York Bight, filling it with the millions of tons of seawater the storm had brought along to the city like an unwelcome guest. As the bight filled, the water began to spill over. Tiles popped *off of the Holland Tunnel as water forced its way through. The subway tunnels filled with salt water that corroded their already weakened tracks and pipes. The water surged up over the streets, over the tires of the cars parked there, into the basements of buildings, into the buildings' lower floors, then up into the higher floors. The people left behind scrambled to carry their possessions higher and higher, up stairs, down hallways, up stairs again, until finally it became obvious that there would be no place high enough, that the waters would keep coming, unrelenting. A force.*

PART ONE

MAKAYLA—NOVEMBER

1 A week before Superstorm Bernice, I was walking home from the 24/7 when I saw it. It was in the spot where the old bodega had been for ten years, years in which I'd gotten to know the owner, Abdul, and in which he'd always let me know when the oussies had come in. Abdul had told me a while back he'd be closing up, that he couldn't afford the rent anymore, not now, not since the neighborhood had gotten a new name from the chum slingers that made it sound more like an extension of the nearby, more fashionable neighborhood. It was sinking more smash in to make it the kind of place that the new neighborhood residents (the kind of people who never knew to ask about the oussies, or even needed them) wanted, or pack up and leave. And he'd decided to pack up.

The *it* I saw that night was another store. But when you've slagged all day for smash enough to barely pay your rent and not do much else, there's the bodegas like Abdul ran, where you can maybe go and get little bits of something, a cup of noodles or a dollar bag of chips, and then there's places that make you feel like you're too poor to walk inside. And feeling very poor, *being* very poor is like going down a street and realizing that all the beautiful places you walk by, places that have wine and good food and music, are locked when you try to walk through their doors. And so, after a while, you stop looking at them and start looking down at your feet, hoping maybe to find a hundred-dollar bill that will act as a key to one of those doors, or a drug or a dream that will make you forget those doors are there at all.

The store I saw that night was not open to me, I could tell you that. I could tell, looking in, seeing the dim lights, seeing the woman who looked like she'd just come off some decorating magazine cover, looking dap even in her slag clothes, that it was not a bodega. I saw a little sign inside. I saw it next to a little bowl of dog treats that the sign told me were made of traveled ingredients from the finest places in the world, the cost of getting them there be damned. And my head started feeling squeezed together like my brain was expanding and taking up too much space. In all the years I'd lived in this neighborhood, in all the times my family had helped organize block parties, in all the times my dad had volunteered to talk to kids in school about street violence as someone who barely got out if it alive himself, in all the times my mother cooked food for the old lady who lived down the hall and struggled to get by on her piddly-shit sienty disability check and whose kids never came to see her, no one ever, *ever*, offered us a damn thing that could be called "traveled."

I reached into my bag then. And from all the things that slipped through my fingers, my keys, my wallet, my sunglasses, I grabbed one thing. A combination lock that I kept on my locker in the break room of the 24/7 and took home with me at night. The metal weighed heavy in my hand there inside my bag, but only for a moment before I whipped it up and back behind me, then over my shoulder and through the dimly lit window.

The glass broke and fell like bells. I heard the woman in her slag clothes scream, and I ran.

2 I've heard that years ago they didn't know just where a storm would hit. Now they know. There's no maybe paths, no loose science. There's no "somewhere along the Eastern seaboard." There is: Duluth will be hit by 100 mph winds. There is: Sarasota will face torrential downpours. There is: New York City will have pieces of it knocked into the ocean.

So we all knew Bernice was coming and where she was coming. She wasn't the first storm, and I didn't think she would be the last, not then—New York didn't seem like a place that could have an end. We would all wake up to our coffee in Greek paper cups and be furious about the train delays no matter what happened.

It had gotten bad, though, even I had to admit. After the last one, there had barely been time to rebuild the worst hit coastal areas like Gravesend and Sheepshead Bay. Of course, all the smash had been poured into Manhattan and the wealthiest parts of Brooklyn, as it was every time. They had things back up and running there in a few weeks, but even then you could see people getting restless. How many more times? Why hadn't more been done to prepare? There was jaw on the news of Hesco bastions and better power grid protection, and they were building a buffer and a barrier that kept getting destroyed every time a new storm hit. They couldn't build fast enough. The subways still had those sienty sandbags protecting them, and the lines at the gas stations were blocks long.

My grandma was living out in public housing on the edge of Gravesend, and last time her twelfth-floor apartment was fine but she didn't have heat or lights for weeks. I went over there to try to get her out before the storm came, but she just sat there in the dark with the TV on and say, "Makayla, where'm I gonna go?" And I said, come back home with me, back to the neighborhood, back where she lived all those years before my mother and father checked, before she had to live on what the government gives her, before I had to live in some 'trosh basement that I *still* can't afford. I kept jawing. Come with me, Granny, the water almost never gets in that far, it's better than being out here alone. And she said, "No, Makayla. I stay here." And she did.

She said the same thing before Bernice. But then I didn't fight her, because then my sienty basement apartment was all packed up in boxes. I didn't want to move. But the rent had gone from $2,000 to $2,500, and I couldn't make that extra five hundred dollars come from anywhere. Same old story that anybody who'd lived on my block ten years ago could tell you. I knew that the minute I was out, my rentboss would have the chum slingers showing the place before he could even slap a new coat of paint on it. Then he'd make promises, gut everything, make it the sort of place he could charge three or four grand for. But there was nothing I could do. There was no such thing as security in the city anymore, not for people like me.

So I didn't fight my grandmother's decision. I just made sure she had a shit-ton of gallons of water, food that didn't need to be cooked and wouldn't go bad, and a case of slurree. As soon as the subways were back up, I'd go back out there and take care of her.

I got up the morning of the day of Bernice and went to slag at the 24/7. I stood on my feet all day, moving boxes of shit from one place to another, ringing up coffees, donuts, bags of chips. I worried about what I was going to do if Bernice was real bad and the 24/7 closed for the day. I couldn't afford lose a fifth of my smash for the week. I started to worry and bite my nails. I went outside and smoked one of my oussies, even though if I finished my pack before work was over, I'd have to buy the full-priced cigarettes we sell upswing at the 24/7.

After work, I went back to my place. I sat there in the boxes with my television on as they began calling for evacuation. I thought about my grandmother, and the hallways that smelled like piss and shit the last time I'd had to go over there and make sure she was okay. I thought about my sister who nobody'd heard from in months, who, last I did hear, was living in the streets, scoring drag any way she could. And I thought, *Where would I go?*

As I was sitting there in the middle of all those boxes, my phone rang. I looked down at the screen and saw that it was Jaden, a guy who I'd pretty much grown up with, who still lived a few blocks away.

"Where are you?" he asked me.

"Where do you think I am? I'm in my apartment waiting to start floating to the ceiling," I replied. I guess I sounded short, but I don't like jawing on the phone very much, and I was in the middle of having a crisis.

"Well, get your ass over here," he said. "I'll sleep on the couch and you can take my room."

"What about your roommates?"

"Gone. I could use the company."

Jaden, he's practical. He's hung on to the apartment his family lived in long after they didn't live there anymore, long after the landlord stopped doing repairs, hoping he'd leave. Jaden started doing them himself. He found three guys who wanted to live in the new, hot neighborhood and charged them what they could pay (and what he couldn't) to live there. Sometimes I get jealous of how well he gets along in the world in ways I can't bring myself to.

I hadn't yet packed up my toiletries for the move, so I went into the bathroom and began tossing them in this dissat backpack I still have from when I was in high school. I packed up my glasses and my contact solution and my toothbrush and toothpaste and all the things I might need. I even packed some of the things I probably wouldn't get to use if the power went out, like my straightening iron and my Mixplayer. I grabbed all the beer out of my refrigerator and threw it in there, too.

The wind had picked up outside, and people were walking down the street with their clothes pulled back tight against their bodies and billowing out behind them like sails. Some people looked worried, some looked like they were having a good time, drinking out of paper bags. But there were a lot fewer people on the street than there usually were. Cars were rolling by, nice-looking ones, and it was clear they were getting out. I noticed lots of people were going down into the subway, but nobody was coming out the other set of stairs, even when the train rumbled by beneath the street.

The front entrance of Jaden's building has been all redone for the people like his new roommates that live there, so where there used to be a busted lock and a broken security camera, there's now two locked doors and an intercom that rings up to each apartment. I'm just waiting for them to bust down the walls of the downstairs apartment and make a lobby out of it, with a doorman just standing there smiling as you go in and out, greeting everybody by name. I don't know if they'd lose smash by taking out that apartment, or make more by raising everybody's rent because now it was a doorman building. Figuring out ways to make smash has never been my strong suit. Just ask the people who sign my checks at the 24/7.

I pushed the button under Jaden's apartment number. He's the only one who doesn't have his name up there. It's like the rentbosses at that place are hoping that if they just will him out, he'll go. But Jaden's not going anywhere, not with the kind of rent he pays, and the laws in place that limit how much they can raise it. What's he going to do, I always ask, when those laws go away, like they're always threatening to? He doesn't know, just like me. But for now, he's okay.

Jaden answered right away, buzzing me in without even calling down to see who it was. Who else was crazy enough to be out there? The wind was blowing a little harder now, I felt it pushing into my face, drawing my skin back just a bit. The cans of beer in my book bag jangled and sloshed together as I went through the double door and ran up the stairs.

The door to Jaden's apartment was open partway when I got up to the third floor. I pushed it open farther and saw his bike hanging up from the hook in the front hallway. Jaden loves that bike, has had it since he was a kid and takes care of it like a baby. He learned how to fix it, he oils it and replaces parts himself. His first slag was as a bike messenger when he was just a teenager because he could ride faster and better than any of the people older than him. I walked by the bike then, pushing one of the pedals in a slow circle with my hand. Jaden was still a bike messenger, for this company in Manhattan that caters to rich people who can't be bothered going somewhere to pick it up and can't wait for things to be shipped. They do it from anywhere to anywhere, so he ends up delivering the craziest things sometimes. Once he delivered a kitten to a five-year-old who lived on Central Park West. Turned out the kid had just had a play date with a friend who had one, and couldn't wait to get his own. So Jaden had ridden from a pet store to this kid's house with this scared little kitten in a box in the basket attached to his bike. Other times, he didn't know what he was carrying at all; there were simply locked boxes. Jaden didn't ask too many questions about those.

Because of all that biking, Jaden's in amazing shape. He's got these legs that I bet could kick through a brick wall, like in those old kung fu movies. He's always got girls around him and some of the guys on the block flirt with him, too. Even though Jaden's straight, he flirts right back with everybody. He's good-natured and dap, and a lot of people love him. Sometimes standing next to him I feel like an angry ogre from a fairy tale.

"Hello?" I called, walking past his bike. The hallway I was in had a room off to either side, and led out into a living room with another bedroom on the far side of it. That bedroom was Jaden's. It had a big window that faced the street and a huge tree with speckled bark stood outside it.

"Hey," Jaden said, emerging from his bedroom. He already had a drink in his hand, and as he got close and hugged me hello, I could smell that it was a whisky drink. Likely there would be no slag tomorrow for either of us, so before we started worrying about the smash we'd lose because of that fact, we might as well enjoy our night off.

I pulled the beer out of my backpack and took it over to the refrigerator. It was full of the typical stuff you'd imagine for three single guys living together—frozen foods, loads of cans of slurree, an outdated carton of milk that I didn't want to go near. I looked around and looked at Jaden.

"What were you planning on eating if the power goes out?" I asked.

"Don't worry, I got us supplies," he said. He opened up one of the cabinets above the sink and showed me boxes of things. More slurree, granola and breakfast bars, macaroni and cheese, noodles. It wasn't exactly gourmet fare, but it would be enough to keep us going if we needed it.

"And check this out," he said. He motioned over to the living room where he had a small generator plugged in and juicing up. Near it was a camping stove with little propane tanks attached to it. Jaden was ready.

"Great," I said. "Better than I would have done. Who knows how long we'll be without power after this bitch hits."

I popped open a can of beer and started sipping it. Jaden and I sat down in the living room, on the couch, and started jawing about the neighborhood, about people we knew, about people who had moved or checked. By the bottom of my first can of beer, I began to feel a warmth in my stomach and a lightness in my head. It was such a pleasant feeling, a real escape from the heaviness and the pressure that I always feel like I've got inside me. The sun started slipping down over the Manhattan side of the city, and the winds picked up. The door of Jaden's bedroom was open, and we could hear the branches of the tree outside it slapping against the panes. I was supposed to sleep in there, and I kept picturing the tree smashing through the window, through the wall. Jaden slept on a mattress on the floor, and I asked him if we couldn't pull it out into the living room, where there were no windows. It took us some effort, and I kicked over my half-full second can of beer in the process, but we managed it.

"Hey, let's go to the corner store and get a sandwich before we have to eat noodles and drink slurree for days," Jaden said.

"Okay," I said. I was starting to feel hungry, and a sandwich sounded great.

When we got outside, the wind whipped our hair back like we were on motorcycles.

"Maybe we should just go back inside," I said.

"It's just a few blocks away," Jaden said.

Walking against the wind was like walking in sand out at one of the beaches in Gravesend. We struggled down the street, grabbing each other's arms and holding on tight. We had walked a block and a half when all the streetlights went out. And the lights in the buildings. We stood there in total, pitch darkness. I don't like the dark, ever since I was a kid. It's not something you admit to people very often, but my sister used to think it was funny to put me down in front of horror movies when I was little and ever since, a dark corner is somewhere I imagine the world of terrible things emerging from—horrible faces, ghosts, twisted figures, the possessed. I wanted to go back, but I didn't want to say it again. I didn't want Jaden thinking I was a numptie of some kind. Most people believed I was nails, and that's what I wanted them to think. Nobody fucks with you then.

"Scared?" I asked him, poking him in between the ribs.

"Come on," he said, swatting me away, then poking me back. I started feeling this flutter inside me and tried to ignore it.

When we got to the corner store, we saw that it was lit by candles. We were surprised to see a bunch of people in there, drinking beer and eating. They all had pints of ice cream in front of them, and they were shoveling away with spoons. As we walked in, the guy behind the counter motioned over to the freezer.

"That shit's all going to melt," he said. "Might as well grab some."

Jaden and I looked at each other and then raced for the freezer like a couple of kids, pushing each other out of the way as we dug in there, looking for the best of what was left.

"Is the beer free, too?" Jaden asked, joking.

"Beer's twice as expensive," the guy said. "And don't even ask about the batteries."

Suddenly I remember that even though I'd gotten my grandmother water and slurree, I hadn't gotten her any batteries. I thought of her alone in her apartment, with a bunch of the religious candles she keeps around lit and glowing. I thought of her knocking one over and starting a fire. My hand went a little slack on the pint of ice cream. I had to pull my mind out of the hole it started to slip down then, because there was nothing I could do about it. Things get like that sometimes. Everything goes dark and I have to struggle to keep some sort of light and hope in my head. I often think of my grandmother, or my friends like Jaden. But sometimes there's nothing I can think of that will pull me out of the pit I can go down in my head.

Jaden was up at the counter ordering our sandwich. The guy behind the counter made it extra thick, with lots of turkey and lots of cheese. I guess those were going to go bad soon, too.

"Hey, I got my Mixplayer," a guy drinking a beer next to the potato chips said, pulling a tiny square out of his pocket. "You got speakers back there?"

Before I knew it, music was thumping through the store,

and people were dancing with their beer cans in their hands. A guy came up to me and held out his hand. Giggling a little, I let him take mine, and soon we were dancing around the store. Jaden watched, smiling. The dance lasted the whole song, and then another. Pretty soon I was out of breath from moving around the cramped space so much. Damn oussies must be catching up to me.

"Come on," Jaden said. "We should get back." Now he held his hand out to me, and I grabbed it, and giggling, we walked back into the night. As we walked, we dug into our ice cream with plastic spoons.

"I like your new boyfriend there," Jaden said. The guy had been in his sixties, with gray hair and a stomach that hung over his belt. "Neighborhood guy? Known him for long?"

I laughed. "Get hoddered," I said, pushing him with one hand.

"Okay, okay. I won't tease you. I just better get an invite to your wedding."

"Shut up," I said. I was still laughing, shoving ice cream in my mouth.

"Want to take a walk?" Jaden asked. The wind was blowing like crazy. I was going to walk with him, even though I was scared shitless to do it, but then the rain started coming down. And not a drop or two here and there, like the beginning of a thundershower. The rain started coming down like someone had torn off a seal. Without a word, we ran back for Jaden's place. Our boots splashed through the wet streets, and the rain soaked through the hoodie I was wearing.

When we got back to the apartment, I took off my boots. I didn't have a lot of clothes with me, so Jaden offered me a pair of boxers and a T-shirt. I got changed in his room then opened the door up. Jaden had lit candles in the living room, and everything was glowing soft yellow and apricot orange.

"Look at this," I said. We crept over to the window and watched the water fall from the sky like we were standing at the bottom of a waterfall—not that either of us has actually ever been near a waterfall, but you can imagine that sort of thing pretty easy.

We went back into the living rom. I sat on the mattress in the middle of the floor like I was sitting on a life raft. Jaden sat on the couch.

"Where did your roommates go?" I asked.

"Back to wherever they're from," he said. "To their parents' houses I guess."

"Do you think the water will come out here?" I asked. I knew I wasn't being the greatest conversationalist, but I hadn't actually wanted to sit there jawing about the good-breeds Jaden lived with.

"You don't need to worry," Jaden said in a soft voice. I guess it was supposed to be comforting. "The water never comes in this far. We've got a generator and food. We made it last time, we'll make it this time."

I breathed out a big sigh, but I tried to keep it quiet. It ended up sounding like a whimper. To cover it up, I said real quick, "Let's get another drink. Let's get this party going."

We sat there and drank some more. As we were drinking, jawing, Jaden turned to me with a half smile that's been driving the girls and the boys in the neighborhood crazy for decades and said, "Hey, Makayla?"

"Yeah?"

"What's the worst thing you've ever seen?"

Jaden likes to ask questions like that. Not just about bad things, but questions that are supposed to get people to open up, to start jawing to him for real. For all the flirting he does, he can get people down to real things pretty quick. We've known each other for years, but I'm one of the only people who never answers him straight.

"Your mother taking a shower in the fire hydrant," I said.

"Come on, really," he said.

"No, I swear, it was 'trosh," I told him. We both started laughing as the rain pounded the walls.

An hour later, we were a little drunker, and the rain was still coming down just as hard. I kept thinking of my grandmother, up in that piss-smelling building with no lights. At least she had food and water, I told myself. I kept thinking about her in the dark. Would the batteries in her flashlight last until I got there?

"Do you want to go outside for a cigarette?" I asked. Jaden smoked once in a great while, never enough to make him out of breath when he was riding his bike. He looked at me like I was phrenic.

"Just smoke in here," he said, and I did, I lit one of my oussies right up.

After I had smoked it, we snuck back over to the window. The wet leaves were now slapping the pane as solid and loud as slaps right to the face. The streets were eerie in the darkness. If the storm clouds weren't there, you'd be able to see the stars like you never could see them in the city.

Even though the power was out, we hooked up Jaden's TV to the generator for a while and watched the local news. The anchor was standing somewhere that looked alien, with trees whipping around behind her, and her hair blowing every which way. She was telling us that the worst, the storm surge, was yet to come.

We flipped through news from all over New York and

Long Island, and everywhere it was the same: blackness and wind, rain and branches falling into the street. They kept showing the hurricane on the screen—not the real-life effects, but this weatherman view that was all yellow and orange and red and green and white swirls. It was really beautiful to look at, almost hypnotizing. I felt myself being sucked in closer and closer to the screen every time it came on. We looked outside again, and the street looked like a river now, running away.

"Should we have left?" Jaden asked. "This looks worse than I've ever seen."

I didn't say anything for a minute. Then I asked, "Where do you think they all are now?"

"Who all?" he asked.

"You know, the people who left. The neighborhood's empty. Do you think they have other houses?"

He thought about it for a minute.

"The kind of people who live here now? A lot of them, yeah."

"Do you think they're in their other houses having, like, storm parties? I mean, watching all this and ordering food and being comfortable and dry?"

"Maybe."

"And what about their places here? I mean, a lot of these people probably *own* these apartments and condos."

"Yeah, probably. At this point, the ones that do know what kind of gamble they were taking buying a place here in the city, after all these storms. So to them, it was probably like buying a scratch-off ticket. Fun while it lasts, but at the end of the day, you know you're throwing your money away."

I got to thinking about *that*, about how if I had that money, I'd make it last into something that worked for me for a lifetime. Things got even darker in my head. Even with the lightness of all the beer I'd drunk, my head was feeling tight again.

We turned the TV off to save the power, and we were left there in the dark with just the candles. The dark was still spooking me. I kept admonishing myself, *there are real things to be afraid of.* But it didn't make it any better.

Around midnight, a loud crack sounded out, and I must have jumped a mile in the air. The sound was followed by breaking glass and the musical noise of it hitting the ground, just like a few days before with that shop window. Jaden rushed toward his bedroom, leaving me alone in the living room. Even in the dark, I could see through the door what had happened. A big branch had broken off that tree that'd been scaring me and gone through the window. It had ended up directly in the place where his bed had been before we dragged it into the living room. I'd be dead if I'd been in there, or at least seriously hurt. My heart was pounding, and I didn't feel very drunk anymore. Anything that had been fun about the night had ended.

"Stay out of here," Jaden said, and pulled the door shut, coming back into the living room.

"Should we go outside and see how bad things are?" I asked.

"No fucking way," Jaden said. "I saw enough through the window. It's bad out there."

"How bad?"

"Bad. We'll go up to the roof in the morning when the rain stops, but right now we need to stay in here where there's no windows."

"What do we do in the meantime?" I asked. I had begun biting my nails again. They were down to the quick, and still I kept biting.

"I'm going to try to put something over that window, to reinforce it to keep all the water out," he said. "You stay here."

I took my hands away from my mouth and stopped biting my nails. For the first time, I realized how I must look, sitting there on the bed, chewing my hands and scrunched up like a kitten in a thunderstorm. I straightened out, stood up.

"Oh hell no," I said. "I'm not going to sit here like some numptie while you go doing all the manly things to save us. What are we going to put over that window?"

"I'm not sure of that part yet," Jaden said.

I pointed over to the door that separated the kitchen from the hallway.

"If we take that down off its hinges, we can probably cover that little window up. Do you have nails? We can nail it right to the frame."

We went into a closet off the hallway and found his tools, taking out a hammer, some nails, and two screwdrivers. We took the door down while the wind whipped in through the broken window, making the closed bedroom door shake. When the door was down, we carried it toward the bedroom. We opened the door, and the wind whipped our hair back and pulled our clothes tight against our skin. The rain was coming in, too, making the wooden floor slick. We almost slipped, and we dropped the door damn near on my foot in the process. Luckily, I jumped back in time. With the storm busting up the city like it was, I would have been hoddered with my foot broken.

Jaden shoved the tree branch back out the window, and I had my first look outside. Trees were broken and fallen all down the street, and the water was picking them up and moving them along with it as it went. The wind was whipping the rain around like whirlpools in the sky. You could barely see beyond them. Street signs and stoplights were lying in the street, being picked up and carried a few feet by the wind before coming crashing down again. The streets weren't flooded, but the rain was still coming down like mad.

"Come on, let's get this thing up," Jaden said as I stood there staring. The wind was blowing at us like we were on a roller coaster.

We slammed the door up against the wall over the window like we were in a horror movie and it was keeping the zombies out of the house. Jaden held it as I moved around it hitting nails through it into the wood of the window frame. For a minute, I thought how pissed off Jaden's rentbosses were going to be about us damaging the wood, how they would take it out of his security deposit someday. Then I remembered that they were going to be doing a lot more work than puttying up some holes.

When we had the door up over the broken window, the rain stopped coming in except for a trickle. We looked around the dark room at the mess they had left—wet clothes, papers, bags, and leaves scattered everywhere.

"Should we clean this up?" I asked.

"We don't even know if this is as bad as it's going to get. Let's get back in the living room and turn the TV on."

On the news, they were playing and replaying the footage of what looked like an explosion recorded on somebody's phone. They were showing downtown Manhattan, where the water had surged past the half-built Hesco bastions and was tossing cars around like toys. Pieces of buildings floated by in the dark water, and at the edge of the screen we saw what looked like a lifeless body floating there.

I turned the TV off.

"What are we going to do?" Jaden asked. He wasn't biting his nails like I'd been, but he looked kind of like a little boy in trouble, his head hanging down from his hunched neck and his hands clasped in front of him. My moment of fear was long from over, but I knew I couldn't let that show.

"We're going to sit here and make it through the night. In the morning, when the rain stops, we're going to get out of here. We'll go to the evacuation center where they took all the nursing-home patients and old people. But for now, we're going to sit right goddamn here and pretend we didn't see any of that shit outside."

"And how are we going to do that?"

"We're going to sit here and drink beer and talk."

Jaden stood up slowly and went to the refrigerator. He opened the door, and it was even darker inside the fridge than it was in the kitchen. He took us out two beers and brought them back to the living room.

"All right," he said. "I'm always asking questions, and you're always making up reasons not to answer them. So why don't *you* ask *me* a question?"

"Tell me a story," I said.

"What do you want to hear, 'The Three Little Pigs?'"

"No. Just say anything. Tell me about the first time you went to the Museum of Natural History, or had sex, or did something you regretted. Just talk to me, for fuck's sake."

"Okay, something I regretted," he said. "When I was fourteen, all of my friends were going out to do move one night, and I wanted to go with them. But I didn't have any money. It was before I started slagging on my bike. And I didn't know where to get any, so I stole a hundred dollars from my mom's purse. And I went out and split my face off and danced like an idiot, and we went to some party in some shitty old warehouse down by the river, and I thought it was the best night of my life for about ten hours. And then, the next day, the last day of the month, I saw my mom empty out a jar of pennies and start rolling them up into those little paper sleeves. She was counting up change so she'd be able to make our rent, part of which I had gone and shoveled up my fucking nose. She didn't even say anything to me, even though she must have known I'd taken the money. She just sat there, real quiet, and rolled those pennies and nickels. And that's just about the most 'trosh I've ever felt in my life."

I sat there thinking for a second before I said, "That's some pretty deep shit, Jaden."

"You're the one who wanted to hear a story," he said. "Guess you would rather hear 'The Three Little Pigs' after all? Even with the wind blowing our house down?"

For once he did not look like the happy, friendly guy I had known all these years. He looked like he had something deeper in him than smiles and flirting with everybody. I looked at his eyes, downcast and dark, and something flickered in me like lights after the power has just come back on.

3 We could only tell it was morning by the fact that we'd woken up. Without any windows in the room, there was no light to tell us. The sounds of wind and rain had stopped. There was an eerie, peaceful feeling in the room. The candles had burned down to nothing just before we'd fallen asleep. We'd watched each one wink out in the darkness. Then Jaden had gotten the couch ready for him to sleep on, and I'd cov-

ered my head with the blankets and squeezed my eyes shut as tight as I could.

"Jaden?" I said, not long after I'd opened my eyes. "You awake?"

"Yeah," he said, next to me. My eyes adjusted to the dark enough to see him. He sat up and stretched his arms above his head as if it were any other morning, as if we hadn't seen all we'd seen last night. I didn't want to turn on the TV or go outside. I just wanted things back the way they were. Not back to last night, back to years ago when I was a kid, helping sweep up the block after a block party that my mother and father had taken part in putting together. There had been the easy way of hiring the department of sanitation, but there'd barely been enough money to pull the whole thing off, much less hire them. As someone young and able to do little else, I'd always gotten put on the street clean-up committee. It hadn't been so bad, though. While cleaning the streets I'd always found things—money, lost jewelry, treasures shining in the dirt and empty cups and food-stained paper plates. Once, when I was fourteen, I'd found a little bag of weed and slid it into my pocket before anyone saw it and smoked it in the park with my only friend who knew how to roll a joint. Lying there in bed, I wanted those days back. Before the storm. Before any of the storms. There was a longing inside me until that voice that's my reality came back and said, "You don't have time for this shit, and the past couldn't have been that great anyway."

"Want a breakfast bar?" Jaden asked me. Without waiting for me to answer, he got up from the couch and walked over to the boxes and the cooler he'd dragged into the living room the night before. He took out two blueberry cereal bars and handed me one. We ate them in silence, chewing slowly.

After we finished eating, I grabbed my bag and went back into Jaden's bedroom to change clothes. I pulled on a pair of tight-fitting black jeans and my still-wet combat boots. I pulled on an old band T-shirt that I'd gotten at a stoop sale, a band called the Ramones that I'd heard on a light rock station and liked anyway. Next, I layered on a fleece-lined hoodie and a vest that had a million pockets in it for things like my cell phone and keys and wallet. I checked my cell phone before putting it in a pocket, and saw that, though the battery still had some life in it, there was no reception. I walked back out into the living room where Jaden was waiting.

"Let's go see what it looks like out there," I said.

"You're ready? Okay. Let's go up through the fire escape onto the roof."

We made our way toward one of the rooms off the entrance hallways, where a guy named Kyle stayed. There was a fire escape through Kyle's window that didn't have a tree in the middle of it. There was sunlight peeping out through the crack at the bottom of Kyle's bedroom door. I took it as a good sign. I was hoping, really hoping, that last night had seemed scarier from where we were than it actually had been.

We opened the door and stepped through it. The guy had left the room a complete pigsty when he packed up and left—dirty clothes and plates everywhere. We stepped over the garbage, picking our way between piles of it. Jaden opened the window. He put one leg over the ledge and then another so that he was standing on the grating of the fire escape.

"Holy shit," I heard him say from out there.

"What?" I said. "What?"

"The water made it out this far," he said, his voice flat.

Okay, I thought to myself. So there's a little water down there. No big deal. Couldn't be that much. Not this far into Brooklyn.

But when I climbed out into the fire escape, I saw that I'd been very wrong.

The world outside the building looked like a lake. Water was up to the halfway mark of the first-floor windows. We were as far as you could get on any side from water, but the water had found its way right to where we were. The water was murky, brown and green and gray at the same time. I broke up my brain a bit trying to figure out where it all had come from—the rivers, the ocean, the rain? But those things had been there before, and they had never swollen so much that the water came in this far. I mean, I knew the oceans were rising, everyone knew that. But they'd been rising, and still they'd never come in this far inland. I just kept thinking, *How did this happen?*

There was stuff floating in it, too. Wood and branches and clothes and bags and newspapers and shoes and garbage and things I couldn't identify. There were little swirls of these things, as if they were about to be sucked down in some whirlpool. But then they just bunched up together and broke apart and started floating away again.

"My God," I said. "*Mi* fucking *dios.*"

Over an alley as we were, we couldn't see too far beyond the edges of it. Jaden started climbing up the ladder to the silver-painted roof. The ladder went down to the second floor, but no farther. I could see him climbing up above me, just his ass and legs moving up and up. I started up after him, my knees shivering just a little bit in the cold and maybe because heights aren't especially my thing. The last bit of the ladder, where I had to stand on the top and scrabble up to the roof without holding on to much, made me feel queasy. But I made it. I was up there and we were looking down.

All around us was water. It made the buildings look like Legos floating in a bathtub. The sun was shining down, but the air was cold and the slight wind still blowing up off the water was colder. Around us we saw groups of people here and there standing on their roofs, waving over at us. I thought to myself *these must be the people who are left.* Not just left after the storm, but the kind of people who were like us who were still left in the neighborhood, left behind by what had been happening all around us. People who'd been forgotten.

Off in the distance, we heard the buzz of a motorboat heading down what had once been streets, but were now canals of water. There was a smell in the air like rotting, like shit, and I wondered what had overflowed—sewers or some kind of waste treatment facility, or what.

Yet despite the smell, and the garbage, and the looks of fear I could see even in eyes that were buildings away, there was a kind of peace, too. A kind of stillness that made everything seem okay. The way the sun was reflecting in the water and off the buildings as it rose up in the sky. The blue of that sky itself, so untroubled and serene. I almost forgot where we were for a moment.

"Holy shit," Jaden said, and where we were came back to me full force.

"What do we do?" I said. "We can't even walk out the door. The water's too high. The entire first floor must be flooded."

We wandered around the rooftop from edge to edge. It was an island now. Around us, people were waving their arms at us, maybe hoping we had some kind of answers that they didn't. I looked across the alley at a short, brown-skinned man in a yellow baseball cap. I waved back at him.

"Hello!" I shouted.

"'ello!" he yelled back, his accent thick and unidentifiable.

"What are we going to do?" I shouted.

"We have to figure out a way out of here," he yelled back. "My wife and baby are here. We've got to get to somewhere safer. Is your cell phone working?"

I shook my head, then yelled, "No! Do you have enough food for now? Water?"

"For a little while," he shouted. "We have a radio. They said there's a shelter not too far, on the third floor of MS 587. We've got to figure out how to get there."

He stood there waiting for me to say something back, but I had nothing to say. I looked down at my combat boots. They were soaked and felt like wet weights on my feet. I tried to think of something to say to this man who was worrying about his kid's life, and I couldn't think of anything at all. His arms, which he'd been gesturing with, fell down to his sides as the silence extended. We stood there quiet for a few more minutes, looking at each other. I don't know what he saw in me, but I could see his desperation, his fear, all the responsibility on him that he had no idea how to handle given the circumstances. When he finally saw that I wasn't going to say anything else, he turned and walked to the other side of his roof and started shouting off the edge. I couldn't hear what he was saying.

I turned to find Jaden sitting on a dry spot on the roof. His head was down between his knees. He usually looks so smooth and strong and like he's right in control of everything. Right then, he looked shaken.

"They'll come for us, right?" he asked when I got up close to him. "Somebody's going to come for us eventually? They wouldn't just leave us here to die, would they?"

"I don't know, Jaden," I said. "Depends on who *they* are. And who *they* think we are."

"We'll be able to flag someone down," he said. He tried to make his voice firm and failed. It sounded like another question.

All morning the boats went down the canal-streets just near us, but not next to us. When we saw people manning the boats far off, they looked official. Some wore uniforms and caps, some had on army fatigues. We went down into Jaden's apartment and watched the TV for a while. It told us things like "State of Emergency" and deployment of the National Guard. We went back up to the roof and saw birds flying overhead like they do when someone's on the loose. We tried waving up to them. We wished aloud that we had those bright-colored flares like they have in the movies. Of course, we didn't.

I saw the man across the alley again. I yelled out to him, "What's your name?" It seemed important, suddenly, that I know who was there in trouble right next to me.

He yelled back, "Samuel."

"Where are you from, Samuel?"

"From New Jersey," he said.

My face got hot, knowing I'd asked a stupid question. "Why are you still here? Why didn't you get out?"

"I don't get my paycheck until tomorrow."

Well if that didn't just beat all things, I didn't know what did. I walked back to the far corner of our roof where I couldn't see him, where he couldn't see me ball up a fist and punch the ledge of the roof. There were another couple people across the alley on that side, and they waved their hands and called out to me. I ignored them. I couldn't help it. I didn't want to care about any more people until the ones I was already caring about got out.

Before an hour passed, Jaden and I got hungry again and went down the ladder into the apartment. We turned on the camping stove and boiled some water from a plastic gallon jug and made some macaroni and cheese from a box. We realized as we poured the water that there had been one flaw in Jaden's survival plan—there were only two gallons of it in the house. We paused for a moment, looking at the water and waiting for it to boil. We didn't say anything, but both of us knew that it might come down to those scant two gallons being a problem. Finally the water boiled, and we cooked our food. It was processed and gross and tasted delicious. After, we turned the water from the sink on to wash the plates, and what came out of the faucet was brown.

At around three o'clock, a boat came powering down our street, leaving a wake of water behind it that lapped up against the building below us. There were three men in it in combat fatigues. I wanted to make a joke about how I couldn't see them in all that camo, but it seemed pretty stupid, and I was petrified that they might just power away on their boat. There were other people in it, too, people crowding against the sides of the boat looking defeated and desperate. The man in combat fatigues who was piloting the boat stopped it underneath the fire escape.

"We're taking people to the shelter," he yelled up to us as we leaned over the side of the roof. "Come on down."

I turned toward Jaden and we hugged each other excitedly. I could feel his heart pounding against me, giving away how happy he was to be getting out of there. We started climbing down the ladder, me first. We were only a few feet down when I stopped.

"Wait," I called up to Jaden. "Go back up."

"What?" he said. "Are you outside your mind?"

I froze. Here were Jaden and I, who needed help as much as anybody else. Jaden was my friend and had been for as long as I could remember, and I wanted him to be safe. But I couldn't get Samuel and his kid out of my head. I didn't even know what the kid looked like, whether it was a baby or a toddler or a teenager. Did I make a decision for some thought of a kid, or did I let my friend save himself?

"Go back up," I said again.

Jaden listened to me, and in a minute we were back up on the roof, calling down.

"Did you take the people across the alleyway? Samuel? He and his wife and his kid need to go."

"We can't fit them and you," the guy in the camo said. "Do you have enough food to stay here a little while longer?"

I looked over at Jaden. He didn't even look mad, and again that feeling like new lights flickered in me.

"It's the right thing, Makayla," he said. "I'll be hoddered if I want to *do* the right thing, but we know it's right."

"Yeah," I called down. "They're probably inside. You should go in and get them."

One of the men in camo started climbing up the fire escape across the alleyway, and disappeared inside a window. I stood there and watched. I looked down, not saying anything to the guy still in the boat, until Samuel appeared at the window, then climbed out onto the fire escape. Then his wife appeared, a tiny lady holding an even tinier kid who couldn't have been more than five. We watched them go down the fire escape, the boat sinking lower into the water as each one climbed in.

"Thank you, thank you," he said up to me. I didn't say anything back. I sat down on the roof wondering what I'd just done to me and Jaden. As I heard the boat start back up and power off, I wondered if they'd ever be back, or if I'd killed us both.

4 Hours later, the boat still hadn't come back. Jaden and I sat on the roof waiting, but we didn't even hear a boat nearby.

"Why didn't they leave with a kid that small?" Jaden asked, sounding angry.

"You don't know him," I replied. I was mad, too, mad at Jaden for thinking the worst about the guy, that he'd been irresponsible or a bad parent for staying. I climbed down the ladder and walked back into Kyle's room. I slammed the door behind me, because I wanted to hear it shake the walls. In the kitchen, I looked around for something to break. I found a coffee cup and threw it to the ground. It broke in two neat halves, and I felt a little better. This anger happens to me sometimes, rises up in me like heat out of the subway grate when it's winter. I grab something, break something, slam something. When I was a kid, I used to get in fights, grab people by the hair, punch their faces, feel them punching me back. I don't do that anymore, not since I've gotten older. Maybe I still don't have a lot to lose, but now I know better than to hurt people for no reason, or my own lousy reasons that have nothing to do with them.

I went back up the roof when I'd cooled down. Jaden didn't ask about the slamming or the shattering, I think he knows me better than that by now. Anyway, I'd cleaned up the glass with his broom.

We waited there for hours. The stillness I'd felt that morning when the sun shone off the water was long gone. I was cold and I was hungry, and I felt unsure that the boat we'd seen or any other one would come our way any time soon.

As if echoing my thoughts, Jaden said, "What if they don't come back at all?"

"We can't think like that," I said. "Come on. Let's go inside and eat."

"What if we miss the boat?" he asked.

"They know we're here," I said.

Daylight savings time had happened the week before, so the sun was long since down. My boots still hadn't dried, and it was getting colder and colder.

Back inside, I found some packages of ramen in the box next to the cooler and opened them up. I boiled as little water as I could get away with boiling and let the noodles sink in. They lost their square shape quickly. After they'd boiled for a minute, I opened the powder packet and dumped that in, too. My stomach was growling like a stray dog. I stopped and listened to the sound of it, and, as I did, I became aware of another sound. For a minute I couldn't place it, and then I realized that the soft little *slap slap slap*s I was hearing was the water lapping up against the walls outside.

Jaden and I ate sitting on the couch. After we'd both finished, he put his bowl down and looked over at me.

"They're not coming back tonight," he said. "The sun's gone down. They're probably at the emergency shelter, and not leaving until the sun comes back up."

I let that sink in. We had to get through another night here, in the dark, in the cold. I felt a sudden rush of gratitude wash over me that Jaden had called me, had brought me here to stay with him.

"What should we do since we have all this time?" I asked, trying to keep the trembling out of my voice. "My Mixplayer still has charge. If your screen's charged, we could hook it up and watch something. Or listen to something."

"Do you feel like we did the right thing sending that boat away?" Jaden asked me.

"What?"

"Did we make a mistake?"

"I don't think so, Jaden," I said.

He sat back on the couch. There was silence for a moment, then he said, "What's the worst mistake you ever made in your life?" He was back to his questions.

"Once I held a door open for a goodbreed," I joked. "Didn't know until she got close and I saw her designer *every*thing. By then it was too late."

He didn't laugh. He changed tactics. "Yo, Makayla, do you remember when we met?"

"We were just kids," I said. "I don't remember."

"I do," he said. "We were thirteen. It was before I started riding my bike, and I was just this scrawny, goofy kid with big ears. Mike Baylon kept beating me up after school. You remember Mike Baylon?"

"Holy shit, yeah," I said, slapping him lightly on the shoulder. "He always wore his older brother's hand-me-downs until he grew into them, so half the time he was swimming in his clothes. I haven't thought of him in years."

"He kept beating me up after school, until this one day, he was handing me my ass, and you came around the side of the school eating a push-up pop. You had that shit dripping down your chin, and your tongue was blue from it. And you walked up to that bastard Mike Baylon and pushed him down on the ground."

"I did?" I said. If I had, it was just one of many fights I'd been in as a kid.

"Right on his ass. And he wasn't afraid of me, but he was afraid of you, because you took on kids twice your size all the time. And you started yelling at him. I still remember what you said."

"Well? What did I say?"

"'Mike, just because you have mother issues doesn't mean you have to go around being an asshole!'"

"Oh, shit, didn't his mom die when he was little or something?" I blushed remembering.

"Yeah, I think so," Jaden said. "But you know what? He never touched me again."

"So what does that have to do with mistakes?" I asked, coming back around to where he'd started the conversation.

"The mistake *I* made then was that I didn't kiss you the minute you did it," Jaden said. "I decided that I would wait until the block party the next weekend to try. And by then you were going out with Erik Lee."

"You had a crush on me as a kid!" I said, laughing. I couldn't believe I was laughing, not with how bad things seemed. "You never told me!"

"You never noticed," Jaden said. "You had a new boyfriend or girlfriend every week when we were growing up. I was just that kid with big ears."

I noticed that Jaden has stopped laughing. I stopped, too.

"It wasn't like that," I said. Then, I started feeling that tight feeling in my head again. The one that I hated and could never make any sense of. That feeling like the world is always coming at you, and your head, the corner you're backed into, just keeps getting smaller.

"Jaden?" I said, my voice rising. "Why are you telling me this now? What the hell do you even expect me to do with that, right here while we're waiting to see if we're gonna live or die?"

"When will be the right time, Makayla?" he asked. His voice had not risen to match my own; it was still calm and low.

Jaden went into Kyle's room to sleep for the night, leaving me alone in the living room.

5 Ever since I was a kid, I've had 'trosh nightmares. That night was no exception. The dream didn't start out so bad. In it, I was in the park near my house, flying kites with my dad. The kites were high up in the sky, just specks, and my dad was saying that I had to let go of the string. But I didn't want to. I didn't want the kite to fly up and away forever or, worse, take a nosedive somewhere far off where I'd never be able to follow it.

"I won't!" I screamed at my father.

Suddenly, he was clutching his chest. I was screaming in his face, and he was curling up smaller and smaller, as if he was trying to climb inside himself. He was having the heart attack that had killed him in the waking, living world. The one that had taken him right out of my life two years after my mom checked.

"Daddy!" I was screaming, which I hadn't called him since I was a kid. Certainly not in the bad years that had come between when I was a kid and when he had died, when I had run wild and he'd watched me, knowing how easy it would be for me to slip and fall down and never get back up again. But now I was calling him Daddy again, and begging him not to go.

The dream shifted, then, and we were in a hospital with no

lights and no machines. He was still having a heart attack. I couldn't see him anymore, just hear him crying and begging in the darkness that couldn't begin to compare with the darkness that waited for him after the pain was over.

I woke up moaning and tossing and turning.

Jaden was there almost immediately, wrapping his arms around me and telling me that everything was okay.

"I'm here, I'm here," he kept saying.

As I got my bearings, as my mind cleared, one thing remained with me. The image of someone dying in the dark. How many people had had surgery just before Bernice hit? Or were having heart attacks right now and couldn't get to a hospital at all? How many people were gasping in the dark for air? Or checking alone?

"What do you think is happening at the hospitals?" I asked Jaden when my own breathing returned to normal.

"They must have backup generators," he said. "For the patients on life support and things like that."

"But aren't those generators in the basements? And won't the basements be flooded?"

"I don't know," he said. He stroked my hair as he held me close to him.

I thought about all those people in the dark, in the cold. I thought about them dying. I thought about how we're all going to die, maybe not right now, maybe not as a result of this storm, but all someday. That one hits me every now and then. Sometimes, when I'm alone and it's late and I'm very tired, or when I've just spent twelve hours at the 24/7, that thought hits me in the face and makes me feel like giving up. I just think of life as shoveling food into your face and shitting it out, people as weird beings who do strange, destructive things to each other and the world around them.

And it all seems so senseless and foul, like people are just huge intestinal worms on the face of the earth. I think about my mom and my dad, who I loved, who checked. And it's so much pain that I try to make myself angry about something instead, because I know that'll keep me alive so much longer than the pain would.

But other times, I think about dying and I think about nothing being forever, and it makes me feel determined to do something good with whatever time I have left. I mean, I know where I stand. I know I'll never be president, or a doctor, or anything like that. But even to do things like my mom and dad did, to put on stupid, sienty block parties for my neighbors—even those things seem good enough.

I started to catch my breath. "We have to get to the emergency shelter. They'll need us there."

"We'll get there," Jaden promised. He loosened his grip on me, holding me at arm's length. "Makayla, about yesterday—I'm sorry. We'll forget all about it. We'll get to the shelter today."

We got dressed and boiled ourselves some water for instant coffee and ate. We were down to one gallon of water. After we drank our coffee, we went back up to the roof. The cold up there was no longer a deterrent; the apartment was freezing as well.

At around noon, we heard birds overhead. We ran back into Kyle's room and stripped the bed of all its sheets, and then did the same to all the beds in the apartment. Up on the roof we pulled the sheets longways and twisted them up, then taped them down to form the word "help." Every time a bird went overhead, we waved our arms as widely and wildly as we could. It didn't help. Nothing helped.

After a while we went back downstairs. We decided to

drink some of the slurree and eat protein bars because it didn't take water to make. We opened the last gallon jug of water and took small sips out of it, tipping it back carefully. A trickle of water ran out of the side of my mouth and down my neck in a little rivulet, and I rushed to stop it with my hand that wasn't holding the jug. I handed the jug to Jaden.

Just as he was lifting it up to take a sip out of it, we heard the distinctive sound of motorboats nearby. We jerked toward the fire escape, and as we did, the bottle slipped from Jaden's hand. We watched the water glug out of the jug onto the floor, and were torn between it and the window. We chose the window. We rushed up the ladder, to the roof. The boat was close, right on top of us it seemed from the sound. We climbed as fast as we could, and ran to the edge of the roof, waving our arms. But it was too late. That second we had hesitated had given the boat just enough time to pass us. We stared at each other before slowly descending the ladder.

There was a wide pool of water on the ground in Jaden's living room when we got back down there. The jug was mostly empty. We had missed the boat, and now we wouldn't have enough water to make it through the day.

"What are we going to do?" I asked, looking down at the bottle. I righted it, and what little was left sloshed to the bottom.

Jaden didn't have an answer.

6 By noon the next day, the water was gone, and our throats were dry. While the slurree might technically keep us from dehydrating for a little while if it came down to it, the thick

consistency of it only made us thirstier. As did the cereal and protein bars and nuts that we were eating. We had to come up with a plan. We sat across from each other in the living room, not jawing at all.

"We're going to have to go into other people's apartments," Jaden said finally.

"Like, break in?" I asked.

"Well, we can try knocking first," Jaden said.

"We can't just go stealing from your neighbors," I said.

"Neighbors?" Jaden said. Now he had an edge to his voice. "All my neighbors are gone. These people left, they're not my neighbors, or yours. They're just people who left us here to die while they went to their fancy houses in other places. This isn't their neighborhood."

I saw his point, but I still felt uncomfortable. What if we broke into a house where not everybody was gone? And what if those not-everybodies had guns or weapons? And what if they were the kind of people who looked at our brown skin and our dark eyes and shot first and were sorry later?

"It's not like we're looting, Makayla. We need water. We have to get it somewhere. That's all we'll take."

I put my boots on and started looking around for something to carry. There was the hammer we'd used to put the door up over the window, and a crowbar in a closet. Both would come in handy. I handed the hammer to Jaden and took the crowbar myself.

We started with the doors nearby. Jaden had been joking, but we did work our way down the hall knocking. When we got to the third door, someone called back from inside.

"Who's there?" they said, fear in their voice.

"We're ..." I hesitated, thinking of what Jaden had said. "... we're your neighbors."

"Go away! Don't come in here!"

I turned toward Jaden and whispered fiercely, "I told you, I *told* you no one would think we were upswing coming knocking on their door like this."

"Come on," Jaden said.

We knocked on doors all down the hallway. When people answered, they mainly told us to go away, to get away from their apartments. Finally, we came to the last one, a door with a new, fresh coat of paint. I remembered Jaden jawing about the Smiths, a family that had been there for ages, moving out of this apartment recently. There must be new people here now. We knocked on the door and called out again. I put my ear to the door and listened for any sounds, but I didn't hear any. I turned to look at Jaden. He shrugged. I wedged my crowbar right between the newly painted door and the jamb. As I pushed with all my strength, the door screeched open.

It was dark inside. I pulled out my phone and turned on the flashlight, illuminating the darkness with a weird bluish glow. The light bounced off shelves of knick-knacks, figurines and antique bottles and silver statues. It was the kind of stuff you would only spend money on if you had it to burn. I felt that heat and tightness again, mixing up in my head. These were the kind of people who lived in our neighborhood now.

"Come on," Jaden said, pushing me forward. We went through the living room to the kitchen. We rummaged around but didn't find anything useful. There was a rotten smell that came out of the refrigerator when we opened it. All the rich-people food, meats and cheeses and delicate little fruits that were like something in a painting at the Met—they were all rotting away in there.

We went through the cabinets. Finally, in one near the floor, we found a six-pack of water. Not water like they sell at the 24/7, either, but that mineral stuff that comes from springs up in the God-knows-where mountains. Traveled stuff. Stuff in glass bottles. Jaden grabbed the case and we started making our way toward the door.

As we were leaving, I took the crowbar and ran it all along a shelf, smashing the glass figurines to bits.

7 We tried not to drink too much, but two days later, the water we'd stolen from the goodbreeds down the hall was dwindling. Jaden's eyes were beginning to look sunken. We walked up to the roof every morning and stayed there for hours. We were freezing.

We began to fight about little things—who got the last of the cereal bars instead of a protein bar, who had used the last tissue. We were beginning to run out of food and toilet paper. The water still hadn't gone down.

At around three o'clock the third day after our break-in, after we'd spend hours on the roof, gone back downstairs to eat and come back up, we heard the distinctive sound of a motorboat. It came into view, the waves caused by its wake splashing up against the sides of buildings. We leaned over the edge of the roof, waving our arms and screaming. The two men in charge of the boat must have heard us, because they pulled up close to the building. We motioned them toward the alleyway.

We began climbing down the ladder toward the boat. Besides the two men, there were several people in the boat. On one side of the boat was a teenager who looked partly scared and partly annoyed. With her was presumably her family, a mother and a father. They were arguing with each other in a language I didn't understand. Near them was a girl in her early twenties. She didn't look scared at all, but rather looked like she was having the time of her life. She was dressed in a T-shirt with the sleeves cut off despite the chill in the air, and her arms were long and thin and the veins stood out. She was leaning over the side of the boat, looking ahead down the alley. Then, all alone in the middle of the boat was this kid. He had short dark hair cut into a little mohawk and brown skin. He looked shocked. He was bent over at the knees, holding his feet and staring down at them. He didn't look up.

"Swing over and lower yourself down," one of the men in fatigues called up as we reached the second-floor fire escape.

I went first, swinging one leg over the railing on the edge of the fire escape. Then I swung the other over, and was clinging to the outside of the structure. I slid my hand down until they were at the bottom of the railing and stepped off, one foot at a time. For a frightening moment I was hanging there above the boat. I didn't want to let go. I could feel my hands loosening their grip as the full weight of my body hung from them.

"It's okay, Makayla," Jaden said.

I let go. The boat shook as I dropped the last couple of feet. The family near the side of the boat grabbed them, but the young woman in her twenties just laughed and rode the rocking boat like they were the undulations of a rushing subway car and she didn't have a bar to hang on to. The little boy in the boat didn't move an inch even as the boat swayed from side to side. Jaden followed me, and I hung on to the sides of the boat as he dropped down.

For the first time, I got a good look at our rescuers. One

was white and one was black, but they wore matching fatigues and stony looks. They looked at me like they were looking through me, both of them. I tried to be friendly, anyway.

"I'm Makayla," I said, "and this is Jaden."

"Why the hell didn't you evacuate when you had the chance?" the man at the back of the boat, the white guy, barked at us. I didn't like that. A look slid over my face, I could feel it.

"I'm sorry. I didn't know I was invited to your house," I said, all venom.

Jaden stood up from the crouch he was in and put his hand on my shoulder.

"She's upset," he said, trying to smooth things over. The two guys looked through him, too. All the other people on the boat just stood back and watched.

The man at the front of the boat said, "Well, you're stuck here now. We're taking them," here he pointed over at the other people in the boat, "to the rescue shelter. We'll take you there, too, if you want."

For the first time I noticed all the voices echoing down the alleyway. Other people. Other people who would have given anything to be in this boat, even with these two ories. I made a promise to myself, for Jaden's sake as much as my own, that I would keep my mouth shut, no matter what they said.

A gust of wind kicked up and blew the water into a little whirlpool right in front of us. The wind had died down since the superstorm hit, but it was still strong and cold as blades. I turned away from the soldiers to where Jaden was kneeling down next to the little boy.

"What's your name?" he asked him.

The stared down at his feet, at his little black sneakers.

They were the kind that project holograms onto the sides if you step down on them, and every time he rocked back and forth, his little shoes lit up. He didn't even glance up at Jaden or me.

"Do you know his name?" I asked the family at the back of the boat. I kept myself from shooting the man in the back of the boat a dirty look.

"No," they said.

The man at the back of the boat spoke. "We found him alone on the roof of a building. Don't know where his mother and father are, if he has them. He was just up there alone, doing what he's doing now. We found some bodies down the street, floating nearby, but if they belonged to anybody he belonged to, he didn't react one way or the other."

I reached down toward the little boy. He jerked away as if my hand was made of fire. Moving a few feet back, he resumed his crouched stance, his eyes down.

"Leave him alone, Makayla," Jaden said. He had backed away. I wanted to. Who was this kid to me? I just wanted to get to the shelter, and then, when the water went away, get my grandmother. But I just kept staring at his shoes. Somebody had bought him those shoes, somebody had loved him enough to want to give him something that would make him happy like that. And that person was gone now. I remembered the things I had kept after my parents checked—my mom's hair scarfs and my dad's old flannel. Things that brought comfort and pain every time I looked at them. I wondered if this boy was feeling those feelings as he looked at the shoes someone who had loved him gave him. I sat down next to him. I didn't reach out for him again, but I stayed there.

With the roar of the motor behind us, we began making our way down the waterway that used to be a street. I knew these streets, but now they looked like an alien landscape. Trees were torn down, windows broken, bodies floated in the water, bloating. In the wake of our boat I saw the wet fur of a drowned street dog, wrapped up in a downed electrical wire. What had killed it, the water or the electricity, I couldn't say.

I smelled smoke, and up ahead of us I saw the dancing orange of a fire. I wondered how there could be fire in all this water, but, as we pulled up, I saw an old factory building blazing, black smoke billowing out of it in clouds so thick they were almost solid. It looked like something out of a movie, like the kind of thing you don't see in real life. I had barely started taking in that scene when I heard a steady *pop pop pop* off to our right. I knew gunshots when I heard them.

"What the hell?" I said aloud. Jaden didn't even look at me. He was looking out back behind the boat, watching all the garbage that was going up and down in our wake. The man at the front of the boat answered me.

"Oh, it's worse than that," he said. "We've seen women who were raped, people beaten within an inch of their lives. Some people take the worst and they make it even worse than that."

The man at the back of the boat made a noise in his throat. "Fucking animals. You people who stayed here are all like animals."

"What the fuck did you say?" I asked, breaking my resolve to keep my mouth shut. "Say it again, go ahead."

"When you get thrown in the with rest of the animals, don't blame anybody but yourself."

I took a step toward him, my hands balling up into fists at my sides. I hadn't been in a fight in I don't even know how long, and the guy had a gun. I was ready to jump him, though, and hodder whatever happened after that.

"Makayla, look," Jaden said, grabbing me by the arm.

He turned me around to the front of the boat, and I saw a school submerged in water with the wide, high front doors thrown open. Whatever was inside those doors, we couldn't tell, because all we could see was blackness.

The captains of our ship piloted the boat through the double doors and then inside. They took us to where the stairs emerged from the water.

"Take the boy," the man in the back of the boat barked.

"Did you think we were going to leave him with you?" I shot back.

The family reached over for him. They didn't seem like bad people. Maybe it was just better to let him be with them. But then the boy moved just a bit toward Jaden and me. I put my hand on the boy's shoulder. He didn't move again. I placed my hands into his armpits and gently pulled him up. He was limp like a rag doll, and I was surprised he could stand on his feet. Those little shoes kept flashing their silver pictures up on the sides: basketball players jumping, cars racing, motorcycles roaring by. The boy stood, and I linked my arm in his. Standing, the top of his head came up to my chest. That made him just about four feet tall. I helped him over the edge of the boat, onto the first stair that rose out of the water. He slowly placed one foot in front of the other as I pulled him along. The other people in the boat followed us.

At the top of the stairs, there was a landing that looked down over the pool of water that had forced its way into the school. Floating in the water were test papers with red grades on them, pencils, pens, markers, art projects. A papier-mâché head was floating in the water like a decapitation. Off of the landing, there were two double doors, one on either end, without any windows. They were closed. As the men in the boat roared off, Jaden and I pulled the boy toward the one on the left. We stood in front of the double door in silence. We all stood there listening.

"Do you hear that?" I said.

"Yeah," Jaden replied.

Behind the door, there were sounds of chaos. Moans and yelling and a kind of wild laugher that didn't come from anything resembling joy. What was back there?

I placed my hand flat on the door, spreading my fingers wide and seeing the chipped polish on my nails. The door was ice cold, like the air all around us. For some reason, I had expected it to be as hot as fire.

"Do we go in there?" I asked.

"What else can we do?" Jaden said. "We can't exactly swim to safety."

I took a deep breath and pushed the door open.

The smell was the first thing that hit us. It was 'trosh, worse than garbage day on the hottest day of the summer. It was worse than a sewer backing up. It was both of those things at once.

It took us a minute to get our bearings after the smell hit us, but when we did we looked up and realized that there were lights on. I could hear, under the sounds of yelling and moaning, the sound of a machine hum, a big generator. I could hear other machines buzzing away.

After blinking in the light, I looked down. There were people everywhere. The ones from the boat faded into them. There were blue rubber mats on the ground, kind of like I started seeing slung across people's backs when the Jillian Studio opened up in the neighborhood. But these weren't fancy Jillian Studio people's mats, they were some state-issued variety, thin and dirty. People were lying on them and sitting on them. They were lined up all down the hall.

I felt resistance on my arm. The boy was standing dead still, pulling me back. He didn't want to go any farther. I couldn't blame him.

"It's okay," I leaned down and whispered in his ear. But I was sure it wasn't.

On either side of the hallway were classrooms. We peered into the high window on one of the doors on our left and saw hospital beds on wheels and people in them and machines next to them. The people were old and wrinkled and looked like they were completely unconscious, except for one who kept repeating, "Let me go home, let me go home, let me go home." In the corner of the room, there was an empty bed with bloodstains on it. There was one person dressed in white moving from bed to bed, checking tubes, checking pulses. I turned the handle of the door and opened it slowly.

"What's going on here?" I called to her.

She turned to me with a scowl on her face.

"Can't you see I'm *working*? Do you think I have time for questions? Find somebody with a uniform on and try to ask them."

Suddenly a scream erupted from the throat of one of the patients. It was long and drawn out and high pitched. It went on and on. I backed out of the doorway, pulling the kid with me. I shut the door behind us. I turned to see Jaden looking wide-eyed around the hallway.

"We have to get out of here," he said. I looked down the hallway where he was looking and saw two people waling away at each other with their fists. As I watched, one man's face bloodied as he took hit after hit to it. He fell to the ground where the other man started kicking him. Nobody came to break it up. In little pockets in the hallway, there were families with children trying to pretend it wasn't happening, looking down at games set up before them, or at phones that were still working. The kid at my side burrowed his face into me. I rose my arm up and put it around him as the man on the floor's face became unrecognizable as anything human.

"We have to get out of here," Jaden said again.

"Where, Jaden? Where are we going to go?"

8 We ended up huddled up in a room that had science projects along the ledges of the broken windows, soda bottle tornados and attempts at perpetual motion machines. I wondered if the children I had seen in the hallways trying to block out the fight were the same ones who had made them.

The kid we'd found on the boat still wasn't talking. He had gone into a corner and was crouched down again, staring at his little shoes. I stayed close to him, my arm around his shoulders. I felt like I had to protect him. Why, I didn't know. He wasn't my kid, he wasn't my responsibility, I kept telling myself. But I knew I couldn't think that way. This kid belonged to me as much as I'd belonged to my neighbors as a kid, when they'd watched to make sure I got in my door when I was walking home late at night and they were out on their stoops.

I looked down at the watch on my wrist. I wore it because the 24/7 had a strict no-cell-phone-on-the-floor policy. I was glad to have it now. It read just before six o'clock. Hours had rushed by while we had wandered from room to room looking for some kind of order. There had mainly been people everywhere who knew nothing. The ones who did know a little were too overwhelmed trying to take care of the sick that they had no answers for anybody else. Jaden and the kid and I had walked by a room where a woman was screaming, giving birth. As we stood there, the head of her child pushed itself through the bloody hole between her legs, and came screaming into a world that was screaming right back at it. I had stood there awestruck, watching, the birth just another part of the chaos.

I tried to get the blood and the disorder out of my mind as we sat there warily eyeing the people around us. Who knew who they were? I realized with horror that anyone could be a murderer, a rapist, the guy in the neighborhood who mugged old ladies. The girl in the cutoff shirt from the boat had ended up in our room. She kept disappearing, looking enthusiastic instead of horrified when she came back. She started a conversation with me about how this was the twelfth disaster zone she'd been in the last few years, and there was always so much to see and do. She looked almost excited. I decided that I hated her.

Jaden's voice shook me out of my anger. "Are you hungry?" he asked. We hadn't eaten since early that morning, and we didn't know when the boy had eaten last. Jaden looked down at him. "Are you?"

"I'm starving," I said. "I wish we ate before we left the apartment. I haven't seen any food here at all."

"Maybe they have some in some of those locked rooms," Jaden said. "They must have brought supplies here before the storm."

We looked around the room, as if there might be something there we hadn't seen. But we had examined the whole room when we came into it. This time, as we looked, I saw someone I hadn't seen before. An old lady was huddled in the corner farthest from us. Her dark skin was lined with deep wrinkles and, jutting out from her heavy sleeves, her wrists were so thin they looked like they would break as she reached to pick up the rapidly emptying bottle of water in front of her. I felt a wave of remorse for thinking the worst of everyone around me.

As I sat there, I felt my anger bubbling up in me again. Here was this lady with nothing, and who was to blame for it? Her family who'd left her? The rentbosses who'd driven them out? The goodbreeds who'd come in and taken their places before they were even gone? As I thought about it, I looked down and saw that I'd been making fists and digging my nails into my palms. There were angry red little half-moons cut into them. I tried to loosen them, but every time I looked down, I was doing it again.

I sat there for an hour, and my stomach started rumbling louder and louder as I did. Jaden came over to me.

"I'm going to find out about food," he said. I figured it would be okay. Jaden cracked the door open and edged his body out, opening it as little as he had to to do so.

Twenty minutes later, he was back. He looked shaken up and pulled the door closed tight behind him. He walked over to me and crouched by where I sat.

"I found some soldiers. They said they have some slurree and water they're going to pass out. Maybe we can get the kid to drink some."

Even though I was expecting the soldier, I froze when the door cracked open again. I heard the shouts and moans outside. It opened slowly, and all I could think of was all the 'trosh things that could be behind it. I squeezed my knees close to me, bracing myself to attack and to run. Would I leave behind Jaden and the kid if it came to that? I didn't know. Two guardsmen walked in with a plastic milk crate full of cans.

"Come and get it," one said. His voice was laced with disdain, like he was talking to a room full of dogs he was throwing rotting meat to. They left the crate on the ground and were gone again.

We all moved toward the crate. The slurree was off-brand, and when I looked at the nutritional content on the back, I saw that it didn't have half the stuff as the name brands have. If we drank just this, it would keep us alive for a little while, but just barely. It probably would have been better if they'd given us white bread sandwiches with a piece of bologna and orange American cheese, like they used to in the summertime for kids who relied on school lunches over the rest of the year and wouldn't eat otherwise.

I quickly counted the cans and measured the number against the amount of people in the room. There was enough for all of us, and a few left over. A mother who was in one corner with her two kids grabbed enough for all of them, then went back and grabbed the seconds. She got a few glares from the other people in the room, but she plastered a look on her face that was high and above, like what she'd done couldn't be considered anything but upswing.

"I got children here," she said to the glaring eyes around her. "*Children.*"

Her two kids popped open the slurree cans and slurped at them. They looked like they hadn't eaten anything all day. When they finished, their mother handed them another. She looked around the room hard as if she dared anyone to say anything.

The boy had come over to where I had the cans of slurree. He turned his dark eyes up at me, and they were shy beneath their heavy lashes. He reached out his hand and I handed him a can. He grabbed it away and ran back to the corner he had come from.

"Wait," I said. I went to the middle of the room where all the desks had been pushed into a haphazard grouping. I pulled a few of them together into a large rectangle, and pulled some chairs in a circle around them. "Let's sit down together."

Jaden came right over, but the boy stayed in the corner. After a little while, seeing he wasn't going to come to us, I went over and took him by the hand. His other hand clutched the can, which he still hadn't opened. His sleeve pulled up a little where he held out the can, and I saw long red welts going down his arm. I pulled the sleeve up farther and saw that the scratches stretched all the way up. He looked up at me, then down. I pulled up the other sleeve, and saw them on his other arm. Where they had come from, I didn't know for sure, but I hadn't seen them earlier. The likeliest scenario seemed that he was hurting himself when no one was looking. I had a moment of panic, trying to figure out how I would keep him safe from himself. I decided that if I could keep him safe from everyone else, we'd work on this later.

I took the boy over to the desks. Then I went back to the wall where there was a paper towel dispenser that you turn a little handle and those thin, brown paper towels come out. I ripped one about a foot long off for me, the boy, and Jaden. I took them to the desk and placed them next to our cans of slurree.

The slurree tasted awful, worse than usual, which often isn't the greatest taste in the world. The stuff is strictly to keep you alive; there is usually little pleasure or enjoyment to be had from it. Which I guess was what made it even more of a slap in the face. I didn't feel lucky just to have it. I've never felt lucky for the scraps I've gotten handed my whole life, from the meager food stamps my mom fed us all on to the sienty holiday extras we got at the food bank. Ungrateful, some would call me. But those people are the same ones that are dining on things like steaks and caviar when I'm getting government cheese and cut-rate slurree. Those are the people who think when I save up my goddamn food stamps to buy a steak, too, that I am living too well. Those are the same people who forced me and my family out of the places they thought were too ghetto for the longest time, before they weren't and then they were too good for the likes of me. The can of cut-rate slurree in front of me was what they gave you if you spent the night in jail, or had the misfortune to end up in a city-run mental hospital. Those cans on the table in front of us didn't make me grateful, no. They just reminded me that like so many times before, I was among the forgotten.

9 The wind was blowing through the broken windows as the sun went down. There were some blankets in the room, bunched up by the blue not-Jillian mats. The boy had gone back to the corner to crouch down after he'd drank his. He'd gulped down the contents of the can, then pushed his chair back and moved faster than I'd seen him move yet to the corner. As the night fell, and the wind grew stronger through the windows, I walked over to him and wrapped him up in a blanket.

His hands were shoved into the front pocket of his hoodie, like they'd been for most of the time since I'd found him. It was a pullover hoodie, so it just had that one big pocket in the front. It looked from the bulge in the pocket like his hands were clasped together. As I wrapped the blanket around him, he must have lost grip on what he was holding there, because something crashed to the ground.

I knelt to pick it up. It was a cell phone. The glass of the touch screen hadn't broken in the fall. I turned it on, hoping that maybe in the phone there was someone marked "Mom" or "Dad." Maybe there was some way we could get in touch with someone who knew this boy and was going crazy wondering what had happened to him. How we would do that with no reception didn't cross my mind at the time.

With the phone on, I came to a password screen. I tried swooping some geometrical patters between the numbers, but nothing worked. I leaned down to the little boy and showed him the screen.

"Do you know what to press?" I asked. The boy went into a cower, his head down. I could see little splashes of water on the floor from where the tears were dropping out of his eyes. I put the phone in my pocket and sat down next to him. I didn't say a word. I put my arm around him and rocked a little back and forth. After half an hour or so, his body went slack and heavy against me. I lowered him down to a mat on the floor and walked back across the room. There was mostly silence around me. The girl in the cutoff shirt was gone, and nobody seemed to want to say much to each other. The old lady was there, still looking weak and frail, haunting me with thoughts of my grandmother. After a while, we heard a yell and something slam against the wall. I wanted to go see what was happening.

"Don't go out there," Jaden said, grabbing my arm. "When I went to look for food, I heard about people getting shot. You need to stay in here."

I heard a howling like an animal was being killed. I stayed where I was.

I stood there, dazed, until I felt a tug on my shirt sleeve. The boy was next to me.

"What?" I said, looking down, not expecting him to be out of his corner. He had tears in his eyes again. "What is it?" I asked.

He pointed down to his crotch. A wet spot was spread all over the front of his pants. I noticed then that he smelled like urine. I pulled him close to me. I wanted to tell him it was okay, that I would change his pants, take him to the bathroom. But it was too dangerous outside, and I didn't want to wander the halls with him. And there were no more pants.

"What are your kids peeing in?" I asked the lady who had taken the extra slurree.

"Here," she said, She shoved a bucket she must have found in the closet at me. It was filled up halfway with urine. "I don't know what we'll do when they have to go number two."

I stood between the bucket and the rest of the room, letting the boy know that it was safe to use it. Finally, as I stood with my back to him, I heard the sound of him relieving himself.

"Jaden, what about you?" I asked.

We took turns. When we were done, the bucket was almost full.

"What do we do with this?" I asked.

"Give it here," the woman with the children said. She took the bucket and upturned it out one of the broken windows. I wondered how much shit and piss was out there floating in that dirty water that still hadn't receded.

As the night got darker, Jaden and I curled up together on a mat. I was so much less angry with him for what he had told me. He wrapped his arms around me as we curled up in the spoon position, kissing the top of my head. I was starting to feel just the tiniest bit safer when the thought of us all falling asleep at the same time flashed through my head. I jumped up. I hit the bottom of Jaden's jaw with the top of my head. Knowing I was disturbing the people who'd already fallen asleep, I rushed toward the door and pushed all the desks we'd sat at while drinking our slurree against it. If anybody was going to get in, they at least weren't doing it without making some noise.

"I need a weapon," I said, crawling back over to Jaden on my hands and knees. "What can we use?"

"It's a children's classroom," Jaden said. "It's designed to *not* have things you can hurt people with in it."

I rummaged around in the teacher's desk. I found a plastic ruler in there, and some masking tape. Take them back over to where Jaden lay on the ground, I sat next to him and began wrapping the tape around the ruler. It wasn't until it was thick and stung when I slapped my hand with it that I crawled back under the thin blanket with Jaden. I knew I was being a real numptie, but I felt better with that little piece of reinforced plastic in my hands. Like I could disarm somebody with it, or shove it down their throat if it came to that.

Jaden put his arm back around me as I laid back down. I didn't realize how tight a ball I was rolled up into until he began to stroke my hair and rub my shoulders. As he continued doing so, I relaxed bit by bit until finally I fell asleep.

As I slept, I dreamed that I was in a pitch-black hallway. I could smell the death and the shit and the piss all around me. I walked with my hands out in front of me, stretched as far as they would go, hoping they hit something before it could hit me.

"Granny?" I said. "Grandma?"

Nobody answered, and I just kept walking forward in that blackness. It was like nighttime like I'd never seen. They say, and I don't know if it's true because I've never been far out of the city, but they say that walking in the woods on a night with no moon is that black. But even a few nights prior, when Jaden and I had walked in the dark, it hadn't been as black as that dream was. It was a black night, and I was in a window-less space that made it even blacker. Something brushed my hands, something soft and light and almost not even there, like a spiderweb. I shuddered.

"Granny?" I called again. I didn't know why I was jawing like that, drawing attention to myself from whatever else was in that blackness.

A red light flashed on briefly. In it, I saw a man with a huge snake, like the guy who, when I was a kid and Coney Island was still there, was always posing for pictures down at the boardwalk. But the snake was wrapped tight around his neck and must have been choking him. It was wrapped around his arms and torso, squeezing. He had a wide smile on his face, as if he was actually enjoying the checking he was doing. It was a phrenic kind of smile, with hell in it. The light went back out.

"Granny?"

I heard her moaning off to my left. Her or someone that sounded just like her. I couldn't tell in all the blackness. I went down on my hands and knees and started feeling the ground. I felt nothing, just the cold floor, for the longest time. And then my hands hit something.

I felt her face, wet and slick with blood. The light went on just in time for me to see a hole in her head from a gunshot, and my hands right on top of it. I woke up moaning and making a lot of noise.

"Shut up, you phrenic bitch!" someone in the corner said.

"What the fuck do you think you're doing waking everyone up? I'll fucking cut you."

"You shut the fuck up," Jaden said. He put all of the strength I knew he had into those words. "You come near her and you're going to regret it."

Jaden wrapped his arms around me tighter, his hands resting on my shoulders and pulling me close to him.

"I have to get to Gravesend," I whispered to him. I was shaking.

"Tomorrow, baby," he said. He had never called me "baby" or anything but Makayla. "Tomorrow."

I tried to get back to sleep, but the night was cold and the cold was coming through the broken windows. At some point, the boy came out of the corner and curled into me where I was curled into Jaden. He was shivering. I reached into my back pocket and handed him his cell phone, which he clutched like it would make everything okay.

10 I woke up with early morning sun coming through the windows of the schoolroom. The day still seemed gray and ominous, even with the golden sunlight. Someone in the room was leaning down over some sleeping people, rummaging through their possessions while they slept. When he saw my eyes open, he stopped and went back to the spot he'd occupied before on one of the blue mats. He laid there staring at me, glaring. I clenched my hands tight around my sienty weapon.

Jaden and the boy were next to me. None of us had showered in days, and it was clear. We stunk. My long black hair hung down greasy around my face. Normally, I would have put some shit in it and went on with my day, but none of my hair products besides my now-useless straightener had been on the list of things I'd jammed into my bag when I'd packed. I thought of the things I had brought with me—a toothbrush and toothpaste, my cell phone charger, my contact lens solution. Most of them weren't worth their weight in my bag and I'd probably have to discard them. I'd taken to wearing my glasses on day two, with no running water to wash my hands before taking out the lenses. Likewise, I'd given up on the idea of brushing my teeth because the sink was out in the dangerous hallway. I could feel a scum of tartar building up on them when I ran my tongue over them.

I'd been avoiding the hall at all costs, but, sitting up, I knew I had to go out there. My dream came back to me, and my resolve to find my grandmother came with it. If we were facing this, here, who knew what she was going through out there, alone in her apartment. The housing project she lived in was not the safest place I'd ever seen on a good day. What it was like now, with all the power out and all the chaos the storm had brought, I couldn't even imagine.

I slowly extracted myself from Jaden's arms, and from between him and the boy. I didn't see how I would get all of us out to Gravesend. Where had my resolve to help people here gone? It had disappeared when I saw the reality of the place. I guess in my head, it had been some clean little emergency room, and I'd been wearing a candy striper uniform. Numptie, I was always such a goddamn numptie.

I stood up straight. Jaden would know where I went. And he would be there to watch the boy until I came back. I wished I could say goodbye, in case things went wrong, in case we never saw each other again. Then I realized that I could. I leaned down and kissed him on the forehead as gently as I could. Jaden smiled in his sleep, but, other than that, didn't stir. I quietly made my way to the door. A wave of tenderness washed through me seeing the same smile that had been making me happy for years. That smile was for me now, just for me, and maybe I was phrenic to leave it behind.

There were more people out there than there had been when we came in. I could barely walk down the hall for all the people. I fit my combat boots into spaces around the edges of mats and blankets. I passed by a man who was lying on the ground, restrained in zip ties. He squirmed toward me as I walked by, and I tried to look cool while I was getting away from him, but it was impossible not to jump and scamper. I passed by a nook off the hallway filled with shit and piss. The two were running in a puddle toward the rest of the hall. The smell was 'trosh.

"Hello?" I called into a room. I was looking for someone upswing, someone who might help me figure out a way out of there and to Gravesend.

I peeked inside the room. There were people huddled up all over it. As I looked around, I realized that the people I saw around me in the emergency shelter were the people I had thought were disappearing from the neighborhood. The people I had known the whole time I lived there. We were still there, it seemed, and in some fucked-up irony, we were the ones who had stayed after all. Well, here was the old neighborhood I'd been looking for. Here were the people. And all it took was a natural disaster hitting and everyone forgetting about us to bring us back out.

Taking a deep breath, I went back into the hall and made my way into another classroom. This one had fewer people in it, but it also had a stench that wasn't shit and wasn't piss and wasn't old food. It was death. These weren't just the bodies of living people huddled around on the floor, they were people who'd checked. I looked over in one corner and thought I saw motion under one of the blankets. What living person would stay in this room, I wondered, with all this death? Then I saw the blanket fall away and saw that there were two huge rats gnawing away at one of the bodies. I saw the light flash in the rats' eyes as I jumped back, pulling the door shut behind me.

After looking inside a few more classrooms, I finally found one filled with people in army fatigues. They seemed to have set up in there, with glowing wristscreens and boxes of water and slurree. I tried to turn the handle on the door to get in, but it was locked. I knocked.

At first they ignored me. But I kept knocking. And knocking. Finally a man with a handlebar mustache and a cap over his brown hair came to the door.

"What?" he practically yelled in my face.

"I need help," I said.

"You all need help," he replied, and went to close the door again.

"No, I need help getting out of here," I said, jamming my leg in the door so that he couldn't close it. For a minute he tried to anyway, and I felt pain in my thigh and calf. "I need your help."

"Nobody's getting anywhere," he said. "Not until the water goes down."

"My grandmother is all alone out in Gravesend," I said. "I know this storm must have hit hardest out there. You've got to help me get to her."

He laughed derisively, but he had stopped trying to close the door on me. "Nobody's going anywhere."

I pulled my leg out from the door. He slammed it behind me and I heard the lock click into place. Sure enough, when I tried to turn the knob again, the door was locked.

"Motherfucker!" I screamed, slapping the door with my hands. One of the soldiers inside turned his eyes to the door, but that was it. Much as I yelled and hit it, the rest of them didn't even bother looking at me. I was going to have to find another way.

I made my way through the halls back out to the landing we'd come up on when we first entered the building. Maybe if I waited there long enough, someone would come along who would help me.

At first it was just more soldiers, and though a few were kind, most were as dismissive as the ones inside had been. My stomach grumbled as I sat there waiting. I didn't want to go inside to try to find slurree for fear I'd miss someone who would help me. I kept thinking of my dream, of my grandmother lying there with a hole in her head. How did I know that someone hadn't attacked her, broken into her place already, and that was what was waiting for me out there? I tried to tell myself that she had survived a lot in her time. But it didn't help me overcome the fear that the dream had put in me. As I stood there, I started biting the little bit of fingernails that had grown back since the last time I'd bitten them all down.

Finally, a man who wasn't in fatigues came along in a boat with several people in it. He wore a truck driver's cap, and old, paint-splattered blue jeans. He had on a flannel shirt with a puffy black vest over it.

"Hey," I said, as he was leaving people off at the stairwell. "I need your help."

"That's what I'm doing," he said, almost cheerfully. Disaster brings out the best in some people, I guess. This guy seemed thrilled to be piloting around in this boat bringing people to and from the shelter. I guess he hadn't seen what he was bringing them to.

"I need to get out to Gravesend," I said. "My grandmother's out there."

"That's where I'm from," he said. "It's a disaster out there. Houses destroyed, blown away, trees through them. Won't get rebuilt for a long, long time. I hope she's okay."

"She's up in a high-rise," I said. "I need to get out there and bring her back. I can pay you. Not much, but I can give you something for helping me."

"Don't worry about it," he said. "Just get in. We'll see if we can bring her back here."

I got in the boat after the people who were already in it got out. The man's name was Peter, he said. I looked at his clothes, then down at mine. His looked a thousand times cleaner. I wondered when I would be able to change mine. Then I thought of my basement apartment with everything packed up in boxes. That was the first moment it hit me. It was all gone. Everything was gone. I sat down in the boat.

"Where in Gravesend are we going?" asked Peter.

"Far Gravesend," I said. "The Ocean Way Apartments."

We went along the water with his boat churning up water behind us. We went down long corridors of what were once streets, but now felt like canals. We could have been in a picture I once saw of Venice in a book, if everything didn't look so broken down and destroyed. Buildings loomed up on either side of us, their windows looking dark and haunted. Many were broken, and I thought back to the winds and rain just a few nights before. Now, with the sun shining through the cold air, it was hard to believe that night had ever happened. But all around us was evidence that it had.

Peter kept up a steady stream of words about the things he had seen, but I didn't talk. I sat back in the boat and tried not to see what was around me. I tried to be in the sun, in the reflection of it on the water, away from the hard metal on the bottom of the boat. I leaned back and closed my eyes. The rumbling of my stomach kept me from disappearing inside my head.

Then, through my closed eyes, I could tell that the light had gone away. I opened my eyes, and we were going down an alley between two high buildings. The alley was dark and floating all around us was garbage and shit.

"What's going on?" I asked. "Why are we here?"

Peter cut the engine on the boat. He walked toward me, the smile still on his face. It was a wide smile, one I had not noticed before was not just kind and helpful. It was a bit wild. I suddenly felt like such a numptie, thinking this guy was upswing.

"Remember you said you wanted to pay me?" he asked. "To give me something?"

I saw where it was going right away. But all around me was filthy water. He had positioned the boat so that we weren't even near any fire escapes.

"Stay away from me," I said. For the tenth time I cursed myself for not having a weapon. I'd even left the stupid tape-wrapped ruler in the school room.

"Nothing much, don't worry," he said. He was coming closer, and his hand was reaching for his zipper.

Where was I supposed to go?

PART TWO

EVANN—NOVEMBER

1 It was getting late in the day, but I couldn't make myself get out of bed. Even as my wristscreen lit up with messages from my dad. Even as my Cavachon, Pollock, stood next to the bed whining those little whines that broke my heart. He wanted to go out so badly, but I couldn't get up. I looked at his little brown-and-white face, practically a teddy bear's face, but I *still* couldn't get out of bed. Bernice was coming and I couldn't make myself do anything at all to prepare.

I had to get in a car soon to go to my dad's in-state compound. I knew. I *knew*. But, like a lot of days, I couldn't make myself do anything.

Where are you?
What are you still doing in the city?

My dad's messages kept lighting up the screen as I reached down to scratch Pollock behind the ears. He made tiny grunts of pleasure and for a second I felt a little less guilty about making him wait to walk.

My dad worries about me a lot, like I'm a child or something. Actually, when I was younger, he was even worse. I remember when we first moved to New York. There were neighborhoods that my dad told me not to go to, ever. He said that the kind of people who lived there would take one look at my clothes, my shoes, my hair and kill or rape me or something. I remember those days. Once, when I was thirteen, because I thought my dad was wrong and everywhere was good and everybody was equal, I went to one of those places on the subway. I got off the train and smelled urine. There was this guy pissing, just pissing in a corner where the doorway was. I looked over and caught a glimpse of his cock, and it wasn't even studded with pearls like anybody who has any bodmods has. I ran away. I couldn't believe any of it. That people lived that way. And I didn't think my dad was *right*, necessarily, that these people were all bad, but I realized he was right that there were places I shouldn't go.

But the nice thing was that the older I got, the more those places disappeared. The whole city became nice, and clean, and everywhere around me crummy old buildings started getting ripped down and new, *remarquable* buildings, the kind with swimming pools on the roof and *magnifique* doormen, went up. The poor people went away. I didn't know where they went, but I guess things must have gotten better for them. You didn't have to feel bad about people asking you for money on the street when you were just out trying to have a good time with your friends. There were never any of those awkward moments when you didn't know if someone was homeless or just dressed way down—they were just dressed way down, ten times out of ten. I was so happy that the city had cleaned up, and the homeless shelters weren't full, and everything was good for everybody who lived there. That's progress.

I wasn't thinking about progress, though, as I got ready for the storm to hit. A lot of things were going through my head as I lay in bed, with Pollock whining, breaking my heart. The city hadn't progressed much in a way that could combat the storms. All of us knew to get out, most of us had places to go. The ones who didn't, I felt bad, but I didn't feel that bad. I mean, when the last storm hit, I felt this twinge because my friends from the city and I went to my dad's in-state compound and had a *fabuleux* time, weathering the storm, drinking mojitos, doing move. I felt kind of bad, later, having had a party when people were suffering. But people who stayed in the city were doing the same thing. When I got back I asked the guy who does my laundry what he had done, and he said, "Had a storm party." We talked for a while. I talk to everybody, I'm just that kind of person. And his party wasn't so much different than ours—drinking, drugs. The only difference was that he had stayed, and we had left. I *still* felt a little bad, though, when I realized that things had been a little worse than I'd thought they would be. I gave one of my paintings to an auction for charity. It was a painting that I loved, too, but I felt good helping people who had less.

I'd *tried* to get ready for Bernice, throwing things in boxes that I would have driven in-state with me. Then I thought back to the second storm, Maxwell, that had happened after I bought my little apartment in the Lower East Side. That's when I laid down.

My apartment is the dream space I've always wanted to have since I moved to New York. It's a *beau* ground-floor two-bedroom in a historic building. It's just so quaint that I couldn't resist buying it when it came up for sale. My dad said it wasn't the greatest investment, that I should have got myself a condo in a newer building, or a place in somewhere up-and-coming, like Allentown. But that's totally hypocritical, because he invests in these buildings all the way out in Brooklyn, which he says are safe because they're so far in. But, anyway, this building that I bought my apartment in had this brown brick facade, and a big kitchen that I redid (not that I cook a lot, but I'm always hoping that someday I'll meet someone who does), and two bedrooms with windows that let in the morning sun and open into this raggedy little garden below that all the neighbors are crazy for and take care of like we're in the suburbs or something. It's so cute and quaint.

The first storm when I lived there, Fiona, wasn't so bad. Water got in a bit to the basement, and the apartment owners had to have the mold it caused professionally removed. So I didn't think that when Maxwell hit there would be much more damage besides that. I was wrong. Water got into the ground floor and ruined a lot of my things. The antique mahogany headboard on my bed that had belonged to my grandparents got waterlogged and warped. It was really sad because it was the first gift my grandfather had bought my grandmother when he got his first real job that actually paid him more than what he needed to live on. I had wanted to keep it forever, then give it to my kids. But it got destroyed. The same thing happened to my all-organic-material mattress. I had taken the rare books I collect off the bottom few shelves of the bookcase in my living room and placed them in boxes up higher, but the water had still risen high enough to destroy my signed first-edition *Fountainhead* and some of my first-edition lithograph books. And, worst of all, it traveled far enough up the wall to damage the Basquiat my dad bought me as my first serious piece of art when I graduated from Parsons. I loved that painting so much. It was the first thing that ever made me feel full. When my dad gave it to me, this kind of *whatever* feeling I have a lot of the time disappeared in this wave of color and emotion. It was so bold, so jagged, that I couldn't help but feel so much. That's the way it's been every time I get a new piece of art, but never quite like that first time. God, I love Basquiat. I kept kicking myself for not taking it out of the apartment, but it was my home, you know, my home. I didn't think something that bad could happen in my very own home. I laid there thinking of that painting, how beautiful and irreplaceable it had been, and how it was gone now. I started to cry a little. That's when Pollock started to cry, too. He's very attuned to my feelings. Sometimes even more than I am, I think. He pressed his wet nose against me, digging it into my arm, my armpit, my cheek, as I lay in bed crying.

The parties in-state stopped after that storm. When my friends and I saw each other back in the city after Maxwell, we all wondered the same things. Why were we staying there? Why were we hanging on to this city that was falling into the ocean? There were so many other places we could be. And, sure, New York City had always been a mecca of arts and fashion and food and *magnifique* things, but the more storms hit, the less it was. One of my favorite restaurants, this little place with brick walls and old oak tables and waiters who are about a hundred years old each, closed up because of storm damage, and the last I heard their chef had opened a place inland in *New Jersey*, because he said it was a safer bet.

I had learned my lesson during Maxwell, and was going to get most of what was valuable out with me. The things that really mattered most: my paintings, my more expensive clothes, things I couldn't stand the thought of losing, or that wouldn't be okay if they got wet.

I started to get frustrated as I went along packing. I don't have a great attention span because of my ADHD, and I couldn't get my prescription filled again this month because of all the business types who use the drugs to work long hours. I laid down, feeling overwhelmed, and I didn't get back up.

Finally, Pollock's cries were just too much to bear. I think that's why my dad got him for me. I can tend toward the depressive side (my dad calls it ennui), so sometimes I think he bought me Pollock so I'd have to get out of bed. It never fails. I love that dog, and I'd never let him go too long being hungry, or thirsty, or having to use the bathroom. So finally, I stood up, got his leash, and called someone to come and pack my boxes for me. I'm so fortunate that there are services for everything in New York these days.

So Pollock and I had a bit of free time before we had to leave the city, and I tried to think to myself what I'd really like to do with that little bit of time. I would walk Pollock, of course. But also, I'm not so far from Brooklyn, and the car services hadn't closed down yet in preparation for the storm. So I figured we would take one out to Brooklyn, to see Basquiat. Pollock would take a walk in Green-Wood.

The first time I went to see Basquiat was kind of a disaster. It was before I had Pollock, so I was all alone. Basquiat's buried out in Green-Wood Cemetery in Brooklyn, which, if you don't know, is the biggest, oldest, richest cemetery in the city. I mean, there are huge monuments all over the place, mausoleums bigger and nicer than some people's apartments, *beau* flowering trees in the springtime—the whole place is like a *magnifique* park, but with dead people. It's where I'd like to be buried, someday, and have people walking around enjoying themselves, having picnics near me.

I thought it would be nice walking around Green-Wood looking for his grave, but even with a map, I got terribly lost. My wristscreen decided to update, so I didn't have it to guide me for about twenty-five minutes. By that time, I had walked in a huge circle and was back at the front gate, this huge castle-like brown brick structure. I gave up, really sad, because I love Basquiat and everything about him, and I had just wanted to see him and I'd failed.

But it was almost like that failure was meant to be. I went back again, a few weeks later. This time I was less stressed out about finding his grave and thought, even if I don't, I'll just walk around thinking about him. And that's what I did. I thought about how cold and alone he must have felt, sleeping in Tompkins Square Park when he was a teenager, but also how it must have been okay, because even then he must have known how great he was and that it was just a matter of time until everyone else saw it, too. I thought of him alone, at night, in a hospital bed, looking at the copy of *Gray's Anatomy* his mother gave him after he was in that terrible car accident. Then I began to think of his mother— how she had gone crazy, been institutionalized, when he was just a kid. It made me think of my own mom, who had died when I was very young. I knew him in that moment, I swear, even though there are all these *obvious* differences between us, I knew what that pain of losing a mom was. I stopped and looked around me. I was under a bough of a cherry tree, on a path lined with them. I swear, right then, I knew Basquiat.

I looked down at the map I was carrying, and realized I had been walking on the right path, not as some silly metaphor or anything, but really, truly walking the right way to find him. I would be there soon.

Finding his grave was hard in a lot of ways. I thought it

would be one of the huge *fabuleux* ones, one of the obelisks that reached to the sky, or a stern angel. But no. I searched and searched the general vicinity on the map before it suddenly dawned on me—the row of low, square, plain graves that looked like pauper graves—that's what marked this man who had so obviously loomed above all the other people buried here.

I started to cry a little. As I walked down the row of inconsequential graves, I spotted one that appeared to be covered in garbage. The sobbing came full-on when I realized it was his.

For a minute, the tears blurred my vision as I thought, *This is it. You live your life in the hugest way, you make the most* magnifique *art, and this is the way it ends. Under a pauper's grave somewhere, covered in trash.* But then my eyes cleared, I saw the little items on the grave had all been placed there so lovingly. A cigarette, a paintbrush, a piece of malachite, a paper with a crude crown drawn on it that said SAMO underneath. I wondered about all the of the people who had come looking as I had come looking, who had left here all these little garbage-treasures of theirs as an offering after walking the path to the grave, and maybe even understanding him as I did. The tears started again.

I almost started crying then, on my way there in the car with Pollock, as the storm was about to descend on New York, thinking about it. But I pulled myself together. I patted Pollock's soft fur. My therapist often says that I should pick him up when I'm sad because touch is a wonderful antidepressant. I patted him and looked at his soft brown eyes. And I started talking to the driver.

"Where will you go?" I said.

"Excuse me?" he said, turning down the radio.

"I'm sorry to pry," I said, "but I talk to everybody, just about everybody. Where will you go when the storm hits?"

"I don't live here in the city," the driver said. I peered at the license in a plastic sheath on the rear of his seat. His name was Hameen. His English was slightly broken, but my wrist-screen was translating what he said onto the screen so I'd have no difficulty understanding. "So I will go home."

"Where do you live?" I asked.

"Out in New Jersey, about an hour away. I drive to the city every day, then drive people around all day, then I drive back. Then I drive my children to their sports, then I drive my wife to her work. It seems like I live behind a car wheel sometimes."

"You'll be safe there?" I asked. Pollock was making low noises of happiness as I scratched behind his ears.

"The storm shouldn't hit us too hard. Things are safer out there in many ways. When I was younger, people were afraid. There were so many reasons, they sometimes wouldn't get in my car, they called me names, they did not like my name, or where I was from. But ... things have changed a bit for us. My children are safer, now, than I was."

"Things do get better," I said, sitting back. And it was nice, that this man believed that, too, after what he'd been through. The Water Wars have given us so many immigrants that it's hard to believe that, even when he was younger, things were that bad. I mean, people should be *used* to people coming over. I thought for a second, *maybe I should start a nonprofit for these issues.* Then I thought of what he said, that his children were safe out in New Jersey, playing sports and having fun even. Things always get better, they have to. Pollock yipped once, as if in agreement.

We got closer to Green-Wood. Normally, I walk to Basquiat's grave from the main entrance, which is through the entire cemetery. I like experiences. But today, I had the driver take me to the entrance nearest where he's buried. It would be a brief walk for Pollock, but there was really no time for strolling through the whole place.

I handed the driver an extra twenty dollars and asked him to stay put until we came back out. I hurried to that little gravestone nestled in the row of people he was so much greater than, Pollock running to keep up. The wind had blown a lot of the little gifts people left behind off the top of the grave. I knelt by the stone, my hand on the ground. I could almost feel the greatness his poor body had contained radiating out of the ground. Pollock was pulling at his leash.

I always struggle with what to say when I get there. Usually I just end up thanking him and going, but this time felt different. I felt like I might never be back. I cried a little, for the first time since initially finding the grave. Still, I could not figure out any words that would match what I felt for him, for his art, for the life he had lived.

I took a hundred dollars out of my purse and put it on top of the headstone with a little rock holding it down so the wind wouldn't blow it away. I do that every time I come. Maybe someone who was so much like him will show up one day and need it. I wondered if they would take it, a person standing there with nothing, but feeling it had been left as a tribute to him. Probably it just blows away, eventually, every time.

PART THREE

JESSE—NOVEMBER

1 In my dreams, we were huddled up in the zero-degree sleeping bag, back in the squat. The fire was burning in the oil drum, bright as a thousand mother-fuckers, warm like summer on a beach. Lux and I had our hands up against each other in the dim light, just fucking around, measuring them against each other, wishing out loud that we could switch.

I was just settling into the warmth and the serenity of that scene when the shit-ass douche-jockey nurse woke me up. Me, José, and Sebastian were not in the squat in the old IRT station, but the dark-as-fuck lobby of the hellhole hospital we'd dragged Lux to, nodding out from the pills we'd taken. We were all covered in her blood from lifting her body off the street and dragging it there while she moaned this horror-film death-rattle moan that scared the nut sacks off of us.

The nurse's mouth was in a hard line, and the circles under her eyes were dark. She shook me fully awake roughly.

"Your friend," she said.

"Yeah? What's happening?" I mumbled.

"She's not in great shape," she said. "She's lost a lot of

blood. We should airlift her out of here first thing when a helicopter comes, but even if we do . . ."

"Is she going to live?" I asked.

She looked at me hard then. The pompous ass-herpe of a jerk looked me up and down in that way that makes you want to puke all over someone. She took in my dirty, patched-up clothes stitched together with dental floss, my black eye makeup, my nodding-off slouch. I had my coat off, and her eyes didn't miss the scars up my arms from when I lived in a shitty abusive house in a fucked-up little town and cut myself over and over to get my head out of there for fifteen seconds.

"There are a lot of people here who are clinging to life for everything they're worth," she said. Her mouth was still in that hard line, like she smelled something terrible. "There isn't a lot of room on the helicopter. So I'm going to ask you something. Does your friend want to live? Or would it be better just to let her never wake up?"

2 I woke up in a cold-as-tits sweat, even though I was wrapped up in Lux's zero-degree sleeping bag and was right next to the woodstove. It was the middle of the night, and the twins were unconscious nearby. It was still dark outside, and it was dark as pig shit inside the abandoned elevated IRT station. The only light was from the dying embers of the fire. They were still giving off the heat of being chased by fifty cob rollers, but wouldn't be for much longer. I got up out of my sleeping bag and walked to where we'd, months ago, stockpiled wood from construction sites along one of

the walls of the station. The night was cold away from the fire, but it could have been worse. Years ago, we wouldn't have been able to be out here at all. But I barely remember those years. I quickly took a couple of square scrap pieces, ran back, and threw them into the drum. I blew on the embers, the boards blackened then caught, and soon the fire was blazing harder than a neo-Nazi at a white supremacist rally again.

I had been having dreams that had made me toss and turn and sweat. We'd been back in the hospital. José and Sebastian had been nodding out on the Valium I'd given them and were in the wrecked waiting room, no goddamn use at all. The lights were out, and nurses and doctors were running from place to place. People were moaning on gurneys. Machines were running, on backup power, in the dark. I was trying to find Lux. Where the fuck could she be? I looked in rooms with dying people, dead people. I tore blankets off of corpses, looking to see if she was underneath. But I couldn't find her. Finally a nurse grabbed me.

"Does your friend want to live?" she'd said. She said it flat, like a robot in an old sci-fi movie.

In the dream, my voice had frozen. I tried to say *yes*, but I couldn't say anything. She waited there, and I struggled to make words, a voiceless animal. I couldn't make any words come. I knew Lux's life was dependent upon what I said, but no matter how hard I tried, I could not make any sound come out of my mouth.

That's when I woke up.

Every other night or so I have these nightmares, sometimes less. Sometimes I fall asleep, wake up from a nightmare, fall back asleep and have another one. I wonder sometimes if they'll ever go away. Trauma. It's a motherfucker.

In the dark, I tried not to think about Lux. I tried not to

think about the sleeping bag that I wrapped myself up in, which used to be hers. I tried not to think about if she was alive or dead. I tried not to think.

I stood up again and walked over to one of the walls that ran down from the opening of the station to the far-back where we were set up. Several plastic shopping bags with handles hung from nails we'd driven into the wall. It had been a dirt-ass bitch finding them, no place still uses them, but we'd needed them because they were so easy to hang and seal. I pulled down the one closest to the opening of the station and rummaged around in it for a while before finding a small chocolate bar amid the other food stored in there. Keeping the bags up off the floor like that kept the rats out of them, and keeping them tied shut kept out the bugs. Underneath where the bags hung were our cans of food, and, even though it was dark, I knew exactly where the peaches in heavy syrup were. The chocolate was going to taste great with the peaches, and the Xanax in my pocket. Breakfast of motherfucking champions.

Shivering, I hustled back toward the fire and dumped my breakfast there. The fire began to warm me right away, and I felt like never moving from in front of it again. My bladder was fuller than if I'd drank five forties, but luckily, the piss bottles were right there, and José and Sebastian were sleeping. So I pulled down my pants and squatted over the one with the top cut off and let go. I didn't have to shit yet, which was great, because it was a crotch-ugly sand-fuck to carry the newspaper I did it in down to the street and out of the squat when it was this cold.

Moving the piss bottle off to the side, I pulled my pants back up and sat down in front of the fire. The concrete floor was icy, and I could hear at least one big rat moving around down in the gully that cuts through the station, where the train used to run a long time ago. I've definitely lived in worse places than this. In fact, with the oil drum woodstove, all the food we started stockpiling long before the storm, the warm sleeping bags, the set of cooking pots and pans we found in the trash, the alcohol stove that Sebastian built out of a beer can and a large coffee can, and the bottles of rubbing alcohol that we'd lucked into before the storm when a supply truck was unloading at a pharmacy, I'd say it's a pretty good place to live. Well, it was a pretty good place to live when we were all here.

It had been a few weeks since the storm, less than that since the night Lux disappeared. We'd been ready for the storm. The moment we heard it was coming, we raided the richest neighborhoods only, dumpstering outside the best grocery stores until we had enough food to last us for months. Good food, too, cans that were maybe a little dented, boxes that were just a little raggedy-ass, but good stuff. We got a stack of five-gallon bottles of water. We took the money that Lux had made dumpstering and reselling the barely used electronics that people in this town are always tossing out and bought her enough hormones to get through a while and the rest of us enough Olde English 40s to last a week. Or a couple of days. Or maybe two really wild nights. In any case, we were toasting with the booze and congratulating ourselves when the storm came.

It was more novocaine than hurricane. A lot of water blew in the open end of the station and pooled in the gully where the tracks used to be, but we were far back and stayed mostly dry. There was no power in the station, so we couldn't freak ourselves out watching the news or anything. Lux kept bugging out because she was worried that her pile of Mixplayers and wristscreens were going to get ruined, which was later kind of funny, but not in a laughing kind of way, because they stayed dry and the whole city got ruined. But we hung out and drank malt liquor, and I tried to play guitar and sing this really old song by this guy who's been dead forever, Woody Guthrie. I learned it from some traveler kid when I was moving around more. But I kept fucking it up because I was drunk and José yelled at me the third time I tried to sing it, said I had a shit voice, and I couldn't play guitar. So Lux glared at him and picked up the guitar and said, "I dare you, you piece of shit, to make fun of my voice." And then she sang it, and I sang along. Her voice sounded fucking great. I knew her when it was different. She'd worked a lot to change it, to make it more what she wanted it to be. We sang together, and laughed, and José and Sebastian laughed, too; we weren't really mad at José anyway.

Sitting in the station, I remembered her voice singing. Breathy and soft and beautiful. "My brothers and my sisters are stranded on this road, a hot and dusty road that a million feet have trod; Rich man took my home and drove me from my door, and I ain't got no home in this world anymore." I missed her voice singing and laughing and echoing through the station.

Lux. Fuck. Where were those fucking Xanax?

I pulled the lid off the can of peaches and swallowed a few pills with the syrup. Then I ripped open the foil on my chocolate bar and started to eat it. Slowly, a bit at a time, smelling it and letting it melt on my tongue. A few feet away one of the twins (I couldn't tell which one in the dark), moaned in his sleep. Maybe he was dreaming about Lux, too.

I'd met her in the middle of a riot. It was a global summit in Chicago, the kind they have where a handful of first world leaders meet up and decide what they're going to do about the rest of the world, how money is going to be spent, if they should forgive debt and let other countries put their money into fighting their AIDS epidemics and famines. I hate that sort of horseshit on principle, a bunch of fuck-ass old white men in suits sitting around in a room and calling the shots about who lives and who dies, all with a dollar bottom line. So there I'd been, all in black, with a hood up over my head, a bandana over my face, and a hammer in my hand, surrounded by hundreds of people who looked exactly the same. If we were real with ourselves, we would have admitted that the tactic hadn't worked in decades, no matter how many of us were there, no matter how many Molotov cocktails we threw. No one had stopped one of these meetings since last century. They'd been ready for us every time since then. But we were still out there in the streets, and as I swung my hammer through the front door of a 24/7, I thought, *We won't stop them, but at least they'll see our rage.*

All around me, there was the smashing of glass. When I turned back around and looked in the crowd, I could see that the cops were firing something at us, probably rubber bullets. A sound cannon was blasting through the air. People were running away, and pepper spray was being fired off at their receding figures. I looked to my left and saw a kid up on the roof of a cop car, and then, as he jumped off, I saw flames coming up from it. I looked down and saw this tall, skinny girl curled up in a ball at my feet. She was wearing Doc Martens and this thin, tight, pretty hoodie that barely covered her head all the way. She was kind of queer and punky looking, she had shoulder-length blond hair that looked like she had grown it out from a short cut and never had it evened out. I knelt down next to her.

"Are you okay?" I shouted.

She was hyperventilating. "I'm going to die," she said, in between breaths. "I'm going to die."

It was pretty clear to me that she was having a panic attack. I leaned in closer.

"Deep breaths," I said. I put my hand on my diaphragm. "Breathe from here."

She was gasping, but she did as I told her. I reached back under my hood and pulled the rubber band off of my black hair. It fell all around my face as I reached down and slipped the hair tie over her wrist.

"Snap this against your skin," I said. "It'll focus the pain on one spot. Just do it like this." I pulled the band back as far as it would go and let it hit hard against the skin of her wrist. She winced, then reached her hand up and did it again.

"Keep breathing," I said.

All around us, the bodies in black were swirling and smashing. Everything was loud, everything was broken. We were a little oasis in the middle. People were stepping around us. The police were far away, we were safe from them for the moment, but the line of them was always moving closer. I tried to judge the time we had left before I'd have to run to get the fuck out of there, whether this girl could stand or not. But when I looked down again to the girl, she seemed to be coming out of the ball she'd scrunched up in.

"Is it going to explode?" she asked, looking at the burning cop car.

"It's not like in the movies, I swear," I said. "That fucking sphincter-socket will just burn."

She got up to her knees. I grabbed her hand and pulled her up to her feet. The slightest smile seemed to play on her lips as she looked back at the cop car. I squeezed her hand

and we ran away from the line of riot cops, into the mass of black-clad protesters.

That was how I met Lux. And when I'd come back to New York, I found this station, the perfect place for a squat, and I convinced Lux to ditch the overcrowded punk house she'd been living in in Jersey and come live with me. And it had been good, too. Lux, José, Sebastian, and me, building the place up together, making something like a crew or a family. Only better than my shit-bag family because they were all assholes and fuck them. All of us in the squat looked out for each other, we took care of each other, and that's the most you can really ask for when you're living like we were. It was better than I'd ever thought to ask for.

Nearby, whichever one of the twins had been moving in his sleep started making noise. Scary-ass horror film shit. I dug one of the peaches out of the syrup with my fingers and tried to ignore the creepy sound he was making. It was definitely Sebastian—the light from the fire had grown, and I could see his slightly smaller frame. Not that either he or José was tiny. They were both ripped as fuck, but José more so. Every day he stacked the boards in our woodpile together and lifted them to keep his muscles strong. Every morning, he and Sebastian went running together. Well, some days when Sebastian was hung over, he skipped. But José never did.

I had never thought those two would come out here and live with us. They weren't squatters, they weren't punk at all, they lived with their family who was a little crazy but pretty close and all, they went to the last community college left in the city and got good grades. Straight-up upstanding moth-erfuckers, even though I knew them from radical politics. Good kids. Not who you expect to be living in squalor in an abandoned train station. But about two weeks after Lux and I started gathering things for the squat, they left their house. I didn't know it, but it had been a long time coming. Their mother and father had brought them into the country without legal documentation about five years before. With the new immigration laws that had been passed, the two of them could have become citizens if they turned their parents in. They became activists instead. They left home to protect their family from the scrutiny they were sure they were bringing on them.

I'd met them years before at a May Day march planning meeting. Meetings, especially ones for big marches, can be so fucking balls-biscuit stupid. I was giving the permit committee shit about us not needing a permit at all, and everyone was really annoyed, except for José, who thought I was funny and made Sebastian come get stoned with me in Tompkins Square Park later. I've seen them in meetings and at activist houses way out at the edges of the city for years since then, on trips I took here before I settled down in the station. When they said they needed a place to stay, I thought about it for a minute. Like I said, they didn't seem like the type I'd expected to be living with up there. They were friends and all, but I kind of didn't want them around. But Lux said, *good people help good people.* If there was anything I wanted Lux to think about me, it was that I was a good person. I wasn't always. I'm not. But she had this kind way that I don't know how she'd never lost with all she's been through that made me want to be kind, too. So we let them stay.

We all lived together in the months before Bernice. It was kind of a weird-ass arrangement. The twins woke up early every morning to go running while I slept until noontime. When I did get up, it was to chug dumpstered coconut water to get rid of my hangover. Lux disappeared for hours every day, searching out the garbage cans of rich people so she could scrounge up last year's wristscreens and computers. It was stuff that wasn't good enough for these rich people anymore, but which Lux listed on message boards out in Jersey and sold to people who weren't rich. She gave them good deals, most of the time, and sometimes she just straight up gave them the stuff because she'd get to the meeting point and there would be a middle-aged couple who didn't speak any English and their kid whose eyes lit up like a pinball machine when they saw whatever she'd dug out of the trash. José kept telling her she couldn't do it, that we needed the money, so she said, "Go ahead, *you* go out there and get this stuff out of the trash, *you* figure out what's good and what isn't, and then *you* can tell me what to give to who." I knew, and José knew, that the toughness was partly an act, but when a really nice person gives you a hard time, it often shuts you up more than when an asshole does.

The peach syrup was dripping off my fingers, so I flicked them toward the fire and listened to the moisture sizzle and disappear in the flames. Next to me, Sebastian's moaning turned into coughing. Real, heavy-duty coughing that was shaking his body. I shook the rest of the syrup off my hands and turned around just in time to see him raise his body up and power puke across the ground. I jumped back, pulling Lux's sleeping bag with me.

"Sebastian?" I said. I stepped closer, avoiding the vomit. It stunk like an ass blossom. "You take too many pills?"

In response, I just got this quiet sort of wail. I really couldn't tell in the dark, but he might have been really pale, and a little green. I stepped closer to him.

"You okay, man?" I said. The Xanax was starting to make me feel warm and relaxed even as my tension should have been skyrocketing. As it was, I just felt this kind of dreamy spaciness. *Oh, my friend is puking everywhere. Will have to deal with that at some point.* I walked a little closer and knelt down next to him. I put my hand on the back of his neck.

He was burning up with fever. The heat of his skin against my hand warmed me more than the fire had.

"Sebastian?" I said again.

"Jesse? What the fuck?" he murmured. "I feel like shit."

The puddle of vomit was spreading across the floor. I put my hands under Sebastian's armpits and pulled him up and away from it.

"Come on," I said. "Let me move you and get this cleaned up."

I half walked, half dragged Sebastian over to the edge of the platform, where the gully was, so that if he puked again, it would be down there. Then I took one of the jugs of rubbing alcohol and spilled it over the puke, and, with a broom we kept in one of the corners, sluiced it all down into the gully. As I was doing this, José woke up and asked why I was making so much noise.

"Your brother is sick," I said. "Wake the fuck up."

I was really goddamn pissed off that I had to deal with this. But I went over to the food area and grabbed one of the few bottles of coconut water I still had and brought it over to Sebastian.

"Drink this," I said. I knelt down and put one hand behind his head and brought the other, holding the bottle, up to his lips. He took little sips and immediately puked them back up, down into the gully. José was next to him now, looking alarmed. We all care about each other a lot, okay, even if I was pissed, I still did care. But I've never seen anybody care about each other like José and Sebastian do. Right then, José had this look on his face like he was the one projectile vomiting everywhere.

"Sebastian? Bash?" José said. "What's going on?"

"So ... fucking ... sick," Sebastian managed, curling deeper into a ball.

José looked up at me, pleading in his eyes. "What do we do?"

"I don't know," I said. Around me the empty station felt hollow and enormous. Beyond that, the city felt feral and dangerous. And here we were, with a sick comrade, and no one to help. Even the hospitals, which had been a nightmare when we'd had to take Lux, were abandoned now. "I have no fucking idea."

3 Before the storm, when Lux and I used to walk down the street together, I mostly gave everyone dirty looks. I was never sure if they were staring at me or her, gawking with their mouths open. For a while, it looked like things were going to get better for people like us, or so I'm told. I mean, the laws are there—they can't technically refuse us health care or fire us from jobs. But what about people like us, people who could never afford health care, people who wouldn't even be allowed in the door for the job interview? That's a lot of us. And the violence has gotten worse and worse. The people who hate us shoot up clubs, they shoot our sisters, TWOC get beaten to death every dirt-ass shit-fucking day walking down the street. I've never done sex work, but most of the trans kids I've ever met will fuck for a bed to sleep in on a rainy night. The ones who don't get murdered get so worn

down by living in a world that wants them to stop existing that they do the bigots a favor and save them literal blood on their hands by offing themselves.

So we'd walk down the street in our dirty clothes, with my jailhouse tattoos, looking filthy and fucked-up, and people would stare. I was never sure at who. Sometimes I barked at them, not, like, snapped or yelled, but actually barked. And most people, when they see some amorphously gendered crusty street punk growling and snarling at them, stop staring. They walk away.

Some people don't. They're the ones you have to worry about.

I got read all different kinds of ways. Butchy lesbian. Young dude. All-around freak. It was complicated, even for me. I hated the facial hair that I grew because I'm naturally disposed toward it, but I also bound my breasts and hated menstruating. I wore men's clothes, and women's clothes, and so much eyeliner that sometimes Lux called me "the punk raccoon." Lux got read as a woman, except by people who were assholes, who would rather look at things like her barely noticeable Adam's apple, the fact that she sometimes had some facial hair that she didn't have the money to get lasered off.

That was all before the storm, when we were walking around this New York City that didn't want people like us anymore—poor people, non-socially-acceptable gender-fucking people, radicals. Lux was from Jersey, so, at least geographically, living here wasn't too far a stretch of the imagination for her. But me, I'd been all around the country, to every city you could imagine. The small towns were like death for me—not even figuratively, because once in West Virginia, I'd had a bunch of ass-douche bros chase me down the street with a baseball bat. The big cities, a lot of them were good to disappear into, but it was New York that I really loved. I guess I fell in love with it this one Christmas before I'd met Lux or José or Sebastian. I was fifteen and I'd just left my shitty, abusive home, I was traveling around with these dudes who were older than me, and we got to New York, and they had a place to stay, but they said I couldn't come, and suddenly I wasn't traveling with anybody anymore. I was by myself. The city was empty, because, as I later found out, the city's always empty on Christmas when everybody who wasn't born here goes away to their families and lots of the people whose families are here go away on skiing vacations and shit like that. All those rich people were gone, and I didn't have to watch them scurrying around the streets with their little dogs in bags, and their purses that cost more than anything I've ever owned in my life, and their shoes from Milan and Paris. It started to snow, which never happens anymore, and I was walking down a street in Chelsea, and there were all these lights in windows, and nobody but the people who came in from out of town to work, and even they were closing things up and going back to where they came from. And I (just a kid, remember, and probably not nearly as cynical as I am now) felt like I was in this perfect snow globe or something. Everywhere I walked there was something beautiful to see, buildings and bookstores, and museums. The sun set down a long street, glowing behind the snow clouds, and the river glistened at the end of the street, and I thought, I could just stay here forever.

New York would be great, if it weren't for all the assholes that live in it.

After wandering the United States for years and always coming back to the city again and again, I'd finally found that abandoned station. And suddenly it was like I could have a place here. It had to be somewhere that nobody else wanted, and by that time, mostly everyone who lived on the streets had been shipped out with one-way bus tickets provided by the city government.

The first couple of days after the storm had been almost a relief. Once the water receded, the streets were empty. There was no one to harass us. We raided a pharmacy for drugs and more hormones for Lux. We raided corner stores for booze and we holed up in our little abandoned station home and drank and got high and played guitar and one night Lux and I made out and then the next day we pretended that nothing had ever happened and went back to being friends until we made out again a couple of days later, then forgot about it again.

Those post-storm days weren't bad. Until the night when they were. The night that we ended up in the nightmare hospital and Lux was gone, maybe forever.

Things seemed pretty scary again when Sebastian got sick. José and I kept trying to get him to drink water, and he kept throwing it up. He had really bad diarrhea, too, and even though I kept trying to clean out the bucket he was shitting into with lime, the whole place stunk like death. I washed my hands with rubbing alcohol every time I touched him or the bucket. José was worried sick and wouldn't leave his side. After the second day of it, we decided we needed to do something.

"You have to go to a pharmacy and try to get some antibiotics," José told me.

"Alone?" I asked. None of us had left the station alone since that night that Lux had disappeared.

"I can't leave him, Jesse," José said. There was a softness

and a pleading in his voice that I don't think I'd ever heard before. He's always so brash and hard-ass; Sebastian is the mellower one.

It was nighttime, and the puking and shitting was getting worse. We were seriously worried about Sebastian making it through the rest of the night. I wanted to help. I was also scared out of my mind to be out in the streets by myself.

"Okay," I said, finally. I leaned down and laced up the boots I always keep untied when I'm walking around the station, and I went over the place where we keep our crowbars. I picked it up and felt its weight in my hand—a great weapon and a useful tool. I grabbed a duffel bag in case I found anything we needed besides the antibiotics. I walked over to the fence that separates the station from the outside world and climbed up it.

Down under the station, I looked all around me, paranoid as fuck. I stepped quietly, listening everywhere for any noise. The wind blew down the empty streets. There was a full moon above me in the night sky. It was so bright that the buildings and the dead streetlights cast shadows down on the ground. The asphalt streets were covered in the dirt and garbage that had been left behind when the waters receded. I turned in a circle, looking, listening. I didn't hear anything.

I walked south. To the west, there wasn't much, the Major Deegan Expressway and the Hudson. To the east was where all the stores and pharmacies were. That was where I walked, my boots crunching garbage and glass beneath me.

The first pharmacy I found was mostly ransacked—we had been there before, but apparently lots of other people had been there since. The things that hadn't been taken were dry now, but had clearly been waterlogged—swollen boxes of cereal and mashed potato flakes, filthy packages of socks, little ruined pots of blush and eyeshadow. There were still a few bottles of juice and water around, and I stuffed the few that I could carry into my duffel bag.

The next store I found was the same. Most of the water-proof things were gone, except the cheap perfume and the shaving cream. Looking at the shaving cream made me think of how regularly Lux had managed to shave even though we were living in a squat with no running water. Every morning and afternoon, she'd put a tiny bit of water in a bowl, lather up, and shave, running her hand behind her razor. Twice a day, no matter what, even after there was nobody around to see her face. She said it wasn't about being seen by others – it was about how she felt. Standing in the pharmacy, I sighed audibly. Even here, filled with fear and not far from danger, I couldn't keep my mind off of her.

I shook my head, trying to get the thoughts out. I had to keep my mind on the task at hand, or I could end up dead. I walked out of the pharmacy quietly, carefully, listening all around me. Down the street, the dark facade of the line of buildings loomed menacing over me.

The next pharmacy was mostly the same. I found a few more bottles of water and juice, but nothing much. The floor was scattered with crayons, a rainbow of little sticks that cracked underneath my boots as I walked on them. I moved through the store quickly and went on, looking for the next place.

It took some zigzagging down empty streets to find another pharmacy, but finally I did. I hit the jackpot in this one. There were pills that had clearly been up above the flood line scattered all over the floor. Someone had gone through them pretty well, taking most of the ones that I recognized as Xanax, OxyContin, and Valium. But it didn't look like the person had been able to recognize one of the manufacturers' kinds of Klonopin, so I scooped those up and put them in my bag. As I was picking them out, I saw a bunch of purple and pink capsules, which I knew were antibiotics. They were the prettiest ones on the floor. I grabbed a bunch of those, too, and stuffed them in my bag.

As I was walking out of the store, I heard a noise in one of the ruined aisles. It sounded like a clicking at first, something hard hitting the floor. My heart started beating fast, remembering that night Lux disappeared. The group of prick-goblins who had overtaken us in the street, calling us homophobic slurs, swinging their fists and beer bottles. A flash of something silver. Running, running. And, when we realized Lux wasn't with us, circling back and finding her there on the street in a pool of blood.

As the clicking got closer, there was a low growling. I looked over and saw this dog there, dirty and mangy-looking with matted orange fur. Its lips were drawn back and its teeth were bared. I raised my crowbar above my head and crouched at the knees. It leapt at me. I swung the crowbar down, aiming at his head. I missed, and it latched on to my leg with its teeth. I kicked at it, trying to get loose. Soon we were rolling around on the floor, and my crowbar clattered away from my hand. I was bleeding, which only seemed to be making the dog crazier. It was lunging for my face.

I pushed with all my might and sent it flying back a few feet. In the space of those few feet, I reached out and grabbed my crowbar. Jumping up, I swung it over my head and brought it down on the dog's head with all my might.

The dog was dead, its head cracked and bleeding. I was standing there looking at a formerly living creature's brains, my body shaking, my breathing heavy. I don't give a fuck about animals, I really don't, and this one had been trying to kill me. After a minute, the adrenaline left my body, and my pulse was back to normal. I popped an antibiotic, and searched around until I found some gauze that had been above the flood line and was still clean and some peroxide. I pulled up my pant leg and poured the peroxide on the wound on my leg, then wrapped it up. It wasn't too bad. I pulled the leg of my pants down and tried not to think about it.

Then, I went back to where the pills were scattered on the ground. I searched around and found a lone Xanax. On second thought, I grabbed a random handful and shoved them in my mouth. Something was bound to happen if I ate them all.

4 Back at the station that night, I stared into the fire as José slept fitfully and Sebastian tossed and turned and puked his fucking guts out. The pain in my leg was throbbing, and it was almost like it got into my head and made it raw and bloody there, too. I couldn't keep my mind off of the night that Lux disappeared. I kept replaying it over and over.

Lux, José, Sebastian and I had been down in the streets. We were pretty lit, and we were yelling at each other, goofing around, throwing rocks we found through windows down near the ground just because why the fuck not? We didn't even hear them coming.

Suddenly, they were all around us, a bunch of guys. As soon as I saw them, I almost shit myself. It was obvious that they wanted to fuck us up. Hell, they must've known we didn't even have anything to steal. We were in the streets of an abandoned city, and we were surrounded.

"What's that?" one of the guys asked. "A bitch? Or a faggot?"

"It looks like a faggot to me," another guy said.

I grabbed Lux's arm and tried to back away, but one of the guys pushed me from behind.

"You got a pussy or a dick, faggot?" another guy said, laughing. "Wanna show us?"

My heart was beating so fast that my head felt tight. Putting my hands up in front of me, I feigned surrender, all while backing up. As soon as I ran into the guy behind me, I bent my elbows and swung them back, hard, into his stomach. If I'd had a gun, I would've killed him. Ass blossoms like that, they don't deserve to fucking live, it's them or us. But I didn't have a gun or anything, and I was fucked up and didn't even have a crowbar.

He fell down and we pushed through the circle of them. I saw flashes, something making a quick motion in the dark. I ran and ran and it wasn't until blocks later that I realized there were fewer of us than there were supposed to be.

"Lux? Lux?" I said. Her tall, thin frame was the one that was missing. I leaned over my knees and tried to catch my breath. "Where the fuck is Lux?"

"I don't know, Jesse," José said. "We gotta get outta here. We have to get back to the station."

"No, we need to find our goddamn friend, you shit socket," I said. Would I have done it for someone else? Even José or Sebastian? I didn't know. But it was Lux that was missing. "Come on."

We circled back around, going a block out of our way. The guys were gone from the spot, but Lux was still there. Laying on the ground. Bleeding everywhere. Unconscious.

"Is she dead?" Sebastian asked as we knelt next to her.

I felt for a pulse in her neck. It was there, but just barely.

"She's alive," I said. "She needs to get to the hospital. We have to carry her there."

She was heavy. We had to keep stopping every couple of blocks to put her down, even though the twins were pretty strong. After a while, she started making these horror-movie noises in her throat. Scary as it was, at least we knew she was still alive.

We thought we knew where the hospital was, but when we got there, we were wrong. I was getting sweaty and frantic as a pig fucker on a goat farm. The feeling reminded me of when I was a kid and my mom used to get too drunk to cook before my dad got home, so I'd try to do it. And after about an hour, standing over the heat of the stove, knowing how my dad would react if he came home and there was no food, I'd start panicking and sweating. That was how I felt right then. Fucking trauma.

We circled around some more, until, finally, José went off looking for the hospital by himself. We put Lux down against a wall, sitting up. Her head hung from her neck like it was broken. I took her face in my hands and pulled it up so that she looked like she was sleeping with her head leaning back against the wall.

"Lux?" I said. "You're gonna be fine. I promise this will all be fine." But even as I said it, I could feel the blood soaking her coat. Was I lying to my dying friend? I had to. I didn't know what else to do.

After what seemed like forever, José came back. He had found the hospital. We picked Lux up and carried her there, not stopping once. We knew we were there when we saw a giant building with a mural on the side. Even in the dark, the pastel figures of nurses and doctors helping patients shone. I'd taken someone here once before, a traveler kid who had been staying in our squat and OD'd. I swear, the nurses and the doctors hadn't even seemed like they judged us. They saved his life, then a nurse talked to him a little about getting clean. She didn't even push him, just asked him if it was something he saw himself doing. They hadn't even asked me much besides what he'd taken so they'd know what to do right away. Right then, with Lux leaking blood everywhere, I hoped they would be able to help her as much as they'd helped that kid.

We walked through the front door of a completely empty waiting room. The lights were out, and the only glow came from a flashlight that had been left at a desk. The room was entirely abandoned. No screening nurse sitting behind a desk, no one waiting. There were still marks on the wall where the water had gone up to before receding, and there were chairs scattered all around the room.

I stepped over to the flashlight. In its glow, I could see the blood all over José and Sebastian's clothes. I couldn't see it on my or Lux's black clothes, but I could feel its wetness on me. José leaned back against a wall, and he and Sebastian let Lux's body slump against him.

"There has to be somebody here," I said. "It's a fucking hospital. I'll look around."

I grabbed the flashlight, leaving them there in the dark, and started looking for a way to get upstairs, above where the water line had been just a few days before. The elevators were obviously out of order, so I searched around for a staircase. After looking for a bit, I found one. I hesitated before opening the door. What would come out if I did in this dark, creepshow place? A serial killer? A wave of blood like in the movies? I took a deep breath and pulled the door open. Nothing. Just an empty, dark staircase.

I climbed up to the third floor. I paused again before opening the door back into the hospital. What if there was no one there? What if I was going to have to watch my best friend bleed to death while no one helped her?

After a minute I realized that the possibility of help was better than doing nothing, and pushed the door open. I found myself in the middle of chaos.

On this floor, there were beds full of people all along the hallways. There were more flashlights and a few camping lanterns sending their eerie glow into the darkness. I heard the electronic sounds, beeps that sounded in crescendos, like the chirps of crickets on a dark night in the country. There were people moaning and begging. Machines were blinking, probably on battery power. Between the beds, nurses in pastel colored scrubs ran around. They were obviously doing their best to help who they could, but it was also obvious that there was only so much they could do.

"Where is the fucking helicopter?" I heard one of women in a stained white coat yell. "We need to get more people out of here!"

I ran up to her.

"I have an emergency!" I yelled, grabbing her arm.

She whirled on me, her near-hysterical eyes flashing above the deep bags underneath them. It was obvious she hadn't slept in days.

"Get in line," she snapped.

"My friend got stabbed," I insisted.

She pointed. "Well, there's another stabbing. And three shootings. Not to mention the people who were here before the storm. So get your friend up here and we'll get to them when we can."

"She's fucking dying!" I shouted. "You can't let her die! You have to do something. Please."

The doctor didn't seem to have any sympathy. "Do you think these batteries in these machines are going to last much longer? Half the hospital is going to die if these helicopters don't get back here again and again until everyone's out. And it's been hours since the last one was here. So, like I said, bring your friend up, and we'll get to her as soon as we can."

I didn't know what to do. I started crying. Which I never do. Which I hate because I hate feeling weak, I hate letting people see me be vulnerable. But I had no idea what to do. Suddenly life without Lux seemed like exactly what was going to happen, and I just didn't know how that could possibly be. I wiped at my eyes and came away with a handful of black mascara, which was running down my face making me look like a fucking clown or something. I turned away from the doctor, knowing I wasn't going to get anything more out of her. I started back toward the stairs. As I was walking, someone stopped me. It was a nurse with scrubs with kittens playing with balls of yarn on them. She put her hand on my shoulder.

"We'll do what we can," she said. She shrugged helplessly. "It might not be enough. In these conditions, we might not be able to do enough for any of these people. I'm so sorry."

Then she started to cry. Not huge, racking sobs or anything, just a few tears leaking out of the corners of her eyes and splashing down on her kitten scrubs. I don't think I've ever seen someone in her position cry.

I went back down to the lobby to get the twins and Lux. We carried her up the stairs. When we got her up to the third floor, a nurse grabbed a gurney and put her body on it. Her body. I wasn't sure if that was what it was now. Her breathing had gone shallow, and I wasn't sure if she was still there at all. The nurses wheeled Lux away, presumably to some surgery room. They wouldn't let us follow. We stood there in the hallway, listening to the moans, the dark doors of rooms looming around us like open mouths of jack-o'-lanterns with no lights in them. I grabbed Sebastian's hand and pulled him toward the staircase. I couldn't stay there with all those dying people. We made our way down to the second floor.

Opening the door there was a big mistake. I shone my flashlight around the hallways and saw gurneys everywhere with bodies on them. The bodies were covered up past their foreheads with sheets. Some of the sheets had blood and puke and piss on them. The smell was atrocious, even in the cold.

I've only ever seen a dead body once before that. I was out sleeping in a train yard, back when I was traveling around more. I found a body just lying there in the weeds, dead for some time. Nobody had bothered with it, probably didn't even know it was there. The smell had been the same as what I was smelling now, but not quite as bad because the body was old and it was cold outside. It was cold in there, but all those bodies piling up must have raised the stink level. I covered my mouth with my sleeve.

We went back to the staircase and made our way down to the lobby. Shining the flashlight before us, we righted some chairs and sat in them. They were still a little soggy from the floodwaters, but it was the least of our troubles. I had some emergency Valium in my pocket. I didn't want to share, but I figured the twins needed them as much as I did right then. So I offered. They both took one, even though Sebastian doesn't take a lot of drugs and José never does. I took three. I noticed that Sebastian was shaking.

The twins nodded out, leaving me in the dark room almost alone. I turned off the flashlight and stared into the dark, my eyes wide. I started drifting in and out myself. When I woke up it was always to thoughts of what life would be like without Lux. I tried to stay hard. I had been okay before her, maybe I hadn't always had someone to share things with, and talk to really deep, late at night, like the two of us did. But I'd survived. I kept trying to tell myself, *I'll survive this*. It started repeating it like a mantra. But I kept waking up to tears running down my face.

Then the asshat nurse woke me up. That was when she asked me if Lux even cared about living.

"Yes," I said immediately, not even able to believe the words were coming out of this shit biscuit's mouth. "Of course she wants to fucking live. Now do your goddamn job and save her life."

She looked at me for a long moment, not saying anything. She was judging me as much as anyone ever had. Finally, she spoke.

"We take her out of here on the next helicopter. No waiting. Now why don't the three of you get the hell out of here?"

"Not until the helicopter takes her away," I said.

And there we stayed, nodding off and crying, alone in the dark waiting room and huddled together, until the building shook with the copter touching down on the launchpad on the roof.

Even after the water fell, the wind was constant. Its presence was not the same as the gusts that had brought down the power lines, tumbled the street signs, and broken the windows, but it was there in some form for long after the storm passed. After the streets were dry once more, it blew the garbage and the debris around in small twisters on the empty streets. It forced its way through shattered windows, shaking the glass that clung around the edges of the frame. It slid down the necks of the coats of those who were left there, huddling in the streets.

The wind blew and the lights stayed out. The wind blew and the subways refused to move. The wind blew as the gas stoves and heaters clicked and stopped. It blew at the backs of gang members that walked down streets they had claimed. It blew as politicians met in places far from the empty avenues to talk about what was to be done about them. It blew as crews scrambled to make things move, to make things snap and click and whirl, to make things whole again.

There were places the wind felt even colder than it did in the streets. Out near the ocean, near the decrepit boardwalk and the series of lean-tos that had been built near it by those with nowhere left to go, the wind stung. In the dark rooms that people would never return to, the wind howled. In the high-rise low-income houses where the old and disabled clung to their lives and their memories of a city that was now gone, the wind tore with teeth.

PART FOUR

MAKAYLA—DECEMBER

1 After the boat, something broke. I felt like I'd been pushed sideways out of my own head, and was living somewhere else. My mind was a balloon tethered to the top of my skull, pulling behind me as the wind blew.

After raping me, he went back to the front of the boat, whistling, and steered to where I was going. He took me there anyway, as if he hadn't just done what he'd done, as if nothing had happened. I curled up in the back of the boat, shaking. I was a fucking numptie, I thought, and it was all my fault.

In the stairwell of my grandmother's building, there were no fluorescent lights blinking like they usually were. There was no light from my now-dead cell phone. I didn't have a flashlight, so I stumbled up through the darkness. I didn't know I was myself. I didn't know what it was to be somewhere, where I ended and the darkness began. It was only when I tripped and stumbled, fell flat down on my hands and knees, and felt pain that I knew I still had a body.

My grandmother was waiting in her little apartment with just the light of her religious candles burning. She opened the door and sat back down on the couch, looking off into the dimness of the room.

"Granny!" I yelled, hugging her. She squeezed me back, but it was only for a minute. She's never been big on affection; before my father died, he once told me that growing up, my grandmother and her sisters hadn't been hugged or kissed much, and it had been hard for her to show any kind of love to my father when he was small. Now she just squeezed me briefly and said, "Makayla. You came."

I checked to make sure that everything was as upswing as it could be, that she'd had enough food and water, that she wasn't scared or shocked.

"Damn it, what do you think happened here?" she asked. "I was just in the dark, was all." She swatted me away as I touched her face, her arms, making sure she was whole.

After I was sure she was fine, I went into her kitchen and I grabbed her biggest butcher knife and a candle, and I made my way back down the stairs. I looked around outside for Peter's boat. I could still taste him in my mouth. My heart was pounding, my blood slamming through my veins. I was going to fucking kill him. But he must have known, because he was gone. I stared out over the floodwaters that blended into the ocean. He was gone, and maybe he was gone to do the same thing again. Maybe there was someone in his boat right now, and he was whistling and getting ready to pull down some dark alley. Maybe he felt like this sort of thing was owed to him, and now, with no one around to stop him, he was just going to get what he deserved. The balloon over my head felt tight like it was being squeezed and getting ready to pop. I had to sit down and breathe until the squeezing stopped.

I went back to my grandmother's apartment and let her talk to me until the shaking stopped.

"Why are you shaking, girl?" she asked me, half concerned and half annoyed.

"It's just the cold, Granny. The cold and all the bad things out there. I'll be fine."

I couldn't let her know. I could never tell anybody, because then they would look at me and see how broken I was. I could not be broken. I had to make it through this.

It took hours before the shaking stopped. After it did, I got some slurree for my grandmother and me and we drank it. It was the government-issued kind, the kind that would do the bare minimum to keep us alive, and even then, not for long. Then I went down to the fire escape and tried to flag down a boat. I didn't get one that day, and when night started making the sky pastel, I went back inside. I slept on my grandmother's couch and went back to finding a boat early in the morning. I was able to flag one down around noon. There were more of them out here near the coast than there were inland where I'd been. I made sure, this time, that there were more people in it, that I found one piloted by people in uniforms. Not that I was sure any of it would help. In this new terrain, anyone could be the enemy.

They took us back to the emergency shelter where Jaden and the boy were. Jaden was furious with me. He had searched the entire shelter, sure I'd checked, waiting to find my body in a corner or down a hallway. Finally he had found someone who thought they'd seen me looking for a boat out to Gravesend. Then Jaden had known where I'd gone, but still not what had become of me. He didn't know until I came back into the room we'd been holed up in. I threw my arms around him. I don't think he'd ever looked more dap even though it must have been days then since any of us had done anything to look okay. He looked like home. I squeezed him and thought I would never stop.

We hid out in the small room for days, drinking slurree, trying to stay out of fights and away from trouble. Then the water went down and we were able to walk out into the streets. The whole city seemed like it was covered in mud. I wondered, like I'd wondered about the water, where it had all come from. Our shoes squished through it, making noise as we went. The sky above us was clear and beautiful, with pigeons flying through it as if everything below them was just the same as it had always been.

All around us, the city was a wasteland. Nearby was a burnt, blackened building. In the buildings beyond that one, a row of doors gaped open, and above them were smashed windows. As we walked, we passed a car that had been flipped over on its roof. The roof had crumpled from the weight of the car, and the windshields imploded. Downed power lines curled through the mud like snakes.

"Where do we go?" Jaden asked. He turned in a slow circle, his boots squelching in the mud. "They said at the shelter that FEMA was coming, that they'd set up trailers, but where do we go until then? What do we do?"

I opened my mouth to say I didn't know, but then, before a sound came out, I did. In the middle of the 'trosh scene, there were still these high-rise buildings, luxury condos. I found a stone the size of my head that must have drifted in in the water. I picked it up in both hands and walked over to the glass door of one of the buildings. Lifting it high up over my head, I threw it through the door. The whole pane of glass shattered and what stuck in at the edges fell away as I kicked at it with my boots. Then I put one arm across my waist, stretched the other out toward the door, and bent.

"After you, milady," I said to my grandmother. Granny's seen some shit in her day, I know. She kind of giggled in this tired way, and stepped through the empty frame.

I picked up the big rock and we made our way up the dark stairs to the third floor, where the water hadn't reached.

Light was streaming in through a huge window at the end of the hall when we came out onto the third floor. There was a long hallway and only four doors on it. The apartments must have been enormous. I walked over the first door and tried the handle. It was locked. I lifted the rock up and smashed it down. The door moved a bit, but remained closed. I lifted the rock again. I don't know where the strength came from, how I was able to lift it and smash it over and over. I'm not even sure how much time passed. But what seemed like an instant later, I was standing there with my arms shaking, the rock at my feet, and the door smashed wide open.

The apartment was as beautiful as the rest of the city was destroyed. There was a plush white couch in the center of the living room. Placed at welcoming angles around it were white leather chairs. They were so pristine it looked as if no one had ever sat down in them. Off to the back of the room, there was a marble fireplace. I had never seen a fireplace before in Brooklyn, and I wondered if it worked or was just an elaborate show.

I turned around and, behind me, Jaden, my grandmother, and the boy were all standing, staring. My arms were still shaking. They were looking at me like I had just crawled out of the floodwaters and had scales.

"Well?" I said. "Come in. I know I've always wanted to live in a place like this."

Before long, we were searching the apartment, opening every closet, looking in every pantry. In a bedroom, I found a closet full of warm designer clothes. I pulled a thick, woolen sweater down off a hanger and wrapped myself in it, feeling it around me like a hug from my mother. I found a mink coat and ran over to the bedroom where my grandmother stood, pulling it over her shoulders and laughing. She laughed, too. But then the laughter turned into tears, and I wrapped my arms around her, around the fur coat, and held her close. The boy stood across the room, his thumb in his mouth. Jaden had said he'd started that after I left the shelter, and hadn't stopped since. I reached my arms out to embrace him, too, and, to my surprise, he came into them slowly. His little shoes had stopped flashing pictures. As I hugged him, I felt the cell phone still inside the front pocket of his hoodie. We all sat down on the bed, holding on to each other. After some time, my grandmother's tears stopped, and we went back to searching the house.

The place kept amazing me. The kitchen was bigger than my entire apartment had been, with a huge, heavy wooden counter that wrapped around it, and shelves and storage spaces made of the same wood above it. The sink and the refrigerator shone deep silver. There was a walk-in pantry the size of my old bedroom. It was stacked up with all kinds of nonperishable foods—beef, turkey, venison, and ostrich jerky; wasabi peas; dried apricots; trail mix with raisins and little buttons of yogurt in it; cans of soup; cans of salmon, sardines, anchovies; glass jars of caviar; candied kiwi fruit; nuts; dates; cereal; crackers; chips; canned peaches, pineapple, tropical fruit. There was every food I could imagine, and some that I couldn't. I grabbed a jar of caviar. I had always heard about it, and wondered what it tasted like. I took it to the kitchen and tore open drawers until I found a spoon. I opened the lid and dug a spoon into it. It was like inhaling the ocean at Gravesend.

I walked out of the closet and into the living room with the couches and fireplace. There was a big, glorious window where light was streaming in. I walked up to it and put my hands flat on the glass and looked down. All the words that rumble about in my head about life, dissat and 'trosh and sienty, they all flew out. I didn't have words for this. The glass was cold, but from where I was standing I saw a big chest full of warm woolen blankets. We'd be able to stay warm, whether we could light a fire in that fireplace or not. My grandmother and the boy were sitting on the big white couch now. I took a blanket and wrapped them both in it.

"You stay here and get warm," I said.

My grandmother scowled at me. "You think I'm some kind of invalid? I'll damn well walk around and see what's in this place, too."

That was my grandmother. Crying one minute and cursing me out the next. I was happy to see that the time she'd spent in her dark apartment after the storm, alone and maybe afraid, hadn't changed her much.

She stood up, shrugging the blanket off, and I wrapped more of it around the boy.

"We'll get you some food. And we'll find you a bed. I think there are three or four bedrooms in this place. You'll have a nice one."

When the boy looked like he felt safe and secure, I moved onto the next room. It was a dining room, all set up with an oval table made of mahogany and chairs that matched it. There was a candle holder in the middle with a long white candle sticking up from it. The candle was burned halfway down. Each place around the table was set with a place mat that looked like it had been handmade in some faraway country. Off to the side of the room was a tall cabinet with glass doors and shelves. On those shelves were bowls and plates that look like bone china. There were bright-colored iridescent glass goblets and plates that were clearly collector's items. Whatever goodbreeds had lived here obviously liked to sit down to fancy dinners. Well, I wouldn't mind taking their place while they were gone.

I thought back to the fancy apartment in Jaden's building and how I had wanted to smash and break everything. Here I didn't. This was mine, ours. We were home.

I went to explore the bedrooms a bit more. Down a hallway that came off of the living room, there were five doors—two huge bathrooms and three bedrooms. One of the bedrooms, the one I had taken the clothes from, was clearly the parents' bedroom. It was the biggest and had a high, king-sized mattress with a beautiful carved oak headboard. The nightstands on either side of the bed matched the headboard, and so did the huge dresser off to the side of the room. I pulled open drawers. It had been days since I'd had a fresh pair of underwear, and the thought of one trumped the disgust I felt at wearing some goodbreed's undergarments. I found the underwear drawer before long, and after I pulled out some comfortable cotton pairs, I reached in and took out the warmest, thickest socks I could find. They looked like they were made of wool. I had never owned a pair of socks like that in my entire life.

While I was pulling socks out of the drawer, my hand hit something hard and cold. I pulled whatever it was out of the drawer. There was a gun in my hand. A no-joke Beretta handgun. I looked at it for a minute in the light streaming in from between the heavy curtains. It glinted dully in the light. When I was a kid, my dad took me to a shooting range a couple of times, just because he said I should know how to shoot if I ever had to. He never said why he thought I'd have to, just that I should know. If only I'd had that gun out on that ori Peter's boat.

I reached back in my brain to remember everything I could about shooting. Stretching my arm out, I aimed the gun at the wall. The feeling of holding it out like that made my arm shake. Making sure the safety was on, I put it down on the bed.

Closing the door, I unbuttoned my pants and slipped them down. I stepped out of them and stood there in my underwear. They were ripped along one side, near the waistband. As I slipped them off, I saw bloodstains in the crotch. I took them off and shoved them in the back corner of the drawer. I pulled the new ones on. I noticed that my breathing was heavy and my heart was beating fast. The boat came back to me then, and I pushed it out of my head by force. I thought of where I was, of all the nice things, of how I was going to keep the boy and my grandmother and Jaden safe forever. I pulled my pants back on and slipped the gun into the waistband.

I went into the bedrooms one by one. From the looks of things, the kids that had lived in the apartment were a girl and one boy. The girl seemed to be a few years younger than me, probably still in high school judging by the textbooks on her desk and the size of her clothes. The boy's room was filled with Yankee pennants and jerseys, and model trains of every subway line in the city. I wondered if he'd ever ridden the subway in his life. I went into his closet and found that his clothes were a bit big for the boy we'd brought with us, but would certainly do.

As I was yanking his clothes off the hangers, a dissat feeling rose up in me. I was in some kid's bedroom. The kid didn't know anything, didn't know that his family was filthy rich, or that they were forcing people like me and Jaden farther and farther away. He was just some kid who liked the

Yankees and trains and went to school every day, and loved his parents. Here I was, invading his space, tearing apart his room, taking his things. But I only felt like an ori about it for a minute, because we needed to survive.

I laid the clothes out on the bed, then went and got the boy and brought him into the room. I talked to him even though I wasn't sure he understood me, telling him to get dressed.

"This is all yours now," I said.

I left the room to give him some privacy and went back into the kitchen. I started taking food out of the walk-in pantry. I kept pulling food out and laying it on the table until finally Jaden came over and stopped me.

"We have to make this last, Makayla," he said.

"Oh, no, we don't," I said.

"What do you mean?"

"There are other apartments here that I bet are just as well stocked. And besides, I found something back in the parents' bedroom." I lifted up my shirt and showed him the gun. "We run out of food, we go find more."

Jaden grabbed me and pulled my shirt back down, as if the gun would disappear if it wasn't in his line of sight. "What are you going to do with that?" he asked, his hands gripping my arm so tight that they made little circles in my skin.

"Make sure we survive," I said. I pulled my arm away from him.

The boy came back into the room in new clothes, and my grandmother came and joined us at the table. We put the food out on plates and tore into it.

"Caviar," my grandmother said, eating a spoonful. "And cashmere sweaters. Next thing you know, we'll be driving a damn Bentley."

I looked over at the boy. He had a bowl of peaches in front of him. He picked up the slices one by one with his fork and took little bites off of them like a bird until they were gone. He almost looked like he had a smile on his face, too. It was the first time I had seen him look that way since we found him. I stood up and found a box of matches up in the breakfront with the dishes. I lit the candle on the table and brought it in front of him.

"Blow it out and make a wish," I said. He looked up at me with his huge black eyes. I puffed up my cheeks and pretended to blow. A real smile stretched across his face now, and he blew out the candle and squeezed his eyes shut.

"Alejandro," he said. He pointed to himself. "Ale."

"Your name's Ale?" I asked. It was the first time he had spoken since we'd found him.

He nodded and went back to picking at his peaches as if the best thing I'd seen in days hadn't just happened.

We ate and ate. We ate until our stomachs were full and their emptiness back at the emergency shelter was a memory. Someone said something mildly funny and we began to laugh and laugh, big belly laughs. The boy was silent at first, but as we laughed and laughed and couldn't stop, he began to laugh, too.

For the first time in a long, long time, it felt like we might pull through.

2 When we finally got to bed that night, everyone insisted that I take the parents' room. My grandmother took the girl's room, and Ale was in the boy's room. Jaden said he would take the couch.

"Let's face it," he said. "It's nicer than any bedroom I've ever had."

That night, in the huge bed, I wanted to rest. I stretched out on my back, curled up in a ball, laid on my stomach with my arms and legs spread out at angles from my body. None of it worked. I couldn't make my mind stop. All that I'd seen in the emergency shelter, what had happened in the boat. Every time I fell asleep for a minute, I woke back up right away, my mind feeling stretched out and dry. After hours of it, I tiptoed back over to the door, my wool socks not making a sound in the deep piles of the tan carpet. I crept out to where Jaden was sleeping in the living room and put my hand on his shoulder.

He jumped awake and I felt terrible. Then he saw, in the dark, who I was, where we were, that everything was upswing. He smiled.

"Makayla," he said. "What's going on?"

"I can't stop my phrenic brain," I whispered, pushing back my hair and squeezing my forehead with my right hand. "Maybe you could come into my room until I get to sleep?"

He walked with me back across the apartment and into my room where we sat down on the bed.

"Go ahead," he said. "Get under the covers. I'll sit here and talk to you."

I curled up under them. I still didn't feel 100 percent safe, but I felt safer than I had in a while. Jaden. I thought about all we'd been through together since the storm, and even before that. Kids in the old neighborhood. I thought about his crush on me, what a goofy kid he'd been. That had changed so much. The man before me was tall, handsome. For the first time, I admitted to myself that maybe, just maybe, these lights on inside me when he was around meant something.

"Hey, Makayla? Did you used to think about being famous when you were a kid?" he asked.

I rolled my eyes even behind my closed eyelids. I should've known that Jaden would be back to the questions. He'd let them die down in the last few days, but here we were, as safe as we were going to get, and he'd started up on them again.

"Yeah," I said. "Thought I'd marry a prince and everything. Turned out that princes don't come to our part of Brooklyn too often. At least, they didn't used to. I guess if you've got apartments like this here now, anything's possible."

"Always the smart-ass," Jaden said. "Can't you ever answer one of my questions straight?"

"Just get jawing," I said. "Answer your own question. I'm supposed to be the one going to sleep, not the one talking."

"When I was a teenager, I'd get myself to sleep at night by thinking about being an Olympic cyclist," he said. "I would imagine races where no one could even come close to me. I'd think them all the way through—the aches in my legs from peddling, the shortness of breath on the hills, it was all part of this enormous feeling of victory I'd get to at the end. Then I'd imagine the medal ceremony, and standing up at the top of the platform, but knowing that even though there was a second and third place, nobody had been within a mile of me when I crossed that line. I'd think it over and over. It was like what sucking your thumb feels like when you're little—using part of yourself to soothe your entire self—but in this case it was my imagination, not my thumb."

As he spoke, I let the words drift over me. I felt the feelings of excitement he must have felt, the quiet thrill inside me that feel like snuggling down in the warmest bed on the coldest day of the year.

"But you never entered any races, or anything like that," I

said, opening my eyes. "I would've known. I would've come and cheered you on."

He shrugged. "People like me don't get to be Olympic champions. We get to ride around on errands for goodbreeds and get paid for it, if we're lucky. And besides—if I made it real, it would've taken away the secret feeling about imagining it. And that was the best part. I've never told anybody about it until right now."

"Why are you telling me?" I asked. My eyes were all the way open now. I propped myself up on one arm so that I was on level with Jaden.

He shrugged again, but this time the nonchalance felt forced. "I don't know, Makayla. I guess I'd tell you just about anything."

I sat up against the fancy headboard. Our hands were just a few inches away on the bed, and then there wasn't any space separating them at all—I had my hand clasped over his. I wasn't sure how it happened, just that it felt good. We'd slept near each other every night in the shelter, but there it had been for protection. I reached out my other hand and curled it around the back of his neck, feeling the little hairs at the base of his skull. I began massaging his neck with my hand, and then I pulled him closer to me.

Our lips met gently. For a minute I just sat there, doing nothing. My mind was blank, and it felt so good. All I could feel was the sensation of his soft lips. I didn't think of the past, or the future, or anything but their softness. I felt so warm. He began to move his lips just a bit, pressing them against mine. Our mouths opened and I felt his tongue. He tasted wonderful, a hint of the bottle of wine we'd found and drank after Ale went to bed still on his lips.

My hands were in his hair, pulling his face closer to mine.

Our kisses grew longer, deeper. His hands moved over my shirt to my breasts. My nipples were getting harder and more sensitive. He slipped his hands under my shirt and the touch sent shocks through me.

Before long, we were out of our clothes and our bodies were pressed up against each other. He was warm everywhere despite the chill in the air of the apartment. I touched his chest, his ass, his cock. I wanted to touch every part of his body. When my pants were off, he touched me, and for a minute I felt the pain still there from a few days before in the boat. My entire body tensed up.

"Makayla?" he asked. "Are you okay? Are you sure this is something you want?"

I took a deep breath. These were Jaden's hands touching me softly and tenderly, not some attacker's.

"Yes," I said, unclenching my muscles. "Yes, I'm sure."

I wondered for a moment why I had never done this with him before, why I had waited so long. But all the other times had not been right. This moment, safe and secure, warm and happy, was the right one.

3 For days, I woke up next to Jaden, stretched, kissed him, went into the kitchen and ate, and came back and went to bed. It seemed like it would never get old. I filled my belly, then snuggled up in his arms and breathed in deep the smell of his skin and his hair. Sometimes, I ran into someone else in the kitchen—my grandmother, Ale—they seemed to be doing the same thing I was: sleeping, eating, and sleeping some more. I was so happy to have the simple comforts of a

safe place to lie down and food to eat, that it was all I wanted to do.

After I don't know how many days, I woke up feeling like I needed to do more. I sat up in bed and shook Jaden awake.

"Hey, Jaden," I said, shaking his shoulder. "Jaden."

"What?" he said, rubbing his eyes.

"We're going to stay here a long time, right?" I asked.

"Yeah, Makayla, we're gonna stay here until they drag us out."

"What about water damage and things?" I asked. "Won't mold grow on the carpets and drywall downstairs? We'll get sick."

He sat up in bed. He still looked sleepy, but his eyes were open now.

"I didn't even think of that. But you're right. We should get that stuff out on the ground level as soon as we can."

"This place is huge, though, and that ground floor's all carpet," I said. "You and me can slag, but Ale's too young and my grandmother has arthritis in her hands and knees. Are we going to do it all ourselves?"

Jaden leaned back, shifting all his weight onto his arms, and exhaled. Sunlight was coming in around the edges of the heavy curtains. A pool of it spilled on his shoulder. He was silent for a moment, thinking. Then he said, "We can't. We'd have to pull up all the rugs, pull out all the drywall . . . that's a lot of slag, and we're only two people. Whether we want to or not, we're going to have to get more people into this building."

I was shaking my head before I even knew what I was doing. "No, Jaden. We will not. This is *our* place, and we need to keep it that way. We need to be safe, we can't get in another situation like in that shelter."

"Funny you say that, because the shelter was the first place I was going to suggest we go to get people from."

"Are you phrenic?" I asked. "Are you absolutely outside of your goddamn mind?"

"There were some good people there, Makayla," Jaden said. "People who deserve to be safe, too."

Suddenly, I felt cold. My arms were shaking just a bit. I pulled the covers around me. Good people, he said. I thought about the same words going through my mind as I rode on the boat out to Gravesend to find my grandmother.

"How could we ever know who's good?" I asked. Inside my head, my voice didn't sound like mine. I felt like I was somewhere else.

Jaden put his arm across my stomach, cupped my hip, and pulled me just a bit toward him. "We can't do this alone. Remember when our parents used to help put on those block parties? And how everybody had a piece to do? And who were those people? They lived down the street from us, they were our neighbors. These people are, too. Maybe even more than those who used to live here before, because we're the only ones left. Maybe not all of them are good, but we have to trust at least some of them."

I steadied my arms. Jaden was already up and pulling on his clothes. We went into the bathroom and bathed as best we could with the hand and face wipes we had found there. They wouldn't last long. Maybe nothing would. We had to figure out what to do next.

4 The girl in the cutoff shirt's name was Kristen, and she smelled like patchouli so bad I could hardly breathe around her. As we walked around the ground floor of the building

with her and the other people who lived in the building with us now, she wouldn't stop jawing to me about extreme sports.

"I was space diving when I was fifteen," she said, shrugging. "Not a big deal at all, Mach 1 without a craft is only scary if you can't get your spin down, which really isn't that hard if you know what you're doing. I was practically pro by the time I was seventeen. But by then I was more interested in surfing really big waves—which you don't see unless you go somewhere where tsunamis happen a lot. So that was how it started, the disaster thing. And then, the thing got to be the people—that was more extreme than any of these things. People doing all kinds of shit, killing and dying and freaking out. You never know what people are going to do."

"So you follow disasters?" I said.

"Pretty much all the time, now," she said. As she talked, she pulled an elastic band off her wrist and wrangled her tangled blond hair back into a ponytail. "It's been a few years. Place to place, never stopping really because the disasters never stop. You see the wildest stuff. I saw a mother kill a dog with her bare hands, roast it over a fire, and feed it to her children in Oakland."

As she talked, she walked around the lobby, looking the walls up and down. There were grayish water marks on them. She walked over to one and kicked it.

"Drywall's painted," she said, "which is great fucking news. The best you've heard all day. Because that means we don't have to tear every piece of it off the beams."

Jaden and I looked at each other. He nodded his head once and raised an eyebrow at me. Back at the shelter, I had nearly flown off when Jaden suggested we ask her to come back to the building with us.

"*Her?*" I'd whispered. "Jaden, you must be phrenic if you think I'm bringing that girl back to live with us."

"She's a professional at this shit, Makayla," he said. "I guarantee you she'll come in handy."

And he'd been right.

"What do we use to get rid of the mold, then?" I asked.

"I prefer tea tree oil, because I like the way it smells," she said, "but try getting that shit in the middle of a disaster zone. Still, if there were any holistic wellness stores in the neighborhood, we could always raid them and grab some. But really lots of other stuff will do. Ammonia, bleach, or vinegar would all work. I just wish they didn't all smell so bad."

I looked around the room at the other people assembled with us, many of whom we'd found back at the shelter. Some of them I had seen there, like the woman who had grabbed all the extra slurree for her children, Drusilla. Others had been hidden off in corners, trying to survive just as we had. And they'd still been waiting there for help or something when we came along. I wondered what had lead them to believe, after the lives they had lived, which had to be not too far off from our own, that help would ever come. That they wouldn't have to make it themselves. But there they had been, waiting for FEMA or the Red Cross or whoever people had told them to wait for. In the end, it had been us who came to the rescue.

Kristen was still talking.

"Floors are fucked, though. All this carpet. We'll have to rip it up and take it out of the building. If there's wood underneath, we'll treat it the same way we're treating the walls. If there's concrete we don't have to do shit."

I looked once again at the people gathered in the lobby. There were about twenty of them. Most of them were dark-skinned, some had faces lined with age and stress and the terror of what we'd all been going through. Their clothes were dirty. Some had children with them, little ones looking around in wonder and fear. But these people were listening to Kristen talk, and some of them looked hopeful. They looked like they had looked when I touched their shoulders at the shelter, or in the street where we had found them amid garbage and not too far from bodies. Something had come into their eyes then, as I leaned down and rapidly explained the building we had, how it had everything we needed, and how we were squatting it. Some of them had closed their eyes, and a few had cried.

Drusilla stepped forward toward where Kristen and I were standing.

"You mean my children won't get sick here?" she asked. She looked hard, not hopeful. She reminded me of a lion, how fierce she was, and how that fierceness faded when she touched her children's cheeks, or looked down at them. The children were up in one of the apartments, one that I wished we had picked when I saw the antique oak furniture and rows of old books.

"They won't get sick if we do the work," Kristen said. "Not from mold, anyway. But there are other ways they could get sick. Hep A, cholera, typhoid fever—that shit all comes from contaminated water. Now, FEMA should be here with clean water before too long, so we just have to find ourselves some until they get here. And don't let your kids touch anything outside. Leptospirosis comes from rat piss in the mud and dirt and can kill you."

I saw Drusilla tense up. She looked back behind her shoulder, as if she could protect her children just with her gaze.

A man who looked to be in his late thirties spoke up.

"I've been doing construction work for years," he said. "I can look around for tools, I can teach people how to rip up the carpet. I can help."

A tiny woman wearing a filthy sari spoke up in halting English. "I don't know how," she said, "but I will help."

Other people in the lobby nodded, or looked me and Kristen in the eyes. The man who had said he worked in construction clapped his hands together. The sound bounced through the big, empty lobby.

"Yes," he said. "First we go into the apartments and look for the tools. Then we make this place *ours*."

"Yes," I said, almost in a whisper. I found Jaden a few feet away from me and slipped my arm around his waist. I squeezed him. "*Ours.*"

"Wait," Jaden said. "Some of us should be slagging on the carpets and the mold, definitely. But with all of us here, the food and water in this building aren't going to last forever. Or even very long. We have to send people out for supplies, too."

A murmur went through the crowd as my stomach tightened. This is what I'd been afraid of, letting all these people in—all those stores of supplies being gone quicker than anything. And it was obvious that none of us wanted to go out there.

"Some of us have children to worry about," Drusilla said. "If I go out there and don't come back, who's going to take care of my babies?"

I felt like snapping at her, like telling her to shut up. But someone else spoke before I could, the woman in the sari.

"You're right," she said. "Only people who can accept the risks should go."

I softened then. I thought about this woman, this Drusilla. What had she been through? With the way she protected those children, had she had to fight at some time to keep them? How many people had promised her help only to give her nothing? Who the hell was I to judge her?

"We need committees," I said. I was thinking again of those block parties in my childhood. This was a pretty 'trosh excuse for a party, but here we all were, and we had to slag to make it go.

"Yes," Kristen jumped in, but I kept going over her.

"A food and water gathering committee, a cleaning committee, a defense committee. Am I forgetting anything?"

"Clothes," Jaden said.

"Childcare," the woman in the sari added.

"Food prep," said a man we had found in the streets.

"I'll take charge of the food and water committee," I went on. "Anybody who wants to join can go with me."

"But no one should be in charge for too long of anything," Kristen said. "It's better if we all take turns leading."

"Fine," I said. "But for now, everybody who wants to go out there and look for food and water, be ready at the front doors in half an hour. Bring comfortable clothes and boots if you can find them and something to defend yourself with."

5 There was only one other person. Even Jaden wanted to stay behind and do work in the building. I came down the stairs to meet him in a pair of Italian leather boots that I was going to destroy in the mud and the dirt. But there was a whole closet full of them in my size, so I could afford to waste this pair.

He was carrying a crowbar. I had my gun tucked in my belt where no one could see it, and was carrying a butcher knife. I felt like that gun was my ace in the hole, and would protect me against anything if need be—even this guy who was supposed to be on my side.

We stepped out into the chilly air outside the door. The sun was shining down, but the mud on the ground was still wet and sucked at our boots. The bodies we had seen in the streets in the days before hadn't been moved, and there was a smell in the air of rotting and decay. We tried to avoid where they lay, walking across the street to get around them. Cars were slung across the street at every angle, and we had to climb up and over the roofs of some of them, our boots leaving dents in the hoods.

We walked for a few blocks, and found two stores across from each other. One was a corner store, an upswing one from the looks of it. The other was a chain pharmacy called Allen Brewster's.

"We'll get food and water first, then look for bleach and vinegar in the AB's."

The guy I was with was named Mo. He wore ripped jeans and an old button-down blue work shirt. We hadn't talked much prior to him joining me in the excursion, and now didn't seem the time to. He bounced a crowbar in one hand nervously. We looked at each other. After a tentative moment, he smiled at me and jerked his head in the direction of the store.

"Let's go find what we can," he said.

His heavy work boots that looked like he had arrived in them and my fancy Italian boots crunched over broken glass, slid in the mud. We were wearing heavy clothes and gloves, but if we fell in this shit, it would rip us to pieces, and the wounds would be hard to clean. We walked as carefully as we could toward the store.

The store had already been ransacked somewhat, but a lot of good stuff remained. I found a pack of cigarettes forgotten behind some cans of food. I grabbed both. I hoisted my ass up on the counter and ripped open the pack. I found a lighter on the counter near where I was sitting, in an almost empty display of them. I lit the cigarette and inhaled deeply. I hadn't had one since my oussies ran out back in Jaden's building. I coughed and coughed, and then inhaled deeply again, closing my eyes. It was so good that for a minute, I forgot where we were.

When I opened my eyes there was a guy in a uniform standing in front of me, pointing a gun directly in my face.

"Don't fucking move!" he yelled.

"What?" I said. My cigarette dropped out of my mouth and onto my lap. I let it burn there because I was afraid to move. I felt it singeing through my pants and into the flesh of my leg.

"Let me guess," he said, "honoring the memory of people who died in this disaster by looting a fucking store?"

"I'm just hungry, I'm thirsty," I said. "What are you, some kind of cop or something?" My hands were up and my voice was shaking. I was staring down that barrel, knowing it could hold the end of my life. I wasn't ready to die. I was not ready for everything to be over.

"Yes, I'm some fucking kind of cop. Now get the fuck down from there before I put a bullet in your motherfucking head."

I jumped down, my hands still in the air. Then I saw something move out of the corner of my eye. I didn't even hear anything, just saw a flash. Then the cob roller was on the ground, and a puddle of blood was forming around his head on the dirty tile floor. Mo was standing over him with his crowbar, shaking.

"What have I done?" he kept saying. "What have I done?"

"Let's get the fuck out of here," I said.

We ran for the door. We ran as fast as we could, not thinking to drop the precious things we had gathered, even as they slowed us down.

Finally, far away, we stopped. I looked over at Mo.

"We don't know that he's dead," I said.

He was shaking. "Please, please don't tell my wife."

I looked down, breathing hard. As I bent over my knees, I saw that my fancy Italian boots were splattered in blood.

PART FIVE

EVANN—DECEMBER

1 When Bernice hit, the lights were out for the longest time. You watched the news, and the newsmen didn't want to be out after dark in the city, even with the protection of the TV camera on them, broadcasting to the whole world. The lights stayed out in the city for the longest time, except the few solar-powered streetlights that hadn't been washed away. The bridges were ruined, the tunnels were a nightmare, and the only way to get back there was by boat or helicopter. But I had to get back. I had to see what had become of that quaint little place that I loved so much, and the little garden out my window.

Me and Pollock were staying at my dad's compound in-state, and he didn't want me to go into the city at all. We talked about it while I was sitting around in my room, listening to the Lounge Lizards. I have all their albums in my cloud, and also the real, old copies in my physical record collection. I want to like them, I do. I really want to understand their music. It's *nice*, it is. And John Lurie was great. He was at Basquiat's funeral and everything, and he supposedly even had the idea for the boxing photos that Basquiat did with Warhol. I own the original *Bear Surprise* and everything. Their music is *passionate*, which I love. But also frustrating, if you understand what I mean. It's so *strange*. But I want to like it, so I listen to it over and over.

So I was sitting there listening to this kind of wild jazz, and Pollock was sleeping on my bed, looking like an angel, and my dad was really annoying me about me not going back. Not yet, he said, not with the people who'd been left behind roaming around the streets in packs.

"Fath-*er*," I said, screeching the arm off the old record. I only call him that when I'm upset. "You can't just refer to people in terms of animals. They're human beings."

"My little darling," my dad said, condescending as anything, "there is no way you're going into that city without proper protection."

So my dad made some calls, right then and there. He wants me to have what I want, but he also wants me to be safe. I understand. It's not like he doesn't love me. He made some calls and hired personal security guards for me. Problem solved. I didn't put the Lounge Lizards back on after he stopped talking on his wristscreen. The mood had been ruined.

2 I made it to the island one sunny winter morning with a burly guy named Chet who was dressed all in black, and a beefy, bodybuilder type woman named Marcia. I was happy my dad had been progressive enough to hire her, even though she was a woman. She looked like she could keep me safe.

They both had guns and I knew they wouldn't be afraid to use them if it came down to a matter of my well-being. Of course, I hoped they wouldn't use them frivolously. I read the news—I know how trigger-happy cops can get. I just wanted to be safe, but not at the expense of others.

On the boat, I chatted with Marcia. At first she just grunted at me, but I kept talking. I can get anyone to talk, I always have been able to. I'm sort of a charming person, when I want to be. Finally, I found out that she lived with her ailing mom and a slew of little Chihuahuas (which I loved, so I decided I liked her), she had never been married, and she worked out every day.

Chet and Marcia went into my *chou* little apartment first, and I stood out on the street. They had stopped some National Guardsmen, and they were waiting with me. As they went in, these people just scurried out like rats. The guardsmen pointed their guns at them as they ran away down the street and yelled for them to stop. But they ran and one of the guardsmen put his hand on my shoulder and asked me if I was okay, seeing those people like that in my place. I think there was a tear in my eye or something, but I'm not quite sure for what—those people or my house or myself. I told him I was okay.

Chet and Marcia came back outside then. Marcia put her hand on my shoulder, too. It was like they were about to tell me I had cancer or something.

"It's going to be okay," she said. "But I just want to let you know before you go in that it's really bad."

"I think I can handle it," I said, trying to smile a little at her.

But when I walked up my little stoop, and in through the door that I'd walked in so many times, broken now so that

I didn't have to use my keys, I felt like maybe I was really going to need their sympathy. Everything was destroyed. The paintings had been pulled off the wall, the books taken off the shelves, the food raided from the wide-open refrigerator. There was a gaping burn hole in the middle of the living room where somebody had started a fire. There was a garbage can where more fires had been built in the middle of the main bedroom. The toilet was overflowing with shit and piss, and I thought *animals, what kind of animals would do something like this?* Then I felt bad about thinking it, because I *know* that it's really messed up to compare people to animals—hadn't I just yelled at my dad for it? But I had never seen humans act like this, so that was where my mind went. I put my hand over my mouth then, and a little gasp came out of my throat. I started sobbing. Marcia put her hand on my shoulder again as I stood there in my ruined little place that I had loved so much, where I had come back after nights out on the Lower East Side, where so many of my friends had slept in the guest bedroom, where I had sat with my sketchbook and drawn. All these memories came flooding back to me then, and I cried and cried.

I leaned into Marcia's massive bicep and wept like a baby. After a few minutes she patted me on the back and pulled away.

"Is there anything left that you want to take with you?" she said. "There doesn't seem much point in us staying here any longer."

Heartless, I thought. *What if it was your home*, I thought, *and your little dogs?* But I looked around to see if there was anything worth salvaging. Anything that hadn't been burned or pissed on. And that's when I saw it. There in a garbage can that somebody had set on fire, was what remained of the face of my teddy bear, Jax. I'd had Jax since I was five. My mom had given him to me for my birthday the year she died. Her giving him to me in a big box with a bow on top of it is the last memory I have of her before the car crash. I'm close to my dad, I suppose, as close as you can be when years are spent away at boarding school, and summer camp in the Alps, and you only get winter vacation together the whole time you're growing up. But I loved my mom. She died when I was so young, before she had a chance to be anything but wonderful. Sometimes I'd held Jax and talked to him like I was talking to her.

I went and picked what remained of Jax out of the garbage can. Then I dropped his charred fur back into it and sat down on the floor, crying.

"So there's nothing you want?" Marcia asked again.

"I just need a minute to *grieve*, for God's sake."

So I stood there in my ruined living room crying, and I got to thinking how New York City really was heartless. And how I was never coming back.

PART SIX

JESSE—DECEMBER

1 In my trauma dreams, Lux was the one who was ill As I roamed the streets looking for medicine, she was the one who was lying there, sick as some racist ass-clown, vomiting everywhere. What was even worse was that her attackers were out in the streets as I went looking for pills to make her better, and I knew that if I didn't get back soon and defend her, they would find her again, but this time she was sick and wouldn't be able to fight back at all. I always woke up from those dreams covered in my own sweat, halfway convinced I had whatever Sebastian had gotten.

After a few days, Sebastian's fever broke. He stopped puking. He was able to keep down water and food. He looked like he'd lost a bunch of weight, and his face was drawn tight as an Upper East Side lady's after a facelift. But he was better. José was still worried. We hung out in the squat for a few weeks, super careful about what we touched, how we washed our hands. Every time Sebastian as much as sneezed, José was next to him, making sure he wasn't sick again.

"He got sick because it's so dirty in here and we don't have any water," José said to me one day. "We have to find someplace that does."

"I doubt any place in the city has running water, José," I said.

"Then maybe we have to get out of here."

I thought of the world outside of the train station. I thought of having to look for someone that I wasn't sure was alive anymore. Fuck, fuck that shit. I wasn't leaving, not until I could deal with the fact that I might never find her.

We came to a compromise. We would leave the station during the day and look around for places that were more hospitable. Maybe places FEMA had set up in, or some do-gooders with good connections. If we didn't find anything soon, José and Sebastian were out of there, whether I was coming with them or not.

We started out small, just circling a few blocks around the station. Then the circumference grew wider and wider. We were about twenty blocks to the south of our home on our first day out when we saw it.

At first, it didn't seem like much. Just a little splash of bright green on a building. We were walking in that direction, anyway, and when we got closer, we saw it was an apple. It was bigger than real life, but other than that, it looked so real that I wanted to take a bite out of it. I stepped back to look at it, and I saw that there was another green-brown splash of color about fifteen feet away from the apple. I stepped toward it and saw that it was a pear, glowing up off the side of a ruined apartment building. And another fifteen feet from that was a kiwi fruit, with shining black seeds and a green so bright I could almost taste the tartness of it in my mouth.

Now, in full-on motherfucking wonder-mode, I stepped

back to see another painting fifteen feet from the kiwi. It was a honeydew melon, shining pale green, with a slice cut out of it so you could see the darker seeds inside. It looked so real that I wanted to lick the wall. I followed the path that the fruit paintings had set up and saw a huge watermelon with just a hint of red peeking through the greens of the rind.

Not sure if the twins were still with me, I walked and walked, following the fruit from one wall to the next. After I had walked an entire block, I turned the corner of a building and saw a pile of green fruit painted on the wall, and above them, in all the shades of green that I had already seen in the fruit, the word HOPE hung in jagged letters. Standing in front of it was a group of people. They were staring up in amazement. None of them said a word. A few of them were holding hands. Next to them there was someone handing out boxes of food, stuff that looked like it had been pulled from an abandoned store.

"Have you heard about the building?" the man handing out food asked me as I walked up to him to take a few cans of fruit.

"What building?" I asked.

"The building in Brooklyn. You've got to hear this."

One day, the crew on the Williamsburg Bridge came in the morning to see that their crane had been painted. On it was a monster whose dark eyes were hooded over with a shelf of a brow and devil horns. The eyes had a spot of glowing red in them, the color of a candy apple. Whoever had painted the crane had made their way all the way up the arm of it, their hand never wavering, even at the top where they drew a giant fist. Suddenly, the crane looked like it was destroying rather than building. The crew stopped and stared at it as they came in. One by one, each stood before it, delaying the beginning of their workday to marvel.

All around the city, splashes of color were springing up. Someone was moving between the boroughs as if the trains were still running, as if the highways were still moving, as if the bridges had not fallen into the rivers. Here: a monster's arm. There: fruit like the people in the city could not find wherever they looked. There, on a former church: a picture of a saint stretching out her hands to bless all. There, on a former garage: a painting of a car taking them all off into a city-scape sunset.

In every spot they sprung up, there was wonder. There was awe that something so beautiful could be in this city where there had been so much death and destruction. The rebuilding might not be for them, the people who had been left behind. But the paintings were.

People gathered in front of them, weeping.

PART SEVEN

MAKAYLA—JANUARY

We kept going out on expeditions to get food and water. More people joined us than that first day. Each night we would come back to the lobby and spread everything we'd found out of the floor. We divided it up, and passed it out to all the people who lived in the building.

Drusilla came down every night with her two children. It was the only time she came downstairs. She wouldn't let them play with the other children, or leave her side. When they tried, she grabbed them back by their arms or sleeves. She didn't look ashamed as she took the food and water. She looked like it was owed to her. Somehow, though, I got the feeling that she didn't exactly think it was owed to *her* as much as to *them*. She would grab a gallon of water and tip it up for first one, then the other child to drink from. Only after they had drank all they wanted would she drink any at all.

One night after we had distributed food, I was making my way up the dark stairs with a flashlight I had found in our apartment. I was walking quietly down the hall when I decided to keep going, to go to her door. I knocked once.

At first there was no answer, so I knocked again. I waited and waited, until finally the door opened. It was pretty dark inside, except for some candles. Drusilla was on the other side of the door, with a child on each side of her.

"What do you want?" she said. Before I could answer, she lowered the dark lids of her eyes a bit more and added, "We're here and we've got every right to what everybody else has, so if that's what you've come to talk about, you can just leave."

"I know," I said. I paused. "Can I come in?"

"You stay away from here," she said. She blocked the doorway with her ample body. She reached down and pushed her children behind her.

"I'm not trying to take anything from you," I said. I suddenly didn't know why I was there at all. "We're going to have to slag together, you know?"

"I don't care what you or anybody else do," she said. "All I care about is taking care of them."

"We all care about your children. But if you're going to stay here, you're going to have to start caring about everybody else."

"Don't you tell *me*," she said. She was pointing at me now emphatically. "Don't you dare tell me how to take care of my family. You don't know. How could you know?"

I sighed and looked down. I didn't know what she'd been through. I had a bag of chocolate in my hand that we'd scrounged up at one of the empty stores. I had been saving it for Ale, for when he got back from playing in the lobby with the other kids. Some of them spoke Spanish, and he'd been chattering away with them. It made me so happy to see him coming to life after the state we'd found him in. Her kids had been mostly locked away in the apartment she'd claimed. I knelt down and smiled at one of the kids who was peeking around his mom's legs.

"Here," I said, handing him the chocolate. "This is for you."

The kid looked so damn happy. He ran off with the other kid and I could see them tear the bag open in the dimness of the room.

When I stood back up, Drusilla had tears in her eyes.

"Why are you people being so good to us?" she almost whispered.

I shrugged. "We're all in this together," I said. I could smell the sweat on both of us. The unwashed hair and bodies and clothes, cleaned as best we could with what water we had, what sanitary wipes. I leaned in and hugged her tight. At first she resisted, but then she loosened up like a rag doll in my arms and cried.

PART EIGHT

EVANN—JANUARY

1 I was really depressed after I left my apartment. I went
to stay at my dad's house in-state, but even there all I did
was mope around. There was nothing *fabuleux* about the parties friends invited me to, there was nothing *chou* about my
dad's big house, there was just nothing. Pollock knew how
depressed I was. My dad refused to walk him, saying he was
my responsibility, but I knew it was because he didn't want
me lying around depressed all the time. Pollock wouldn't
let me be too sad for too long. His little face, his dark eyes,
his black nose, his little underbite, the happy little grunts he
made—they all kept me going sometimes.

I started sort-of making plans to move to Allentown.
But people who I know who know a lot were saying that
it was over already, that all the good artists had moved out
once other people started moving there and they had to start
worrying about paying more rent instead of just making art.
Which was sad and made me feel even more down about
everything. I still kind of looked into it, because lots of
people wouldn't *know* it was over for a long time, so it might

be worthwhile to buy a house there to rent out. But in the end I didn't have the heart to go through with all the planning. Nothing good lasts anywhere.

My dad was sympathetic at first, but after about a month of me only getting up for meals, to walk Pollock, and to get myself ice cream for another full-season-marathon of old OLED screen shows, he started to get mad.

"You're wasting your life," he said. He had just come into the OLED screen room from his afternoon run, and was wearing his running shorts. He kept glancing at the screen embedded in his wrist to see his vitals. He took a break from video conference calls and whatever else he did every day just before lunch to run two miles. He ran at the end of the day, too, at least five miles. He said it helped keep him Zen.

He didn't intend to be mean, but I still took it that way. I guess I looked hurt, because he leaned down and put his arm around me.

"I know you've been through a rough time, Evann," he said. "But you need to do things besides sit in front of the screen all day. You're not even watching anything that's been on in the last twenty years."

"Fine," I said. "I'll watch shows that came out this year."

"Evann," he said, dragging my name out. "Get it together. You're going to get fat like your stepmother if you sit around all day."

He didn't say that to be mean, either. She's not even fat. He knows it cracks me up when he makes fun of my stepmother, who I don't like very much, and had been avoiding since I got there. Her name is Valentina, if you can believe that, though she likes to be called Tina. She only married my dad for his money, which she spends on clothes and makeup and salons. But I couldn't even laugh at him making fun of Tina.

I stretched my arms out above me and stood up. Pollock started yipping like I was going to take him out, dancing around in little circles. I felt so *neglectful* it almost killed me.

"Okay, I'll make a deal with you," I said. "I'll get off the couch if you promise to stop working and go somewhere fun with me."

He shook his head. "No can do, sweetie. I have to meet Richard Bradley tonight."

"Mayor Bradley?" I said. "Doesn't he *actually* have things to be doing in the city? Should he not *actually* be working on getting things up and running there?"

"He *actually* wants to talk about plans for the city's renovation, my little skeptic."

I rolled my eyes. Since Superstorm Bernice, so many people who ran organizations or colleges or megachurches in the city wanted to have dinner with my dad. Sometimes, they came out to our house and I had to sit through the boring dinners with them. First they'd draw me out about my education and the art I collect. They might even try to get on my good side by being kind to Pollock, but I could tell they weren't really interested. They were just waiting for the right time to bring their big ideas out to my dad, and ask for his big money. Sometimes he was interested. And sometimes the ideas *were* kind of fascinating. One developer, for example, wanted to make parts of the city like Las Vegas— casinos, live shows, disaster tourism with fancy resorts away from the worst of it, a place that people would go, spend all their money, and leave again. My father said that idea was "enterprising," but in the end, he didn't choose to invest.

I sat back down, feeling defeated. Pollock jumped into my lap. "I'll just stay here on the couch," I said, kind of pouting. "And watch *Turner and the Taliban*."

"I think it would be good for you to come into the city with me, Evann," he said. "FEMA has set up a little solar-powered community in Central Park. Old Upper East Side residents are coming to help generate energy by making solar power capturing sand murals. People aren't living back there yet, but they go there for weekends, and I've heard that it can be fun, a real community thing. Why don't you come in tonight?"

I thought about it. I still had all those terrible memories of my little *chou* apartment destroyed. But here I was, sitting on the couch, wasting away. I hadn't washed my hair in three days, and it was stringy and greasy. I guess I didn't smell too great, either, because I hadn't showered in as many days. I hadn't gone out to see my friends, I hadn't done anything, really. So maybe the city wasn't the worst idea. I would just avoid all the places I had loved, that would never again be what I had fallen in love with.

2 There were party lights strung between the FEMA trailers. They cast this *magnifique* little glow over the tiny town that had been built up in the North Meadow. It was really just a bunch of trailers, and of course people wouldn't stay in them for very long, but it was Friday night and people had just come for the weekend, and there was this electricity. Generators, powered by the solar sand murals, and happy people on stationary bicycles, hummed and kept the food cold, the ice cold, the stoves hot, the people warm. We were all outside the trailers in our winter coats, drinks in our hands. I had come alone, but everywhere I turned, people wanted to talk to me.

"My insurance money came in the other day," a woman in a dark, heavy pea coat was telling me. "They say it will still be a while before the disaster assistance money from the government gets here, but who wouldn't have private insurance, the way things have been? It's not what my apartment was worth, but it's enough for a new place somewhere inland."

She lifted her plastic cup full of clinking ice cubes and amber liquid, and I raised my own, full of vodka and soda.

"To new beginnings," she said.

My father had been right—there was a real feeling of community, one like I don't know if I've ever known before. People may have been neighbors in their old lives, but they may have just been overflowing with post-disaster goodwill, I don't know. Everyone seemed to care about everyone else.

After chatting with a few more people, I met a man maybe a few years older than me. He had diamond studs over the arch of one eyebrow, and said he was in acquisitions.

"Oh?" I said, raising an eyebrow. "What sort of things do you like to *acquire?*"

"Small towns, mostly," he said. "The ones that were abandoned in droughts, after hurricanes."

"What do you do with them?" I asked.

He shrugged. "I haven't decided yet. Most of them are still too empty, too run down. But when the coasts crumble, people will want them and they'll come back. Good investments, I think."

We talked for a while, drinking more, then ended up in his trailer. It was so *chou* and rustic, just a little bed in one corner with a sleeping bag, and a cooler and camp stove.

"It reminds me of back when there were still big forests, when I was a kid," he said. His eyes were filled with nostalgia. "It's like camping out."

We were both a little drunk, and I remember our kisses being sloppy. I unbuttoned his shirt, and he had a hard stomach and more diamond studs embedded around his left nipple. They were set deep in the skin, which meant that they'd been done when he was young, which meant he'd come from money. It wasn't like I was going to marry him, or anything, but you still notice these things.

There were smooth pearl studs up the sides of his cock, so he didn't have to take them out, just slipped the condom over them. I felt their texture inside of me as he lowered me down onto the bed. That felt great, but the rest was a little boring, the kind of mechanical pumping that guys who are just looking to get off do. I started thinking about other things. If I would have to spend the night here, which might be okay, but might be boring or depressing, too. If I *should* move to Allentown, after all, or maybe move to one of these little cities like this guy owned and buy a bunch of it up myself, or if it would be too boring and depressing waiting for anything to happen there. Everything seemed pretty boring and depressing. What the hell was I even alive for, really? I mean, food is great, and I like to drink every now and then, and take move or even drag once in a great while, but what else did I have now that my little apartment and my art was gone? Pollock, I guess Pollock is the answer. I thought of how long he would live. It wouldn't be that long, in the grand scheme of things. And what would I have then? I almost started crying, but didn't because I was with this guy and that would be uncomfortable.

He seemed like he was almost done when I heard this noise. I wasn't quite sure what it was at first, because I don't think I've ever heard anything like it before. It was twangy and deep and far away. It was like it was floating through the air, through the party lights, in through the slightly open window. It got faster and higher, then lower, then slower again. I grabbed the guy's hips and pushed him out of me.

"What the hell?" he said.

But I wasn't listening. I sat up in bed, leaning toward the window.

"What is that?" I asked him.

"That?" he said. "Don't worry, babe. Sometimes the people in this little setup pay one of the people from the other parts of the city to play music here. That's . . . I can't remember what it's called . . . some gourd and string instrument. It's pretty primitive, but it's nothing to worry about."

I sat there in bed, listening to the sound. A singing rose up with it, words I didn't understand. The guy kept trying to get me to pick up where we left off, and eventually it just seemed like less of a hassle to let him finish.

Outside the window, the music played until I drifted off into sleep.

PART NINE

JESSE—JANUARY

1 Brooklyn was the end goal, but first I had this idea. One of the things Lux and I used to talk about when we got drunk was where we would go if the world turned into a zombie movie. The place we always decided would be best was The Met. There were those replica rooms from the 1800s that you could sleep in, there was food and water from the cafes, there were weapons, there was the canoe in the Inuit art section that we could cut down from the ceiling and paddle into New Jersey. There were all those paintings, so you would never be bored.

And there were those paintings by Vincent van Gogh. Lux and I had gone to look at them one day, back before the storm. We had never seen them before, and the other paintings were nice, but those were the ones we really saw. We stopped in front of the two dead sunflowers, one looking up and one face down. Fucking van Gogh. I don't know what it was. I started wiping my nose, which had suddenly started to run. It took me a few moments to realize that I was crying.

"What's wrong?" Lux said. She put her arm around me.

"They're so ... like ... dirtfucking *dead*," I said. I knew about van Gogh. I knew about the lifelong sadness, the madness, the severed ear, how his art dealer brother Theo was his only friend and confidant, and even he couldn't sell his paintings. I could see all that in there in those dead sunflowers. The shitty goddamn heaviness his life had been; that even that which he had once seen as bright, yellow, and full of life, ended up facedown, brown, shriveled, and dead.

"But look," Lux said, pointing. "Look at how they're still bright, how there is motion all around them. How much life he saw even there. He was filled with life. Maybe he just couldn't take how much it filled him up, you know? How much he could see and feel of it."

That was Lux. She was light.

I wanted to go there. I wanted to see those van Goghs now that everything else had turned into a motherfucking train wreck. I convinced José and Sebastian that we should go and stay for a little while. That it would be an adventure, that it would be something we could never do again in our lives if we didn't do it now. After that we'd go to this building that everybody was talking about in Brooklyn.

Macombs Dam Bridge hadn't been destroyed, so we walked it, and then down through Harlem. It was a long walk, and we were carrying bookbags with a metric fuck-ton of water and food, some clothes, and whatever pills I'd been able to salvage. It had been hard figuring out what to take and what to leave behind. That's materialism for you: even in those shitty conditions I still wanted to keep all the stuff we had hoarded. I'd taken my bolt cutters and crowbar and lock pick kit like I do everywhere, but a lot of stuff we just left. I had this half-hope that someone else would find it, find the place we'd called home and use it, make it their own. I hoped it would be some family or something, or a kid who had nowhere like we'd had nowhere. The thought of the place empty made me feel so alone, like places could have feelings and this one would *be aware* of its abandonment. I tried not to think about it. Shitty goddamn feelings only slow you down when you need to be sharp and on your game. I didn't have time for that stuff, not now.

We didn't talk a lot along the walk. Sebastian was kind of huffing and puffing, still weak from being sick for so long. But at one point, he touched my arm and I stopped.

"What do you think happened to all the animals in the Bronx Zoo?" he asked.

The street all around me was ruined—overturned cars, downed stoplight, buildings with their doors open like a mouth of a dead person. All around us was destruction. José had gone ahead, his superior athleticism putting distance between us. I thought of the dog back in the pharmacy, and how I had killed it without thinking twice. But that had been different. That had been an attack. And I don't really care about animals, I've always thought all the punk vegans are pretty silly with how much they do, but there was something about those animals in those cages that made me pause.

"Maybe someone got those fuckers out before," I said. "And took them somewhere safe."

"Yeah," he said. "Or maybe they died in their cages. Maybe they drowned and maybe they're still there rotting."

I shook my head. "I don't know, Sebastian. What the fuck do I know?"

There wasn't much else to say, so we started walking again.

It was a long walk down the cracked remains of Adam Clayton Powell Jr. Blvd. The farther we got from the Bronx, the more we saw nice buildings that only looked somewhat destroyed and people working on making them nicer. When we got to Central Park, we expected it to be ruined like everything around us had been. But there were FEMA trailers, and people milling around, working and cleaning. Sebastian wanted to go by the turtle pond. It was clear where it had overflowed, and there were so few turtles left in it. He wondered out loud if they had lived or died, or gotten washed to sea in the storm surge. I told him to shut the fuck up about the fucking animals already. But I didn't feel that way. Some part of me that I pushed down really wanted to know, too, if they were okay.

We came up on The Met through the trees of Central Park, and walked around to the front. It was this beautiful, stately white building, with marble arches and stairs. As we came around the front, we saw all these men in black, with huge guns milling around on the front steps. There hadn't been all these guards anywhere else we'd looked. It suddenly hit me that one room by Frank Lloyd Wright was more valuable to the kind of people who ran the world than ten families in the Bronx. Than a million people like us.

When I saw all those guards, I remembered this day a while back, before I met Lux or José or Sebastian. I was traveling around, and I'd ended up in Pittsburgh. I'd wandered into this museum. I think it was a Carnegie Museum. I had some time to kill and I wanted to stand around and look at paintings and get lost. I wasn't bothering anybody, but people kept giving me these looks, the kind you start to notice if you get them long enough, even if you're just trying to mind your own business. Maybe they couldn't figure out what I was, because I was wearing a skirt, but my legs were super hairy and showing, and my hair was short, and I had on a Brando shirt over a binder and torn-up men's combat boots. I went from one room to the next, and in every room, a museum guard came up to me to ask if I was looking for someone, or if I was lost. After a while, to get them to leave me alone, I'd say things like, "I lost my mom," and give them these outlandish descriptions of drag queens I'd met once at a party in Bayonne.

Finally, one of the guards in a room with Warhols walked up to me. He had these kind eyes, and I could tell he didn't want to fuck with me.

"What are you doing here?" he asked.

"I just wanted to see the shitty fucking paintings," I said, finally honest. "Isn't that what they're there for?"

"You smell," he said to me quietly, as if he was trying to spare my feelings. I knew I smelled bad. I'd been on the road for weeks, no shower, no bed, no change of clothes. "You smell and you're disturbing the other patrons. Please just leave."

I'm not sure why, but I got tears in my eyes. I think it was the way he lowered his voice, like he didn't want to embarrass me. I didn't want him to see that I was crying, so I started making a scene.

"What the fuck are you?" I asked. "The fucking patron saint of odor? Fuck you, motherfucker!"

I ended up getting thrown out. Like, literally. They said that I was lucky they didn't call the cops.

Pittsburgh. Whatever.

So back in New York, looking at The Met, seeing all those guards, I waved for José and Sebastian to cross the street.

"This isn't the right place for us," I said. "We'll try somewhere else."

2 We kept walking.

"What about Ellis Island?" Sebastian asked. "And the Statue of Liberty? I've never seen those."

"How would we get there?" José said, somewhat derisively. "We're going to have a hard enough time getting to Brooklyn with all the bridges down. Should we swim to Ellis Island?"

"I don't know," Sebastian said. "It was just an idea."

"We'll find somewhere cool," I said. "That whole city is ours now, right? There's got to be some place we want to see that we've never seen before."

We walked downtown with lighter steps. We were laughing and joking, and even José who's normally such a miserable jack-off slowed down and walked and joked with us. The destroyed landscape had nothing on us. I hadn't felt this way since that night that we were goofing off and Lux disappeared.

As soon as I thought of her I stopped laughing. What if she was in one of those awful hospitals where people would call her sir and treat her like a man because she'd never had the money to do anything besides take hormones? I've heard of places like that, she'd been in one before. They had taken her to New Jersey, I was pretty sure. What if she was in some awful situation right now and here I was laughing and joking?

I wondered if they fixed her and sent her home. That would be even worse. Lux had tried to kill herself once when she lived there. She'd gotten her exit bag ready and had the helium and everything, and was going to lie in bed and just go, you know? She posted a suicide note to a support group she was part of on LinxUs, and then turned off her noti-fications and sat down to pet her cat, who she really loved and was sad to be leaving behind. Turned out a lot of people cared what happened to a fucked-up sixteen-year-old trans girl, because in the time she petted her cat, someone had found her info on the internet and called the authorities. They took her and locked her up for a while in a crazy house, she told me. They put her in the men's ward, and all the men catcalled and harassed her except for one guy who called her baby and said he wanted to run away with her. She got out and detransitioned for a while to cope. Then she couldn't take it anymore, retransitioned, and got kicked out.

"Hey," Sebastian said, pulling me out of my thoughts. "Aren't we near the Tenement Museum?"

We were walking down the east side of the island, through Alphabet City. There were huge condos all around us, abandoned now, but rising up to the sky like redwoods. Fucking overdeveloped city. All these people were gone, now, though, and their homes empty. We tried scrounging around in some of the dumpsters as we walked, but everything was long since picked over.

"Yeah. It's down on Orchard Street, I think," I said. "We should head over that way and check it out."

We got there before too long. The Tenement Museum was easy to find—it was the only building that wasn't a high-rise or a 24/7. It looked so weird, this little brick building squished between all these behemoth condos. It had a historical landmark protection, I think, or it would have been gone a long time ago, too.

The front door wasn't gaping open or anything like lots of the doors in other buildings were, but it wasn't locked. There wasn't anyone guarding the place. We made our way in, climbed some stairs, and were standing in this room that was made up super old-time. There was an ancient motherfucking monster of a sewing machine. There was a gas lamp and some other old, rusty things that could have been used for anything, I didn't know what. José just sort of stood in the corner, looking around and not saying anything, but Sebastian and I walked through, touching things lightly with soft brushes. It was kinda awesome, being here alone. There were no guards, but nobody had touched the place after the storm.

We made our way around, quiet, talking about things, touching them. I found a room with a bed. It looked like it was made up to look like someone was in it, someone small. Were people smaller back then, or was this lump in the bed supposed to be a child? I didn't know. I walked over and looked down. There was a little doll there, nestled in the bed. Who had put it there? It was old-time, too, with a creepy cracked face and milky eyes. Someone had left it tucked in.

There was a noise then, from another room. José grabbed some long pole from a wall and I pulled my crowbar out of my bag. We inched toward the noise, trying to make as little noise of our own as possible even though we had just been talking.

Crouched in the next room was a family. They were so skinny that I dropped my crowbar immediately. It fell to the ground with a clatter. They looked so scared.

There was a mother, a father, and a tiny little girl, no more than five. The little girl was in the mother's arms, her face hidden in her mother's neck, her black hair messy around her little head. It looked like it hadn't been brushed in some time.

"What are you doing here?" I asked.

"Home," the man said, his voice cracking. "Home now."

They looked so scared. They hadn't even tried to defend themselves, even though they didn't know who we were or what we would do.

We backed out the way we had come in.

3 We walked past the destroyed bridges and the loud crews working to rebuild them. By the time we reached the South Street Seaport, our legs were aching and our backs were tired from the heavy bags we carried. Everything was a wreck down there. There were still ships that had been tossed up onto the ground and wrecked and broken. They were lodged between buildings and down streets. We walked up to one, gaping at the big hole in the side where it had crashed, looking in at the blackness in the hull.

All along the wharf, there were boats that were still in use. Little boats, big boats, rowboats, and motorboats. The ones that weren't moving along the water and slicing up the mirror surface were chained up. I pulled my bolt cutters out of my bag as we got closer. When we found a little rowboat chained to one of the docks, I waited for a moment nobody was looking and clamped the steel bolt cutters down over the chain. It was cut in an instant, and slid down into the water like it had never existed at all. I felt this super-shitty spasm of guilt. I was probably fucking over some guy who didn't have shit but this boat. But what was I supposed to do? Hot wire one of the motorboats? I didn't know how.

After the lock was cut and the guilt passed, I realized I've done a lot of things, I've been in a lot of places, and I've had a lot of experiences. But I'd be dog fucked if I ever rowed a boat before. I turned to José and Sebastian, but they just shrugged one after the other.

"We'll get in and figure it out," José said. "How hard could it be?"

The river pulled us downstream right away, and José grabbed the paddles, struggling to keep us in place. Even with his push-ups-every-morning muscles, we just kept jerking back and forth in the water, turning in circles, whirling around. After a while, though, he got the rhythm. Once he got it, Sebastian joined him and they each took a side.

"Let me help," I said, after a while.

"You have the scrawniest arms known to man," José said, grunting from the exertion of paddling. "You'd be able to paddle for five minutes. Just leave it to us."

"No, to goddamn bullshit hell with that, you fucker," I said. "You give me that fucking paddle."

José handed it over, but just smirked from the end of the boat as I struggled to get it right. It took a while, and I started sweating and maybe my face got red, which just made José laugh even more. But then I got it.

"See, fucker?" I said. "Took me less time to figure it out than it took you."

We started inching toward the opposite shore. Out in the middle of the river, me and Sebastian paused in our rowing. The city loomed up on either side of us. The East River seemed cleaner than I'd ever seen it—no condoms or used tampons floating along it, no beer cans, no plastic bags poking up like the heads of turtles. The skyline reached up on either side of us, the Manhattan side a bit taller, but the Brooklyn side no less full of condos and affluence. Years ago, when I first got there, I met this old guy living out on the street one day. I sat down and talked to him, and it got to be nighttime, and I took what little money I had, and he took what little money he'd spanged that day, and we bought ourselves big bottles of malt liquor that we put in brown bags. We took what little money we had left after that and got ourselves rides on the train, and, to get our money's worth, we rode it as far as we could. We rode all the way out to Gravesend, out to the beach. While we sat on the beach, he told me all about Brooklyn sixty years before, when he had been a bit older than me. He told me he'd had a favorite place to go, one that was just on the other side of the East River in Williamsburg. It was a dirty old bar with dirty Christmas lights in the window, and old fluorescent signs from beer companies, and they had big Styrofoam cups that they'd sell beer in for super cheap. He said that back then, he didn't have much money, but enough that he could always get good and drunk there. He went there year after year, sitting in the red pleather booths, watching as the old Polish people from the neighborhood left or died, and the young hip people came in. Up until the early part of the century, he said, he'd go there and drink then walk down the side of the East River. Back then, it was still mostly populated by factories, old buildings made of brick where they still made things—not like now when all people do is sit around and make things with their computers. He'd go down to the river when it was still broken down and industrial, and he would climb out onto these long ledges of concrete that reached out in to the water. He would look up, and all around him would be blackness, and then there was the city, twinkling above him like a spectral vision. I never forgot that. That guy's probably dead now, but I can still see the city the way he saw it.

Sitting now in the middle of the gray water, with the sun sparkling down and the wind blowing cold, and this huge built-up city on either side of us, I wondered what I was heading to out there. I felt this sense of dread fall over me, which was strange, because all I'd heard of this building that was waiting for us was wonderful things, utopian things. Yet there was this fucking dread. What if? What if?

Lux once said that the things that seemed the best in her head always became completely shitted up the minute they got out of it and into the world. Her transition, for example. She told me once about the feeling of happiness and accomplishment and epiphany that she'd had when she worked through all the shit in her head, all the stuff that had been put there by a lifetime of living in this world, that said *boy*. All the clothes she'd been made to wear, the haircuts she'd been forced to have as a child, the pronouns people had put on her, the things people expected of her. She told me that for a few days, before she told anyone, everything had been perfect. She had walked around with a smile on her face. She had felt like everything made sense.

Then she told her parents and the what-would-Jesus-our-Lord-and-Savior-think started. Then the harassment started. Then she figured out that the thing that could be perfect in your head could be a disaster when it got outside of it.

What if this building was like that? What if?

4 Getting to Brooklyn wasn't the end of it. We still had a long walk, and while I've been to Brooklyn plenty of times, I've always gotten there underground. Things look a lot different above ground. I honestly couldn't tell one street from the next.

José had a subway map, because he's good with things like that. A long time ago, I had made fun of him for having it, called him a tourist and lots of other things. We had cheapo handheld screens and shit and nobody even used maps in a fucking decade. I was glad he had it now. We walked where the trains went, making our way slowly from one station to the next. It wasn't super cold out, Januaries are like that. It wasn't bad weather to be walking, but we'd walked all the way from the Bronx and we were starting to feel it. My leg had been throbbing for a while where the dog had bit me, even though the wound was almost closed. Our bags were heavy.

That little family in the Tenement Museum kept coming back to me, popping into my thoughts. Would they make it? Why would they live there? Maybe they didn't feel they had the right to one of those condos. I started getting mad, thinking about it. I looked down and my hands were clenched into fists.

It probably took us longer to get there than if we'd walked in a straight line, but we made it. We got to this neighborhood where everybody knew what was going on, knew the building. Someone pointed us to where it was.

It was huge. There were these giant windows that went all the way up to ceilings, and the floors were taller than in any building I'd ever been in. There were silhouettes moving against the dark windows, and down near the door.

We got closer to the door. There was a huge man there. Another came outside with him. There were more inside. I didn't know if he had a gun or a knife. I knew I didn't want to mess with him, no matter what I had.

"Who are you?" he asked.

I threw back my shoulders and got up in his face, even though it wasn't *completely* necessary.

"We heard about what you're doing here. We think we can help you. We think you can help us."

The man standing there uncrossed his muscled arms from in front of his chest.

"You willing to slag? There can't be anybody here that doesn't."

"Huh?"

"Work. Are you willing to work with us?"

"Yeah," Sebastian said, stepping forwards. "We've been working to get by alone. We can work here, too."

"You're willing to cooperate with other people?" he seemed to be looking hard at me this time. People are always pegging me for the troublemaker.

"Yeah, of course," I said.

"And you've got nowhere else to go?" he asked. His voice softened at this last question.

"If we did, we wouldn't be here," I said.

He stepped aside, just like that. And we walked in the door.

There was someone painting.

On the hospital in the Bronx, there had already been murals. Those murals had been of saintly people in white, doing good things with their hands, making the world safe and helping people live. Those murals had been lies once the storm came.

He had seen the inside of that hospital. One night, long after all the patients who they thought they could save had been airlifted out and the rest of them left to rot, after the doctors and nurses were gone, after the people who had meant to do good and who had been brought to the position of only be able to do the least bad they could had left, he took a ladder and spray cans and paint tubes and brushes. He stood there all night in the dark. He climbed the ladder with his boot heels hooking over the rungs. He went up and down. The grays and blacks and browns and reds went up. He drew faces with bones showing, long strings of hair, sunken eyes. He drew soldiers with more machine helmet than flesh. There were horses that had lost all their muscle and sinew and carried riders into death on a mount of bone. Hideous insects marched along with the horses, all mandible and reaching legs, eating and tearing what was left. The buildings he drew in the background were sticks barely held together by blackness, destroyed by the weak power of skeleton fists. The sky above the scene opened into cosmos, and the stars were holes that the universe fell into. The planets were rubber bands stretched to the point of breaking. The moon gave off no light, was naught but craters and lonely mountain ranges.

He created the painting in the night. When the morning came, the people who were left behind, the people who roamed the streets in groups if they were lucky enough to find them and alone and furtive if they were not, stopped to see this looming battle scene. They saw what he had seen when he went inside the hospital and found the bodies cold in the freezing night with the life-saving beep of machines far away. The looked upon it and they thought, "death." They thought, "This is what the city has come to." Finally, they thought, "Someone has seen."

Later, when the camera crews came, and the people behind

the cameras began to find the bodies, the news anchors began to recall a time long ago when a cross had been found in the rubble of those famous buildings downtown that had been destroyed by that famous plane. They showed the picture to those who were far away. Those people far away thought, "art," and they began to think again of return.

He heard of a place where an old woman had starved to death up in a low-rent high-rise. He walked until he got there. Over the city, through the broken streets, past parking meters fallen to the ground, past empty, looted newspaper stands, over and through the debris, down the alleys, over puddles with frozen edges. He walked through the night and through the day. He slept in alleys and building doorways. He found supplies along the way. Who would stop for a can of spray paint but him?

He went to the high-rise and he painted a skeleton hugged by a suit. The suit was a picture of precise folds and creases and seams. It draped off the bones like it would on the gym-sculpted *frame of a millionaire who intended on living forever. In front of the skeleton, he painted a banquet so rich and varied that the people left had only seen the likes of it in magazines, if there. He had never seen this kind of food in real life, either, but he knew it was good, so he painted it there. He painted the skeleton's hand digging into it and bringing it up to his bare teeth.*

PART TEN

MAKAYLA—MARCH

1 The new kids, Jesse, José, and Sebastian, kind of drove me crazy. They had a lot in common with Kristen, even though they were clearly from different worlds. The way they thought about things, the suggestions they made for how we run the building—they seemed to come from the same place of having been through this shit almost professionally. I had mixed feelings about all of them. It was upswing to have people around who knew what was up, that was for sure. But when José suggested we use these hand signals so no one talked over anyone else at our meetings, I got kind of annoyed.

"These are called 'twinkles,'" José said, holding up his hand and wiggling his fingers. "They're a better way of saying you agree with something than interrupting the person who's talking."

"What the hell is wrong with agreeing with someone?" I said.

José shrugged like it was no big deal, but I could tell he was annoyed right back at me. "We have a good number of people here. More are showing up every day. The bigger a group gets, the more important it is to be able to effectively communicate. Instead of pausing a meeting for fifteen people to shout, 'Yes, that's right!' we wiggle our fingers and get the same effect. Makes sense, doesn't it?"

I could tell the question wasn't a question.

So people started wiggling their fingers at each other. And circling their extended index fingers around each other to let someone know they had gone on talking for too long. And shooting one index finger, then another, at someone to indicate that they had hard information specifically relating to what was being said.

"I don't like this shit," I said to Jaden, back in our room. "I don't like these kids coming in there and running the building like it's their show. And what the hell are they doing pulling all those big orange barrels into the lobby from the streets that are being worked on?"

Jaden shrugged. It wasn't like José's shrug that tried to pretend something wasn't a big deal when it was. It was a real carefree shrug, 100 percent Jaden. He seemed to like the newcomers.

"José told me he's making shields out of them," Jaden said. "*Shields?*"

"Yeah, shields," Jaden said. "He seems to think they'll be good to have around, even if we don't need them. I guess I'd rather have a shield and not need it than need a shield and not have it."

"When in your life have you ever needed shields before?"

Jaden got serious suddenly. "I would bet that most of the people here have needed defending at one time or another."

That shut me up. But just for a minute.

"Shields or no shields," I said, "I don't like these kids. They slag okay, I'll give them that, but they think this is their place. This is *our* place."

"Yeah, Makayla, *ours*. Yours, mine, and everyone who's slagged for it. Including those kids."

Jaden put his arms on my shoulders and held me away from him. He looked at me for a minute. We were so still that I could feel my left eyelid twitching, something that had only recently started happening.

"You're so nails, Makayla," he said. "You always used to pretend, but I saw through it. Now I barely know who you are. When did you get this way?"

I couldn't answer him. I loved him. Maybe more than I loved myself. But I couldn't let him know how broken I'd become.

2 Things weren't quite upswing between Jaden and me after that. We worked together, we slept in the same room, we still had sex, all that was the same. But there was this space between us. He would stand back and watch me. Sometimes I bit my tongue, like when people started picking up on José's stupid hand motions, and getting really into them. Okay, maybe I was wrong. Maybe it was best. But as I stood there, hands on my hips, not talking on purpose, I could feel Jaden's eyes on me. Watching and waiting. When I looked his way, he looked in the other direction.

The food gathering committee grew as the number of people in the building grew. Finding food grew harder in some ways and easier in others. Scavenging and what José and Sebastian and Jesse called dumpstering became nearly impossible. Most of what had been left behind but still usable was gone in the first several weeks. But FEMA and the Red Cross and the Natural Disaster Fund had all set up around the city and were handing out meals. Mo, who hadn't backed out of the food gathering committee even after that 'trosh first day, made friends with some of the guys who drove the trucks of food into the city once the tunnels were functional. He told them about our building, what we were doing, how we were growing. Before I knew it, we had boxes of nonperishable food and water that the Red Cross didn't have their shit together enough to notice were gone stockpiled in the utility closet of our building. We found a padlock in an abandoned store and I kept the key. Everyone trusted me.

I took that closet full of food seriously. I wore the key around my neck on a chain I found in the apartment that Jaden, Ale, and my granny were living in. We set up times when everyone would come down and the food and water would be portioned out. Some people wanted extra shares, Drusilla being the most vocal proponent of this. She cited her growing children again and again, said they needed more than other people did. I told her the same thing every time.

"Each one of us gets what everyone else gets. It's the only fair way."

Most people respected that I wanted to do the upswing thing. But not Drusilla. She gave me this 'trosh look every time. The rage that was glowing in her eyes was almost frightening sometimes. But anything we did had to be upswing for all of us.

My granny mostly stayed in our apartment, though she did what she could to help around the building. She'd cleaned houses for a living when she was younger, and she took to keeping our apartment and common space of the lobby sparkling. She would get down on her hands and knees and scrub the floors with a brush, arthritis and all. I would tell her, Granny, relax. I can do the slag you would be doing, no problem. But she wanted to contribute to the building as much as anybody else did. It was kind of beautiful, the way everyone wanted to slag, the way everyone wanted to make the place better.

Ale came out of his shell bit by bit, playing with the other kids in the place. The scratches I had found up and down his arms were mostly gone. I saw one here and there, but they were isolated and faded in a few days' time. He liked talking to Sebastian, and that kind of made me like Sebastian more. When I would see him jawing away in Spanish with Ale, and Ale lighting up and looking up to him, and him giving Ale high fives, it made me feel like maybe these kids who had been living up the Bronx weren't so bad. Ale started speaking a little bit of English here and there, and we would talk together as much as we could.

I usually kept it light, talking about games and music and food, but once or twice I tried to ask him questions about where he'd come from, what had happened, who he was missing. He stopped talking, dead, whenever I did. Though we hadn't had electricity in months, he kept the dead phone he'd clutched in the emergency shelter on the nightstand next to his bed when he slept, and in his pocket when he walked around the building. He never let the thing go.

He told me one day he wanted to be an artist when he grew up. I bit my lip and didn't tell him there was no guarantee he *would* grow up.

Some of the apartments had musical instruments in them. The people who could play them brought them down to the lobby, and we would sit in circles while they played.

Sometimes they played Top 40 songs that we hadn't heard bumping out of car stereos in months, sometimes they played old songs that me and lots of the other people around my age had never heard before, and sometimes someone who came from far away would teach everyone else a song they had brought with them across oceans. The little kids danced and some of the adults cried.

Sebastian saw the effect that the music had on the kids and started an entertainment committee. He rounded up all the art supplies he could find, all the games, all the balls and bats and hoops and baskets, and took the kids into the muddy street twice a day to play, or to the lobby to draw when it was bad out. Parents caught onto it, too, and we had more people in that committee than we needed, so we kept rotating them. Ale liked soccer the best, and was so good at it that I knew he'd played before. I wondered once more about his life prior to the storm.

We lost weight and we wore our clothes until they smelled so 'trosh that we couldn't wear them anymore. Some people, when the bridges opened back up, took up the Red Cross on their offers and left the building to head to shelters in New Jersey. But most of us stayed. Most of us had nowhere to go, and what we had built was infinitely more upswing than anything any disaster relief organization could offer us. Some days, where we were, what we were doing felt normal. It felt better than normal. It felt like a whole building, a whole life, of the block parties my parents had helped plan back before everything got sienty for people like us in this city, back before they both checked. I thought about those days less and less, the good times, and more about the good ones we were building now.

Some days, days when dusk would fall on the kids playing

out front in the street, nights when the music we made in the lobby would float out the open door into the dark night, the building was better than anything I'd ever had before.

3 I was in our apartment after the food had been collected and distributed for the day, relaxing. There was stuff to do, stuff to go to, other ways to help, but sometimes I just wanted to sit back and be alone and think or talk to my granny. That day, one of the truck drivers had given us a treat, something he had likely bought with his own money because God knows FEMA wasn't going to think of it—three cases of beer in Styrofoam coolers full of ice. We each got two beers; we even gave some of the older kids one, why not? I had brought mine and my granny's upstairs while Jaden stayed down in the lobby where everyone was drinking them together. We hadn't drank anything in so long; the liquor we found in the apartments hadn't lasted much past our days of removing rugs and washing things down with bleach. After one beer we were giggling like we'd split our faces off.

"Makayla, you go downstairs, there's no use sitting up here alone with an old lady like me," she said. "Before you know it, I'll be telling you stories about dead people and times when rent cost a couple of hundred dollars."

"I don't believe you even would," I laughed. "You've never told me stories about the way things were when you were younger. I don't think before we got to this building you ever jawed to me more than to tell me a bedtime story when my mom and dad were working late. You're nails, Granny, not the kind I expect to drink a beer and reminisce."

"Nails?" she said. "You want to see nails, you go back to when I was your age. I was the hardest thing this side of a diamond. Sometimes I look at you, and I remember back the way I was."

I stopped laughing. I hadn't been kidding when I said that she never jawed to me much. A story here about how my dad was when he was a little boy, a joke there about my parents after they were married, but granny was tough, quiet. She'd lead a hard life and I guess I just assumed she didn't much want to have to live it again in words.

"The city got bad in your life, Makayla, that's for sure, but before then it was bad in a different way. A way that nobody talked about unless they were on the wrong side of it. It was just white here, black there. Rich here, poor there. In the neighborhoods and in the schools, in the way we ate and the way we got arrested, in the parks we went to and the beaches we swam at. That was just how it was.

"I was twelve when the first boy I knew got shot by the cops. He lived down the hall from me in the housing project. He was sleeping on the couch in the front room of his apartment because that's where he slept when his baby sisters were born. They said his daddy was selling drugs, and when the cops came into that room, guns firing, they didn't care who they were shooting. They put six holes in him, and he didn't even die right away. I heard him screaming when the ambulance finally came to take him away, and when it took him away we didn't see him ever again. The only drugs they found in that apartment were a little bit of pot his daddy smoked. That was a hell of a trade, a twelve-year-old boy's life for less than an ounce of weed."

"Fuck, Granny," I said. "I never knew that."

"Why would I tell you that? You think I didn't hear that

boys screams in my dreams for years? You think those were sounds I want to remember? I can hear them now, plain as they were then."

We didn't say anything for a minute, just sipped our beers. We sure weren't laughing anymore.

"I grew up mad, Makayla. Mad like you. Mad about how things were, mad that nothing I could do seemed to change them. But I was older than you are now, old enough to have your father in his crib already when the cops lined up those eight boys, one of whom they said had stolen a pack of cig-arettes, and shot them one after another. One by one. Left that last one knowing exactly what had happened to the seven before him for a minute before doing the same to him. Can you imagine how their terror must have been growing as they went down that line? It was after all the cops had cameras, too, but you know that footage never showed up in the database, and nobody found it for years. Long after each one of those cops who'd done it had long since gone on with their lives and weren't in danger of facing up to what they'd done anymore."

"The riots of '25 followed that, didn't they?" I asked.

"Oh, yes they did," she said, shaking her gray head from side to side.

"Holy shit, Granny, were you in the streets?"

She nodded once, dead serious. "You can believe I was, Makayla. I left your father with my mother, and I was out in those streets with my neighbors and my friends, and I did things I never thought I would do. I made it back home that night. Lots of us didn't.

"And after that night, every time I heard a cop car go by, every time I heard any kind of siren in the night, I would wake up and go into your daddy's room and say goodbye to him, because I was sure they were coming for me and I was never going to see him again.

"I gave up that night on the thought that I was going to see a better world in my life. I hoped for a while that your daddy would. Then I even gave up on that. When you were born, I got to hoping again, just for a little while. But you see how it worked out."

She threw her beer back and took a long drink, as if she were much younger, and much stronger. She put the bottle down and looked me in the eye.

"Makayla, when that storm came, you started something that I couldn't start, that nobody I knew ever could. You started what's happening at this building. This building, my beautiful granddaughter, is just about the best I've ever seen things be."

I didn't want to look like some numptie, but a big fat tear welled up in the corner of my eye and, before I could wipe it away, slipped right down my face.

"We're all just doing good by each other, Granny," I said.

"Makayla, if you think that's nothing, you didn't hear a word I said."

4 The next morning I woke up feeling sienty from the little bit of beer, or maybe from the nightmare I'd been having. It was a mixed-up dream. I think I was high. I was always looking behind my back. My attacker was there, the smile on his face wide and wild. I saw the face of that cob roller in the convenience store when we first came to the building. I saw his head lying on the ground in a pool of blood. Then,

like magic, faces that looked just like his were in front of me, crying. Little kids no older than five or six, his kids. *Was he really dead?* I wondered in the dream. *Did we kill this man who maybe had a wife and children? What the hell had we done?*

I sat up in bed, breathing hard. Next to me, Jaden was still sleeping—since everything had calmed down and we were more settled into the building, he'd sleep through anything. It used to be that he'd wake up to my nightmares, that he'd comfort me, holding me close saying, "Everything is okay, baby." But now he just slept. I felt my shoulders cold where the blanket had fallen off, where his arms were not.

Thoughts like those in my dream plagued me more and more the longer we stayed. Whose lives were we raiding? Were the people we were taking from really that bad? They had made our lives unlivable, that was for sure, but beyond that, weren't they just people like us who wanted to hear music and eat food and love some people and have some things to call their own? I didn't know, and I tried my best to keep these thoughts as far from my head as I could because there was so much work to be done just to keep ourselves alive.

I got out of bed, wandered into the living room, and sat on one of the white couches. My eyelids were twitching again. The couches had gotten considerably less white as we slagged in the building and came back up and sat on them. After I saw the other apartments, I began to wonder about the people who had lived in ours. Everything was conspicuously expensive. Would this be what I did if I ever got a lot of money? Buy things that showed off how much I had? Or would I be like the people who owned some of the other apartments where everything was dark wood, haphazard in a gorgeous way, crammed with little touches of beauty? I didn't know. I'd probably never know. This borrowed luxury was the closest I'd ever get to it.

As I sat at the huge wooden counter that ran around the kitchen, I tried to think of a future beyond the building. Every time I did that particular mental exercise, I came up short. *I might die here*, I thought. I didn't think of how long I could hang on, just that my end might come in some strange disease that none of us could handle, and there would be no way to get me to a doctor. But I was young, healthy, I stayed as clean as I could and sanitized my hands. But what about the older people and the little kids? My granny and Ale? They were the real ones at risk. I worried about them constantly.

As I was sitting on the couch, I stretched my legs and reached my arms above my head. Someone had started an exercise committee, though I never went. Kristen led a Jillian class, of course. I leaned back and started biting my nails. I felt tense all the time, my neck always sore and my muscles tight. What was this day going to bring? I'd go out, gather food, distribute it. Then I'd see if I could help out anywhere else, with the kids, with some improvement project Kristen had started. It would be a full day. These moments, though, when I was doing nothing, these were the real 'trosh moments. The moments when I could feel everything I wanted to forget.

A knock on the door snapped me out of my thoughts.

"Come in," I said. The door was never locked. We had never fixed the lock we broke to get in here that first day. There was no need. Everything we had, we shared; everything belonged to everybody.

The door swung open inch by inch. José stood on the other side. He knew I didn't like him very much ever since the hand motions thing. He'd been up to our apartment maybe twice since coming to the building. I couldn't imagine what he was doing there now.

"What's going on?" I asked, standing up. I stopped biting my nails.

"Makayla, you need to come downstairs to the lobby right away," he said. Then he turned and was gone.

My heart started beating really quickly. Something seriously dissat must have happened for him to come up here like that. I ran to catch up to him, but he was already on his way down the stairs. No matter how I went after him, he stayed ahead. By the time I got to the lobby, he was already down there waiting.

I looked around me. Everything seemed in place except for the ten people or so standing around, looking annoyed. I kept looking, and soon my eyes traveled into the little walkway off the back of the lobby. The utility closet door was ajar. I grabbed at the chain around my neck, feeling for the key. It was still there.

"What the actual fuck?" I said, walking toward the gaping door. When I got there, I could see why everyone was so pissed off. The lock had been pried open and the closet had been raided. A lot of the food and bottles of water were gone. I turned back to the people standing in the lobby. "Did anyone see who did this?" I asked.

People shook their heads, or said, "No."

I stepped back and looked into the raided closet. I punched the door. This had been my responsibility, and I was pissed that it happened at all. But what I was more pissed off about was that someone had come down and taken the things that were for all of us for themself. I was going to find whoever did this, I swore. And when I did they were hoddered.

"Where were the guards when this happened?" I asked, whirling around toward the people in the lobby.

"They were at the door," Mo spoke up. "Nobody got in last night, that's not what happened."

"So it was somebody in the building," I said. My anger was growing at every word.

"It must have been," José said.

"Was it that Jesse kid?" I said. Jesse wasn't around, and that and the fact that I had never trusted the kid was enough for me at the moment to make the accusation.

"Hey," Sebastian said, angry. "Jesse wouldn't do this. Jesse's not an asshole—they're here to do the right thing by everybody as much as you are. You take that shit right back."

"Fine, it wasn't Jesse," I said grudgingly. I kicked the door again. As I was in the middle of doing it, Jaden came down from the stairwell, walking slowly into the lobby. He saw me kicking the door, saw the people assembled, and got what was happening pretty quickly.

I racked my brain thinking of who would do this. When the answer hit me, it hit me hard and I couldn't believe I hadn't thought of it immediately.

"Drusilla," I said.

Everybody looked at each other. José shrugged once and nodded. "Could be," he said.

The nod spread through the crowd. Jawing started up—no one had seen her down here this morning, she had been trying to get extra provisions for her kids since day one, her door was locked all the time, no one put it past her. The voices rose up, accusatory. For a minute everybody forgot about the hand motions José had introduced and talked over each other in a thunder. We all felt pretty sure.

"Hey, hey," I heard a voice say. It took me a minute to

realize it was Jaden. His hands were held out in front of him, as if he were motioning for a person running right at him to stop. "We don't know it was her at all. This is all just a guess."

"So one of us goes up there," I said. "And we find out for sure."

"And what if we find out she did?" Jaden said. "What if we find out she stole all that stuff? You wanna kick her out, Makayla?"

"I'll do what it takes," I said.

"Aren't we all here stealing?" Jaden said. He came walked down the hall, closer to me.

"We're not stealing from each other!" I shouted. "We're just picking up the pieces other people dropped. She stole from all of us!"

"What about her kids, Makayla?" Jaden said. He was still walking closer to me. The room grew silent as he came up in front of me. Everybody looked at each other for a long time. I looked at Jaden. His breath was coming in jagged; he was upset like I hadn't seen him before. "You want to throw them out in the street? This kind of street where people are roaming around killing each other every day? Where there's no place else for them to go?"

We all stayed really quiet for a minute. My heart was pounding and I didn't know what to say. Finally, I said, "The kids have to go, too."

Jaden stared at me, like he had been since that day when I told him how I felt about Jesse, José, and Sebastian. He shook his head from side to side once, twice, real slow.

"When did you become so heartless?" he asked me.

"The minute she decided she was more important than the rest of us," I said.

Jaden looked away from me, disgust on his face. "We're in this together," he said. "All of us."

"That," I said, "is my motherfucking point."

The guards were standing over by the door. I motioned to them.

"Come on with me," I said. "The minute I find that extra food and water, I want her out of here. I'll need your help."

The people guarding the front door came toward me cautiously. A few people's faces in the lobby had shifted to looks of confusion and hesitation.

"Makayla," Jaden said. The disgust on his face was gone, replaced by the kind, sensitive person I had known all my life. A person who had sympathy for both Drusilla and me. I loved him so much right then. But I knew he was wrong. So I pushed that love somewhere away, somewhere I push all the things in my head that don't keep me moving forward. "Don't do this."

"I have to," I said softly.

He shook his head again from side to side. "When you get back up to our apartment, I'll be gone. I'm going to stay in an empty one. I don't think things are working out between us."

My anger flared up in me again. I felt like punching something, maybe him this time. I clenched my fists and held them at my side. He saw me and just stood there, ready for whatever was going to come.

"Fine," I said. "It's not working out. I just need things to stay good for all of us."

He listened to the words passed from person to person on street corners, in looted stores, in the lines waiting for the meager food handouts from the government. In one such line, two old women spoke about the angels they had once seen.

"I was in the hospital once, long before all this," said a woman bent over a cane to the woman standing next to her. They were both old, both had white hair and dark skin, dark eyes and lips painted over false teeth despite how the world was falling apart around them. "I was hooked up to a machine and it was beeping, beeping, beeping, until suddenly that beep became a trumpet, a song out of the heavens. Standing there was an angel, all in white robes with the face of my daughter who died when she was just a teenager. She stood there telling me that everything would be fine, that even if I let go of this life—and she told me it was my choice to let go or stay—but if I did let go, there was a kingdom waiting for me. All I had to do was believe. I told her I wanted to stay, that I wanted to be with her again, but there was my boys and their babies left here, and I had to stay for them. Then the trumpet became a beeping *again, and I was back in the hospital. That's how I know there's more than this life, more than this struggle," she said. "That's how I know that there's something waiting for us all after this."*

"It takes faith to get through this life," the other woman said. "I do believe God does reward us for our faith."

Murmurs like this went all up and down those long lines that always moved too slowly.

One day, in another line, he heard of a teenager who had been shot by a policeman. The cop said he thought the boy had a gun, but what he'd really had was a banana that the Red Cross had given him. He'd waited in line all day for the banana.

That night, he went to the spot where the boy's blood was still on the ground. He took his spray cans. He painted over the bloodstain. He painted a gun with a banana instead of a barrel. He painted the skin peeling back, revealing the body of a child where the banana would have been.

The painting only stayed on the ground a few days before a crew came to blast it off.

PART ELEVEN

EVANN—APRIL

1 It started getting warmer, like summer. That's how spring is, though my dad always tells me there was a time when it wasn't that way. I was still at his house in-state, but it was getting really old. My dad was still on my case, and Tina— well, Tina just wanted to talk about her hair and her clothes and her nails. All those things are important enough, sure, I mean, you can't go around *not* caring about them. But every now and then I would try to talk about art, and she would just give me this blank stare. She didn't even know who Basquiat was, I don't think. It was only when I mentioned that he dated that old pop star that she cared at all. With all her money and all the things science can do these days, I think Madonna'll be alive forever, and that's *fabuleux* because she knew Basquiat, actually knew him.

I tried some painting while I was staying there. Nothing came out of it. I'm a terrible painter, to be honest. I knew that. I was just bored.

There was a time when I thought maybe I had the potential to get better. But I don't. It's so much easier to appreciate beauty than to make it. When I realized that, one night while I was doing move with my friends in my old little apartment before it got destroyed, was when I decided to become a collector. I have an eye for good things, you know. Going from gallery to gallery, drinking their wine and talking to the artists, making quiet little jokes about the awful things and standing in awe like everyone else in front of the wonderful ones, was something I loved so much more than putting on dirty clothes and splashing paint around a canvas. In the end, I was much better at buying what I knew was great than making what I knew was pretty terrible.

I used to make friends with the artists when I started collecting, but that got weird. I mean, they're weird, there's that, just as people. Staying up all hours, making strange comments, never watching the right OLED screen shows because they're too busy being involved in weird things nobody cares about anymore or never did—but that can be entertaining and funny sometimes. I guess the real problem is that they're always broke. Which is fine if you're hanging out and doing move in someone's apartment and one of them needs you to spot them a pill because they're not making any money off of their art yet. That's okay. But when you want to go out and have a nice dinner, and drinks, and go to the clubs, and they show up in their weird secondhand clothes and can't hang out all night because they're too poor—that's just sad for everyone. So I mainly only hang out with the artists that I know are from good backgrounds, or selling well enough. It's less awkward that way.

The time I spent at my dad's in-state house was pretty soul-crushing. I have friends all over the world, of course, from summers abroad and vacations and such, but even the appeal of going to the places they were was diminished. I mean, New York did its work in preparing for droughts with emergency water supplies, but lots of other places, like the Mediterranean, South Africa, and southern China, are all getting pretty dry. I have friends there. Well, a lot of them left, or have little compounds where things aren't as bad, but it's sad, really sad. And with the droughts come the fires. And if it's not droughts and fires, it's floods. The whole world's kind of fucked, in different ways. So most of the traveling I do is to places like my dad's house anyway, little places tucked away and stocked up for any emergencies and out of the landslides of the mountains and near enough water. I guess I felt safe at my dad's place, even if I didn't feel so happy.

Pollock was happy, and that was something. Once, someone suggested that he was an ornament for me, a pretty little teddy bear dog that I keep in a bag on my shoulder. I love Pollock so much; nothing could be further from the truth. I had him registered as my therapy animal a while back, mostly for travel purposes, but it's also *true*. His little face has saved me from the deepest depression so many times. That he had space to run around in my dad's compound was something.

But all this being holed up in a house in-state was death on my art collection, which had been somewhat decimated by the destruction of New York. I'd housed half of my collection in a special storage space in Brooklyn where the waters shouldn't have reached, but they did anyway. Some of it had been in my *beau* little apartment, and you know how that fared. There was a bit at my dad's in-state house. I kept it in a special room where the temperature is always seventy degrees and there are no windows.

Sometimes I would go and look at it, going over every piece individually, appreciating the beauty, remembering where it had come from, what the artists were like, what I'd been wearing when I found it, what my hair had been done like, every last detail. It made me happy for a minute. I don't just collect things like Basquiats; that would be ridiculous. Every last piece there, whether it's by someone who's well known and *magnifique*, or someone who's just coming up, means something to me. Each one of them is inside of me, in a place I can feel moving through me like my blood. I know that sounds kind of stupid, but that's how it feels; there's no other way to describe it.

As I stood there one day, I removed a woodcut from the storage room and propped it up against the wall. It was a picture of a boat on the sea in the rain, done in stormy greens and blacks and muddy blues. In the boat, one man was beating or killing another man, who had his arms raised up above him. It all took place under a full moon, and was very noir-pulp. I loved it for how simplistic yet daring it was. Those men in that boat were really so far removed from life that they appealed to me. It wasn't Basquiat, that was for sure, but it was really, in its own way, *remarquable* and moved me just the same.

2 One weekend, I was so bored that I went for a pedicure with Tina. My stepmom Tina is the worst, so you know I was pretty bored. She's a tall, blond, leggy woman from the Midwest who came to New York City to be a model. She made it, too, for a little while, which I guess is the best you can realistically hope for as a model. But she knew her days were numbered when she got her first wrinkle, so she grabbed onto my dad at a cocktail party and hasn't let go since.

Tina goes to this *chou* little spa that I really do enjoy when I'm up for enjoying anything, which lately hasn't been often. But I wanted to enjoy it, so I put on some decent clothes and got in her little classic Italian car that my dad bought her for their last anniversary, and off we went to this spa where everything's green plants, pale green and white colors, and vague fruit and flower scents. There are these little women who work there from all over the world. They all seem so tiny and perfect and beautiful, even though they're all doing pretty disgusting jobs like digging around people's toenails all day. I guess you have to do something for a living.

While these women were buffing and paring and painting our nails, we started to talk. Tina isn't one for very deep conversation, so it started off shallow. I mean really shallow. She spent about fifteen minutes talking to me about her new sweater. It's a pretty sweater, almost the same pale green as the spa walls, and so soft. But it's a sweater, and I didn't care to talk about it for *that* long.

"Can we change the subject?" I said.

Maybe I said it a bit too crossly because Tina looked hurt for a second. Then she moved on to her shoes, which were placed neatly on a mat near the door.

"*Tina*," I said, finally. "What are you passionate about?" I've found from the many parties I've been to where people are giant bores that the best way to get out of a horrible conversation is to ask something that makes the other person feel very awkward.

"Well, I ..." she began. "I should say I ..."

"I mean *really* passionate about?" I pushed further. "Like, don't say your car or your shoes. Something that really *moves* you."

Tina shifted in her chair like she was uncomfortable. I felt pretty satisfied that she would shut up, so it really surprised me when she said, "You know, I've always been interested in weather patterns. Don't ask me why." She giggled self-consciously. "Don't tell your father! He would think I'm crazy."

I paused. *Tina* had an interest that wasn't shopping or looking good?

"What is it about weather patterns that interests you?"

She was blushing now, and talking fast, like she was telling a secret she was relieved to be free of. "They weren't always as extreme as they are now, you know. When I was younger, big storms were events. But I was interested in them even then! I mean, did you know how rare and beautiful a tornadic waterspout is? Or that hurricane eyes are surrounded by a vertical wall of clouds that are the most destructive part of the hurricane? But if you fly through the wall, you're in the most peaceful, gorgeous place you've ever seen? It's all so *fascinating!*"

"Tina?" I said. I really didn't know what else to say.

She went on in this rushed tone, talking about gigantic Mexican spring-pendulum seismometers and other such oddities. I was so surprised that I didn't say anything.

Finally she stopped. She looked around. The only person she saw besides me was a little woman painting her toenails zebra stripes, as she had requested for her "for-fun pedicure." I wasn't sure quite how many pedicure intentions she had, but I suspected they were numerous. She let out a sigh. I had never seen her look so relaxed. The whole thing was so odd that I was pretty dumbstruck. Then, to be polite, I suppose, she said, "What about you, Evann? I suppose you'll say you're most passionate about the artwork you collect?"

I paused again, this time because I was blown away by the fact that she *did* take an interest in the things I talked about, when I clearly had known very little about her. I felt kind of bad, you know? Like here she was, just waiting to tell someone all this weird stuff she was into, and never had the chance. What kinds of friends did she have that this was her life, holding in the things she really cared about? What kind of marriage? I felt pretty weird all of a sudden.

I guess I waited too long to answer, because she gave me a strange look. Really quickly, I said, "Yeah, of course. Art. Basquiat. Galleries. Collecting."

She tossed her perfect blond hair over her shoulder, but continued giving me a penetrating look that I didn't know she had in her. It was like I had broken the ice on a lake and found the cold waters.

"You haven't done any of those things in months," she said more wisely than I ever would have given her credit for. "You must be miserable."

Then I was crying. *My God, my God*, I thought. *I'm crying in front of Tina.* I wiped my eyes and tried to say something, but there was nothing to say. I was so miserable. Even Tina could see it.

"Evann," she said compassionately. "I'm just your step-mother. I don't give life advice to anyone, most of all you, but you really need to do something to get back on your feet."

"I *know*, okay?" I said. "But what am I supposed to do? New York is destroyed, Allentown is over. Should I move to some foreign country where they don't even have water reserves? Where do I even go?"

"You don't watch the news, do you, Evann?" she asked.

"You do?" I said. The surprises were never-ending.

"Turn on your wristscreen. I'll send you a video."

"Fine," I said.

The next thing I knew, I was watching a newscast. Newscasts are the worst, with all these shaky amateur videos and boring newscasters. The only really good part is that they constantly break for cat videos. But this one seemed different. It was a straight video, done old-style. Which they never do if not to make a point about how real and poignant something is. So I knew I was in for some big schmaltzy news story. Boring. Leave it to Tina to not *really* surprise me.

There was a blasé newscaster in her Business Wearhouse skirt suit talking about something. I turned the volume up, not that I really cared.

"Now, we take you live to the site where we are talking to Mayor of New York City, Richard Bradley."

Oh, Christ. Mayor Bradley. This was getting even better.

But then I saw it. It was tiny, because I was watching on my wristscreen, but I could tell it was *remarquable*. Truly the most *remarquable* thing I had ever seen since I saw my first Basquiat. It was a battle scene on the side of a building, so perfect that I couldn't look away. I could barely hear what Mayor Bradley was saying in the foreground. I could barely hear Tina talking next to me. It was jagged and bold and frightening. It made me feel that thing, that feeling that I feel deep inside me and can never explain. It was like *Guernica*, but a million times more modern, emotional, and terrifying. It was *fabuleux*, it was breathtaking. None of the words I had could match it.

"This is what our city has always been about," Mayor Bradley was saying as if from somewhere far away. "This painting, this amazing artist who is moving from borough to borough doing these beautiful works, just proves that the city is not gone for good. This painting is the spirit of resilience in this undestroyable mecca. This storm has set us back, but it has not extinguished us. Neither will the next one. We will rebuild—bigger, better. We will be, as always, a place where beauty like that behind me flourishes. We will come back stronger than before, having faced many great hardships together. Like the phoenix, New York City will rise above the ashes."

The newscaster in the bad suit spoke. "What about the many people who say they're never coming back to New York?"

"I beg them to look at this painting and remember why they came here in the first place. If, working by night, in the conditions this city is currently in, an artist can create something so great as the image we see behind me, I think the rest of us can be inspired to rebuild condos, restart businesses, and reform the place that inspires us all."

They went on and on, but I turned the video off. There were tears welling up in my eyes once again, but this time it wasn't because I was depressed.

"It was so beautiful."

"Those paintings are all over the city," Tina said. Beneath us, the tiny pedicurist was finishing up her work. She smiled up at us. "Evann, I think New York *is* the place you're looking for."

"Yes," I said.

The winter that had seemed so relentless faded. The winds whipping through the tunnels created by tall buildings lessened. Buds grew on the bare branches of the trees that still remained upright, but had been stripped clean by the storm. During the day, the sun beat down on the asphalt of the streets, and the heat radiated out of it after the sun went down. Soon unbearable summer would be there, and the winter clothes they had layered on all winter to keep themselves from freezing would be discarded. What would they do in the heat? How many more would die?

PART TWELVE

JESSE—MAY

1 The bad dreams got better once we were in the building. I almost totally stopped having that nightmare about Lux in the hospital. One night, I dreamed that she was cuddled up behind me as I slept in the huge bed in the apartment we'd taken over. We'd slept that way some nights in the IRT station, for warmth and because we were really good friends, you know? I woke up after that dream and stretched under this huge white down comforter I was sleeping under and felt good, felt that she was out there somewhere and someday I would find her.

Things were good there. It wasn't exactly utopia, because you could tell there were de facto leaders calling most of the shots. There was Makayla, for one, who had gotten there first, so people would kind of ask her what was okay and what wasn't. They went to her when they didn't know what to do. I guess there could have been worse leaders. Kristin was another leader, but I could tell she was getting bored with the whole scene now that things were running smoothly. One day we were sitting down in the lobby alone, and she started talking about the life she missed.

"Things were cool when there was so much to do," she said, "and nobody knew how to to do it. They're fine now. They don't need me around. Somebody gets sick, the Red Cross is here. Mold comes back, go ask The Disaster Fund. Meanwhile, there are no huge waves, no space dives, no life or death, you know? That's what I need. That's what I have to go find."

Two days later, she packed up what little she had and said goodbye. She had never needed the building like the rest of us did. Some people were sad to see her go, and hugged her and thanked her. Some wanted to throw a party for her before she left, but Kristin said that wasn't necessary and would just waste lots of resources. Makayla stayed up in her room until the very last minute, and when she did come down, she stood across the lobby with her arms folded over her chest and nodded at Kristin.

Makayla was weird, that was for sure, and after the whole thing with Drusilla, she got weirder. I mean, she didn't like me or José or Sebastian, that wasn't the problem—lots of people don't like us. She started staying up in her room and only coming down at night to do the work she was assigned, or to check the supply closet. She checked that thing like fifty motherfucking times a night. She and Jaden fought a lot, too, not huge fights, but little shows of dominance on her part when the whole building was together, to show who was boss. She was constantly undermining whatever he suggested.

Jaden, for his part, stayed cool. He was a pretty rad fucker, I have to say: easygoing and smart and nice to everybody. When Makayla started shit with him, he just walked away, or stood his ground without getting pissed off. He still talked to her the same as when they lived together, calm and chill as a motherfucker.

Eventually, Makayla stopped letting anybody go into the closet at all. She would drag supplies out into the middle of the lobby and let us collect them there.

"It's less of a risk for everyone," she grumbled when someone asked her one night. "I should be the only one who goes near that thing."

The closet situation wasn't exactly horizontal leadership, but in the end it didn't seem like a battle worth fighting. We all got what we needed, and were pretty sure Makayla's intentions were legitimate. So everyone let it be.

In the meantime, José kept up with his street tactic training. He had these zines that he carried with him everywhere. I had always thought it was kind of stupid, intentionally a throw-back affectation, like the map. But now that we weren't plugged into anything, they were pretty useful. He used a really old one called *Bodyhammer* to figure out how to build shields.

But it wasn't just the shields he made. He started making suits out of duct tape and wadded-up old clothes that could be slipped on and off like shirts and pants. He and the other committee members raided stores and found bike helmets in the street and in apartments. They were like goddamn garbage warriors or something. Their shields could be held with one arm, and José showed people gathered in the lobby how to link their other arm with the person next to them to make a wall.

"In tight, shields up!" José yelled. Sebastian was near him in front of the group of people, but stepped back and let his brother do the leading.

The line of shields formed, again and again.

"Will this really help protect us?" someone asked.

José stepped back, scratched his head, and dropped his

leader tone. "Somewhat. If rubber bullets were being fired at us, it would stop them. If we get into a situation where cops are using clubs, it will stop them. You can deflect a taser with this thing, if you know what you're doing. But if they're shooting real guns at you? Well, there's probably not a lot we can do to stop that."

"Who's going to be shooting at us?" asked an older woman who had joined the committee. I had worried that she would get hurt, but José had said she was more likely to get hurt not knowing how to defend herself.

José stopped. He looked at his brother, and at me. They didn't even realize how dangerous what we had in the building was to power. They didn't realize at all.

"There's going to come a day when we all need this," was all he said.

2 José started a library of his zines. There weren't a lot, but he figured that if he was getting information about how to do things like street defense from them, everybody should have access to the same ideas he had. The thought behind it was twofold, he said. Horizontal information sharing was important, but what was even more important was that others might read the stuff and come up with ideas that he didn't. It worked, too. People started reading them and passing them around and talking about them. One day even Makayla came up to our apartment to borrow some. She had gotten thinner, and looked like she wasn't sleeping much. She didn't say more than five words when she came knocked on the door, and didn't stay long. She left with four zines. As

she was headed out the door, I put my hand on her arm. She nearly jumped a fucking mile.

"You okay?" I asked, peering at her. I maybe didn't care; she could be a real jerk. But maybe I did, too.

"I feel safe here. I do," she said, answering a question I hadn't asked. "It's just hard to sleep sometimes."

"Are you eating? Doing things to relax?"

She shook her head. "Eating when I'm hungry, which isn't all the time. I try to read a lot, but I go over the same sentence over and over. Maybe I can read these, though."

I tried to call to mind the picture of her snapping at Jaden, or the day she threw Drusilla out. But she looked so fragile right then. I almost wanted to give her a hug. But that would have been weird, right? I'm not a huge hugger. I was pretty sure she wasn't, either. I patted her on the shoulder, once, awkwardly, like a bro. She closed her eyes like she was barely able to stand someone touching her.

"You're strong," I said. I wanted to add more, about what she did for the building, about what a badass it was obvious she was. But in the end I just shrugged and she went back to her apartment.

While José was leading the street defense committee and starting his zine library, Sebastian was doing his thing with the entertainment committee and the kids. It was the most separate I had ever seen the twins, and they both seemed so happy. They were good guys, you know? Mostly Sebastian, but even José who tried to be such a hard-ass. I never knew guys like that. I mean, the main dude in my life growing up was my asshole dad, who I never wanted to be like, and his fuckwad friends who always came around and drank and made stupid sexist jokes and shit like that. Then, once I left home, I was with these douchebag punk dudes who talk a good game about anti-oppression and equality, but at the end of the day are as sexist and homophobic and everything else as anybody else. I guess maybe if I grew up around guys like José and Sebastian, things might have been different for me, I might have landed somewhere else. Person-wise and gender-wise, too. Like, I always knew I wasn't what they told me, I knew I wasn't this girl in frilly dresses that I had to be before I had a choice. But then I would look around me and see these asshole dudes and think *I'm definitely not that, either*. So I landed somewhere in between, some crusty weird genderfucking person who everybody is confused by and most people don't even think exist, if that makes any sense. I don't know. Being there in the building, I had plenty of time to think about these things.

It wasn't like I was completely idle. I helped clean the place, went out on the food gathering committee sometimes, played with the kids sometimes. Once in a while I sang and played guitar with the music group. But mostly I thought about leaving. It was weird, you know? There was this place, this great place that had come up out of all this misery and despair, and that's what I'd always hoped for. It was like my motherfucking dream of what would happen when the world and capitalism and all that other crap fell. This. But it was nothing, because there was no Lux. I thought every day, maybe I'll take a boat to New Jersey, maybe I'll have the Red Cross relocate me to a shelter there, maybe I'll start looking. Then this dread would come over me. I'd start picking at the pimples on my chin and acting weird and nervous and then José or Sebastian would ask me what was wrong and I'd say nothing. Finally, I'd just stop thinking about her at all, because, you know, having a dream once in a while that she's alive and okay is better than knowing for sure that she's in the fucking ground somewhere forever.

I tried to think more about the building. Everybody was radicalized by being left behind, nobody had faith that anything would save them but themselves and each other. Here was the real dream of it all: we were winning. We were warm and eating, we were happy and free. But how long could it last? For now, we were still under the radar, just another building in a city full of destroyed buildings. But what would happen when they found us here, playing music and playing soccer, stealing and surviving? What then?

It got boring just thinking about all this stuff, and it got boring following the leader at committees. I started making my own zine for the library. I'd never made one before, but I really liked the aesthetic of some of the real old (like last-century-old) zines José had. They were little rectangles typewritten with old machines or handwritten and cut out of a bigger sheet of paper and plastered over a magazine picture before they were photocopied. That's how all the text looked. It was tedious, but it was what I wanted. I started getting people to write things down about the building. About how they had gotten there, their lives before it, what their life was like now. People wrote about all sorts of things, in all sorts of languages. Some of the kids drew pictures. Alejandro drew himself playing soccer with Sebastian.

One morning, I woke up and went down to the lobby with the idea that I was going to get this really old lady, the one who'd been training with José, to write something for my zine. She usually was down there, waiting for something to start, talking to people. I kind of felt like an archivist, you know? I wanted to get everybody.

When I got down there, though, I walked right into the middle of another Makayla/Jaden fight. Or, rather, a Makayla meltdown. It took me a minute of listening to even figure out what they were talking about.

"Why the hell aren't you out there more?" Makayla said. She looked just plain bad. Her jawline was sticking way out, all the softness gone from her neck and cheeks. Her eyelids were twitching. It was something I'd noticed before, but now it defined her sunken face.

"What are you talking about Makayla?" Jaden said, calm as ever.

"I mean it, Jaden. There are a million bikes in this place. You ride faster than anybody I've ever met, and you let other people go out and do the collecting of all the shit we need. That's some sienty bullshit. That's some entitled, sienty bull-shit that you think staying in this building when you could be doing the slag that people out there are doing, but better, is okay."

"What do you want from me, Makayla? I slag hard here. Everybody does."

"I want you to do *more*, Jaden. I want you to do better. Get your shit together."

He looked at her. He probably saw what I did, the hollow eyes, that she was clearly losing her shit as we watched. Since he was Jaden, he probably felt a lot worse about it than I did.

"Okay, Makayla," he said. "I'll get a bike. I'll go out and gather things we need. Does that make you happy?"

"Yeah," she said. She didn't look happy. She looked like she was trying to think of something else to say, but couldn't. Finally, she turned and walked away, back toward the staircase on the other side of the lobby. Jaden took a deep breath and turned around and began walking the other way. He passed by me without saying anything, even though I'd obviously seen it all.

I started to wonder if maybe Makayla needed help that we couldn't give her. Maybe we needed to get her out of the building and to New Jersey. Not like, commit her or anything bullshit crazy like that, but get her somewhere where she could talk to someone. I wondered what had happened to her before we'd gotten there. It seemed like something bad, maybe. It wasn't hard to imagine.

After I saw that fight, Jaden started going out in the mornings and collecting food and water. Since we had the in with the Red Cross truck and all the stores around us had gotten so depleted by people scavenging, anyway, it seemed more like he was doing it to appease Makayla than anything. It was kind of uncomfortable how much he still loved her. We all saw it, even if he was living with new people on a different floor. I guess I used to think that sort of thing was weak and weird, but since Lux disappeared I've been pretty weak and weird myself. It's strange how much people can mean to you. I guess I had never really known before that night of the attack, you know? Before then, nobody meant much to me.

I would think about that for a second. Then I would push my mind to something else.

3 We had pretty much everything we needed in the building, but I was running really low on painkillers. I'd tapered down my use—at first, after finding so many in the pharmacy, I'd gone a little nuts. Then I'd worked my way down to taking them every other day, then every couple of days. It was really goddamn uncomfortable, too, but what are you gonna do? It wasn't like there were any pharmacies where everything good

hadn't been taken. So I started sobering myself up. I kept a couple for emergencies, but mostly I was clean.

That was a motherfucker. But the real bitch of the situation was that my period started coming back. I guess all the anxiety and discomfort I felt around that unhappy event was part of the reason I started taking painkillers. The added bonus was that being strung out eventually stopped the bleeding altogether, my body just couldn't get its shit together enough to have a habit and function like that. I mean, I know nobody likes getting their period, it's not fun for anybody to have blood leaking out of their body, but it induced straight-up panic in me. Having a tampon held inside my body all day for five days made me hyper-aware of my junk, a feeling I tried to avoid at all costs—you don't even want to get me started on what sex is like for me with about 95 percent of the people I've had it with. But you can pick when you have sex or not, most of the time. You can't pick when your body decides to start dripping blood and tissue everywhere.

The first time I got it in the building, I didn't know what to do. I was squatted over the piss bucket in the bathroom of our apartment. My pants were down around my ankles and there was this big bright red spot inside my boxers. My breath started coming in a little jagged. I pulled my pants back up and proceeded to freak out.

José and Sebastian are the only ones I really confide in about anything, but they weren't going to get what I was talking about at all. My hands were shaking a little. After the steady diet of oxys and Xanax, it'd been so long since I'd gotten the fucking thing that I think I had two tampons stored somewhere in one of the pockets of my knapsack. That was it. I tried to think of asking someone if there were any around the building. Then I started thinking about how that would get people thinking about my junk, which, based on the inappropriate questions they ask me about it, people think about more than the average person's junk. Then *I* would be thinking more about my junk, which was pretty much unavoidable in the situation anyway, but sure as hell didn't need to be exacerbated more. Fuck. Fuck, fuck, fuck, fuck.

I took a deep breath and went for my painkillers. If now wasn't an emergency, I didn't know when would be. My lower abdomen was pretty much pulsing with pain. Normally, I'm semi-numb to what's going on in that part of my body, but, with the pain, that was not a possibility. The thing I had to do first was get rid of that pain in any way possible. So, Vicodin it was.

I know it was mostly in my mind, but I almost felt better as soon as I'd taken the Vicodin. My breathing got back to normal and I was able to look for my tampons, which would be a fuckload harder to find than the painkillers had been. I rummaged around in the drawers in my room, in my pockets, in the pockets of my bag. Finally I fished them out. The wrapping was so wrinkled it was almost destroyed, and one of them had popped open. I went back into the bathroom with them and the stupid girly underwear I have to wear to hold the pantyliners in place. I took a deep breath and put the unopened one in. As soon as the painkillers kicked in and I was able to function again, I would have a couple of hours to figure out what to do.

The first thing I did was curl up in a ball. I tried to think of a million things that weren't what was happening in my body. I remembered health classes, talks from adults during puberty, all that fun stuff. I was super-aware of what was happening to me and how much it was absolutely against my conscious wishes for what my body was supposed to be.

So the best thing to do now was put my mind somewhere else. The first thing I did was go through my mind and try to alphabetically repeat the names of drugs I've done. Acid, amphetamines, benzos, bath salts, crystal meth, Dilaudid, DMT, dexies, drag, ecstasy, fast, GHB, h-bombs, ice, jet fuel, ketamine, lazy, move, morphine, nexus flips, OxyContin, opium, PCP, psilocybin, Quaaludes, red light, sativa, trigger warning, trance, ugly Sam, Vicodin, waffle dust, Xanax, yellows, zero. I couldn't always get all of them on the first try, so I went over the alphabet again and again, until I got them all. Then I repeated them until I chilled the fuck out.

By my third go through the alphabet, I felt a lot better, body-wise. The Vicodin had kicked in, and I was able to stand back up. My brain was working a little better, so I figured I had two options for what to do about tampons. The building was half cis women, so I assumed at least some of them got their periods regularly, and they kept supplies on hand. Those supplies were probably in the closet that Makayla kept the key to. So I could ask Makayla. That was option one. Option two was to go look for a pharmacy and hope they still had some hanging around that hadn't been water-damaged. This was an infinitely preferable option for some reasons, and a worse one for others. If I went looking for tampons on my own, I wouldn't have to ask anybody, they would be thinking less about my junk, and none of them would decide I was a girl just because I had to deal with this stupid bleeding. However, the stores had been pretty well picked over by then, and it wasn't very likely I would find something that so many people left in the city needed. And it was getting more dangerous out there by the day, especially for people looting stores for things they needed. Still, the second option was how I wanted to proceed. Definitely.

I tried not to think about the wad of cotton inside me, even though I couldn't feel it or anything. But it was *there*, I knew it was, and it freaked me out in a way that's hard to explain. Did you ever, you know, hurt yourself and everything you do draws your attention back to the part of your body that's hurt? This was kind of like that, only worse, because I generally do my best to make sure I don't think about that part of my body at all. It's a blank space in my mind. Except for moments like now.

My head was a little fuzzy from the Vicodin, but I started rummaging around in my room for the crowbar I hadn't had to use in a while. I grabbed it and stuffed it into my knapsack. My breathing was normal now, and my heart was only moving a little faster than usual because I had to go raid a pharmacy again, something I hadn't done in a while. I got my shit together and walked out the door of my apartment, down the stairs, and through the lobby. I could've told José or Sebastian. I could've asked them to come with me. But I just couldn't bring myself to.

Out in the street, things still looked like a third world country. People wandering around in rags, looking for food and water, garbage piled high down alleys and away from places people were eating and sleeping, rats running to and from the piles of it, mud caking the streets, the sun beating down mercilessly on it all. The motherfuckers with the machines hadn't even come close to where we were yet; they could still be found working away at all the places with the real money, making them presentable for the kinds of people who lived there. We were in a luxury condo, sure, but this part of Brooklyn still had just enough people who nobody cared about for them to be here yet. So it still looked like it had shortly after Bernice.

I went down the block to the first Allen Brewster's. I rummaged the fuck through the place and found absolutely nothing useful. There was another store just like it down the block, but that had been picked over, too. I went into four chain pharmacies, all of which were within ten blocks of the building. Nobody had anything I could use.

"Fuck, motherfuck, goddamn," I whispered to myself. I crouched down and tried not to think of my stupid fucking body and what it was putting me through. I wished for the millionth time that I could have had a surgery and had all these organs and crap removed from me. But that had never been an option for me, not living on the streets, not without any access to medical care even when I was sick as fuck. One day, things were going to be different. But today they were not, and I had to deal with that.

Okay. Deep breath. I was going to have to go back to the building and find out what the women there did when they were in this situation. I was going to have to talk to Makyala.

Just the thought of it made my heart start beating faster. People can't usually make judgments about what they think my gender is. I wear men's and women's clothes, I keep my already pretty flat chest bound down, sometimes I pack, sometimes I don't, I don't shave the mustache on my upper lip that some people pin as male and some as female, I keep my voice pretty neutral. People have a hard time knowing what to think, which is exactly what I want them to think, which is really what I am, you know? This kinda in-between, masc-femme, genderless, genderfuck, person. But the minute Makyala heard about my period, she would always think *girl* from then on. She would start forgetting and using "she" instead of "they" when she talked about me, even if she didn't mean to, even if she had every intention of continuing to think of me the way I really am. Then other people would do it, too.

I walked back to the building feeling kind of dazed. I went up to Makayla's apartment and knocked on the door.

"Yeah?" she said, opening it. She looked like reheated shit. Her hair was all over the place, she'd lost even more weight, and her eyes were sunken. For a minute I stopped worrying about the period thing and started thinking, *holy shit, this girl really needs help*.

"I . . . um . . . I was wondering if there are any supplies . . .I mean, like, I'm bleeding, and . . ."

"Bleeding from where?" she asked, suddenly sounding panicked and looking me up and down.

"I'm not hurt or anything, I just . . . I got my period and I need tampons," I said. I could feel the heat rising up my cheeks, making my face red, embarrassing me even further.

"Shit, girl," she said. *Girl*. There it was, second word into the conversation. She stopped herself. "Sorry, sorry. I mean, I thought you were hurt. I was relieved. I didn't mean . . . yes, they're in the supply closet. I'll get you some."

We walked back down to the lobby. She didn't say much, and neither did I. My heart was going fast again, this time from being misgendered. All the adrenaline from this day was killing my buzz, and I would have to take another Vicodin when I got back upstairs.

Makayla opened the closet door and handed me a box of tampons. I stuffed them in my bag. She sighed.

"There's not a lot left, but this is where they are if you need them. There's not a lot of anything, really." She stepped back from the door and let me look in. There were a few boxes left, but the room was mostly empty. "The Red Cross connection is drying up, and God knows there isn't much left in the stores. I don't know what we're going to do. I worry about it every day."

"Makayla?" I said. I wanted to put my arm out, put my hand on her shoulder. "Maybe you should let go of the closet for a while? Maybe you should take a break and let someone else worry about it?"

She grabbed the key hanging around her neck. "I'm fine. I'm fine. Fine. And I can take care of this. Don't worry about it." She tucked the key away under her shirt. I saw how much her hands were shaking. "If you need anything else, let me know."

"Okay," I said. All things considered, it hadn't gone as bad as I thought it would. One single misgendering, and she'd almost apologized for it the second it happened. And now I had something new to focus my mind on, which was that Makayla was, beyond a shadow of a doubt, losing her shit.

I started wondering what would have to happen to get her out of the building and to somewhere she could get help for whatever kind of nervous breakdown she was in the middle of having. But no matter how I thought about it, I couldn't figure out a single thing that would ever make her leave.

The artist heard of a place they were living better than most. Where there was no violence, where there was something like camaraderie, where there was giving and working together. He heard of this place and crossed the river one day. He waited until night fell. As he climbed a ladder he had dragged out from a ransacked store, a boy came outside. The boy watched as he used his spray cans on the buildings. He brought the boy up on the ladder and let him spray crooked lines and primitive faces. He worked them right into the painting.

On one side of the wall, he painted the city full of dark figures with bones and hooded eyes, scratching and wailing. Farther along, he painted the river, glowing with diamonds of light under the full moon. On the farthest part of the wall, he painted a temple that grew with vines that seemed to move as the paint dried. He painted dawn and a cerulean sky, and beautiful people who were not bones, not skeletons, not death's-heads. Their hands worked together over a ball of bright blue light that burst and shone and flashed like lightning, bringing the dawn ever closer to their joyous faces.

PART THIRTEEN

MAKAYLA—MAY

1 I couldn't sleep at night. Things were real dissat, all the time. I walked through sunlight hours in a daze, trying to figure out what was real, what was upswing, what was distorted by my insomnia. People seemed to give each other looks that meant something I couldn't decipher—but how do you tell what a look means anyway? Or if it's even real? It was so hard to figure out what was real and what was in my head.

When I did sleep, which wasn't often, I had nightmares about the boat and Peter. Or about Jaden leaving the building or checking like my parents had. He was gone now, I knew that, and there was nothing I could do to help how angry I was at him. I yelled at him all the time. But what I really wanted to say all those times I was yelling was *come back, come back*. I wanted back my friend from the neighborhood, wanted back the guy who had made me feel safe and calm again after all the shit that went down on my way to Gravesend. But I'd hoddered it all up, I'd hoddered everything up.

Even Alejandro started backing away from me. He still stayed in our apartment, but he constantly asked where Jaden was, and ran to him when he saw him. It just felt like everything was falling apart.

Then came the morning where Ale came into my room late at night. I wasn't sleeping, I was awake reading one of the zines I'd gotten from José, a photocopy of a real old book called *The Anarchist Cookbook* or some stupid shit like that. It was about all I could focus on. Ale came bursting into the room without knocking. He had smears all over him, I could see it even in the dark. They were on his face and hands and clothes. I lit the candle next to my bed and pulled him closer. I could see that the smears were paint.

"Where the hell did you get those all over you?" I asked. José and Sebastian, who could communicate with him in Spanish, had started teaching him English, too. He didn't speak it so well yet, but he understood what I was saying.

"Outside!" he said. He started pulling on my hand.

I walked with him down the dark stairs, carrying my candle. Flashes of shadow leapt all around us, and I was even more on edge than usual. He pulled my hand down the stairs, through the lobby, out into the strange, surreal night.

I stood across the street and looked up at the building in terror.

The wind was blowing, pulling our clothes back against us. I held onto Ale's hand and he chattered in excitement. All I could see were huge, dark forms, there up against the wall. And I knew what it meant. I knew that it meant it was all over for us. We were hoddered.

2 The next morning, we all stood out there staring. We had heard of this artist, we had heard of these paintings. Words were whispered about them along the streets and the places we went to collect food. And now, there was one on the side of our building.

Ale had seen him. He was talking to José in Spanish, and José was translating for me and other people who didn't speak it. It was the most I had seen Ale speak, ever.

"He says he was a tall guy, with a plain black bandana over his face, so he couldn't see what he looked like other than being tall. Everything was covered, his face, his arms, his hands, Ale doesn't know if he was black or white or Latino or what. There was paint all over him, on his gloves, on his bandana, on his boots. He says he helped him up the ladder to help paint, and he was really nice, and kind, and gentle, and that he was a real artist like in books and museums."

"Great," I said. "That's real goddamn upswing that we've got his credentials. But the fact of the matter is, we're hoddered. First the camera crews come, then the cob rollers come, then they find us. Then what?"

José took a deep breath. Ale was still talking to him, but he put a finger up to his lips to tell him it was time to be quiet. He looked serious.

"We've been getting ready for this day, right? I mean, I know we have in the street defense committee."

"You think your shields are going to stop them from taking this away from us?" I shouted at him. "You think your protest-kid shit is going to work?"

Mo, who I knew better than these kids, who I'd been through shit with, spoke up. "It's something. It's all we have, Makayla. But there's another way."

"What is it, Mo?" I said, softly. My hands were shaking. They wouldn't stop, no matter what I did. It felt like they'd been shaking for years.

"Maybe we leave before they find us," he said. "Maybe we let go."

"No!" I shouted in his face. "No! We can't let this go. We can't."

Mo reached out and put his hand on my shoulder. He had been there with the cob roller, he had saved my life. Still, I jerked back from his touch. "Makayla, many of us will die if we stay. Some of us have to keep living."

I slapped his hand away. "We need to have a meeting. The whole building. Get everyone in the lobby."

⊚ ⊚ ⊚

We gathered in the lobby, but as we stood there, people started to congregate outside our building. At first it was just the kind of people we saw every day, the stragglers, the ones left behind. Then the camera crews and the TV news stations showed up. After that, it was people like Kristen but worse—disaster tourists who didn't want to help, just wanted to snap their pictures and go back to their comfortable lives. José joked that we should start charging them an entrance fee. Jesse said we should just jack them.

We relocated into a rear-facing apartment. There were about fifty of us, and it was like being at a really crowded party. José called for everyone's attention, and reminded people of the hand signals he had introduced us to back when he got to the building.

"Times like these are when it's most important to use them," he said. "When we're all worked up and there's so many of us here. Makayla, you've been here longest and I think you have a lot to say, so do you want to start us off?"

"No," I said. "Everyone knows how I feel."

That kid Jesse started taking what they called "stack" of people who wanted to speak. They suggested that we do "progressive stack," which they said meant people who generally don't get to speak go first. Then they looked around and laughed.

"I mean, I guess that's everyone. I guess none of us are exactly the ones behind the bullhorn."

It broke the tension for a minute, but then José, who was first in line, got to jawing.

"It seems like one of two things has to happen," he said, serious as fuck. "We stay and fight or we leave, go to the shelters in New Jersey, give up the building. I can't say which is best. I personally want to fight. I've never had anything like this, and I don't know if I ever will again, if any of us will. I think that's worth fighting for."

An older woman spoke up, out of turn. She was about my granny's age, but was hunched over. "Some of us been fighting our whole lives," she said.

Mo was next in line to speak. "For every good committee we have here, we've spent a night hiding in our apartments hoping the gunshots don't come through the window. For every person who cares about us in the building, there are five more roaming around out there who would see us dead. For every meal we share with each other, there is a time when we have to post guards at the door. For every nice piece of clothing we take from the closet, we agree that we will not shower for one more day. I am tired. I love it here, I love that we have built what we have. But isn't it time to go back to life? Won't we get that? Won't we be able to start again somewhere where we have a chance at that?"

Jesse raised their finger to denote that they had a point of clarification on what Mo was saying. "We go to the shelters if we leave here. Some of us know what that's like. They'll do everything they can to clean us up and throw us back into the streets. They will make us feel unwanted, and convince us that we are worth less than what they're paying to keep us there. There will be prison food and you will have to watch your children like a goddamn motherfucking hawk because of the people there who would do them harm. That's where you'll start again."

"Yeah, start over for what?" someone yelled from the crowd. José tried to remind him of stack, but he didn't care and kept jawing. "For the same shit all over again? For poverty, and being pushed out? I'm tired of scrambling to eat, but I'm more tired of it when there are rentbosses breathing down my throat, and never enough smash for anything. Stay and fight, I don't care if we die, it's better than living the way we've been living!"

"You want to stay here and rot?" someone else yelled. "That's what we're doing! Rotting! I can smell our bodies rotting away!"

José tried to get the discussion back under control, but it had gone completely beyond his abilities. Heated voices yelled at each other across the apartment. My granny was standing near me, looking like she was about to faint. I pulled her aside, down a hallway where nobody was standing.

"Do you want to go to New Jersey?" I asked. "To the shelter?"

"Hell no," she said, forcefully.

"Granny, I'm worried you can't take the heat here come summertime, even if we make it through this next part. It's pretty bad in New York without air-conditioning these days."

"You think I ever turned on air-conditioning in my life? Do you know how that stuff skyrockets the energy bill? What am I, a Rockefeller?"

Around us, the argument raged on. The heat rose and rose.

"Granny, I just think . . . I can't let you stay. You're the only one I have left. I have to know you're okay. Please. Please go to the shelter before things get bad here."

I put my hand on her shoulder. She could feel me shaking. For a minute, she softened. I had never seen her that way before, and suddenly she looked old, so old.

"Will you come with me?" she asked.

I shook my head. "I stay here, Granny. I'll probably die here."

The voices around us reached a crescendo, and then I heard José's cut through all of them.

"We don't all have to stay. If you don't want to stay, now's the time to leave. Just go and be done with it. The rest of us will stay here and fight."

3 When we made it back to the lobby, there was a line of cob rollers outside the door. One of them had a bullhorn and was yelling through it. They knew we were in there, they said, making it sound like we were robbing a bank. If we came out calmly, they would help us to the shelters. About half of us had decided to leave.

Mo was among them. So was my granny.

"I'm never going to see you again," I said, hugging her in the lobby. I felt so sure. It had been my idea, and I still wanted her to go. But this moment was too much.

"You don't know forever," she said, and at first she said it harshly, like I was a numptie for even saying it. Then her voice softened. "You don't know forever, Makayla."

"I just want it all to work out," I said. Tears were starting to leak out of my eyes.

"You don't let them take it, Makayla," she said. "You, you haven't been fighting as long as some of us. So stay and fight. And don't you let them take away what you made."

People were lining up at the door, saying their goodbyes to people they had lived with, worked with, built their lives around. But in the end, those things were not enough to keep them here. For them, whatever was waiting in New Jersey was the lifeboat that had never come, the rescue helicopter they had waited on their roofs for, the house farther inland. I said nothing. I hugged them and kissed them. They took my face in their hands and thanked me for everything. But they did not stay.

The rest of us stood our ground. Ale had clung to my leg, refusing to leave if I wasn't leaving. Outside, the cops kept yelling through the bullhorn. They knew we were there. They knew we had stayed. They gave us one last chance to come out. But we did not move.

"Okay," José said, to those of us left. "We're going to defend this place. And I think it goes without saying that we can't leave the building, so whatever supplies we have left are what we have to use until they're gone."

Jaden had stayed, and somewhere inside me, I was so grateful for that. He spoke up. "There's not that much. We'll be able to hold out for a week, if that."

José shrugged. He was just a kid, really, still a teenager, but he looked more nails than I had ever seen him look before. I wondered what these kids had been into before they got to the building. I'd read some of their zines—there was street combat, and weaponry, how to build bombs, things you didn't need to know if you were living an easy life. I was suddenly so glad they were there.

"We'll see how many of us are left to worry about it then, I guess," he said.

"This is crazy," one of the men said, shaking his head.

"Well, we're all crazy," I guess, Jesse said. "So let's not talk about it anymore, let's just make a plan of attack."

We retreated to my apartment. It was empty now except for me and Ale. Ale curled up on the couch, suddenly looking tired. The rest of us pulled out José's zine library and began to talk. If they tried to rush the boarded-up door, we used our shield, we used our strength. I still had the gun I had found early on, though I only carried it sometimes. I didn't tell anyone about it, even as many of them, one by one, admitted they had found guns, too. Mine was tucked into my belt, as always, under my baggy shirt. If anyone could see it, they didn't say anything.

"Do we use them?" Sebastian asked. "Or will they only make it worse?"

"Do we have to decide that now?" a woman asked. She was the woman in the filthy sari, who still wore it despite its holes and dirt.

"We can put off talking about it all we like, but I worry that when we need to make the decision, there won't be time to talk," José said. "If we have to use them at all, we use them as an absolute last resort."

As we were talking, a sound started rising that I didn't know the source of. It was a low sound that was almost like a machine grinding to a stop. By the time I realized the sound was coming from Ale, he had already sat up and vomited all over the white couch.

"Ale?" I asked, rushing over to him. He had been clinging to me just a few minutes before, but in the heat I hadn't noticed what I realized just then as I touched his head. He was burning up with fever.

"Oh, Jesus," Sebastian said, running over, too. "Ale? Not now, not now."

"I still have antibiotics," Jesse said. "If he's got something bacterial, it'll help."

Oh God, this was 'trosh. The tightness in my head swelled until I thought it would burst. But watching those kids hover over Ale, offering him their help, my chest felt tight, too, like my heart was getting so big it might explode out of me. I was cradling Ale in my arms. I lifted him up off the puke-covered couch while Jaden started wiping up the mess with some old clothes that we'd worn into rags. I picked him up and carried him to his bedroom. As I did, Sebastian told Jesse to get the antibiotics.

All the thoughts of street fighting and guns were out of my head. All I could think about was how we were going to get things back to upswing for this boy that I'd taken in months ago, taken care of, this boy that I loved with all my heart. I was shaking again. I tried to stop it, but I couldn't.

"Ale?" I said.

"Sí?" he murmured.

"You're going to be fine. I promise. You'll be okay. You'll feel better in a couple of days. And after that, no matter what happens in this building, no matter what happens to me, you're going to hide out in this room, and nobody will hurt you. You're just a little boy. Nobody would want to hurt you. You're going to grow up and be a real upswing person, I know it. And a real upswing artist, just like you want to be. Better than the one who painted on the side of our building. I know it. You will be safe. You will be safe. You will be safe."

I was rocking him back and forth, saying it over and over.

◎ ◎ ◎

The antibiotics that Jesse had made Ale's skin break out in a rash. As he burned up with fever, and itched at the bumps that had sprung up, I walked over the window. I couldn't breathe. Jaden tried to put his arm around me, and I flew off, telling him to leave me alone. The line of cops was gone, but would be back, I was sure. What I wasn't sure of was why they had left in the first place. It might have had something to do with the news camera crew that had shown up. There was a silver police fence surrounding the building, the kind they put around places where they want to pen lots of people in. Tomorrow or the next day, the fight would go on, whether Ale was sick or checked or what.

Checked. With the rash all over his skin, it suddenly seemed like a possibility.

"He's allergic to it," Jesse said. The kid was like a walking pharmacy. "He needs a different kind, and that's all I've got."

"Fuck," I said. I punched the wall next to the window, but not hard enough to break my hand. I didn't care about me, not so much. But Ale needed me. I tried to get my head together.

"Somebody has to see the Red Cross," I said, "get some medication for him, bring it back."

"Nobody can go out there, Makayla," Jaden said. He had been sitting at Ale's side, cleaning up his puke as best he could, taking care of him. He loved the kid as much as I did, I knew that. But it didn't stop me from flying off.

"*You* could go out there, Jaden," I said. "You can ride your goddamn bike faster than anybody, you could be gone and back in no time. You could save the kid's life. But you're a goddamn ori, a fucking numptie who's too worried about his own self to save a little boy's life."

Jaden stepped back, like my words had punched him in the face, and he was stunned. He stood next to me and looked out the window.

"The cops aren't here," he said softly. "They could be back any minute, in bigger numbers than before. But there's a chance."

"So stop goddamn talking and *do* it," I said. While I was saying it, I had this moment of remembering our first night together. How gentle and kind he had been, how being with him had felt like the home I hadn't had in so long. I wanted him to put his arms around me. But I wouldn't allow it. I couldn't. Not now. Not ever again. He had hurt me so much that day he walked away.

"Makayla," he said, real slowly. Jesse and José and Sebastain stepped back, not wanting to get in the way of whatever harsh kind of jawing we were about to do. "I got a question for you. I want you to think real hard about it, and answer me for real this time."

"Fine, Jaden. What's your question?"

"After all we've been through, after growing up together, after surviving the storm, after being your lover, I still don't know one thing. Why did you ever let me be close to you?"

I wanted to answer that I had loved him. That I still did. That he had just about killed me that day he walked away after us growing up together, after we survived Bernice, after we were lovers. But I couldn't. I had to be nails. I had to be nails. It was all I had.

"Let me tell you something, Jaden, tell you something real," I said. My eyes were narrowed as I leaned in close to him. The kids had left the room, and I could say whatever I wanted. "When I left the shelter, I got raped. Some ori forced his cock in me on a sienty boat floating in the middle of a pool of garbage. When I came back, I needed to push that shit out of my mind. Fucking you was the easiest way to do it. So there you have it. That's why I let you get close to me after all those years. To get that shit out of my head. Now get the fuck out of here, and do what you need to do to save Ale's life."

Jaden sucked his lips in and pressed them together and he stepped back. He looked like a deflated balloon. Every piece of me wanted to take back what I had just said. But I had to get through this, I had to survive. I couldn't be weak.

"Okay, Makayla," he said. "I'll go."

Jaden walked around the room for a minute. He was picking things up and putting them down, things that he'd left behind, things that were mine, things that were Ale's. He seemed like he didn't know where to put his hands. He seemed like he didn't know where to put his *self.* He stood in the corner for a moment, every bit the big-eared kid from the block party in middle school. He'd shrunk back into himself. He let out a big sigh.

"Makayla," he said, "Makayla. You could have told me. You could have told me anything. I would have . . . I would have done anything to make you feel safe, to make it be okay."

I wanted to tell him it was a lie. Not the rape. That part was real. But that I'd used him to push it out of my head. I had wanted to be close to him so much. I still wanted so much to just take his hand, to put it against my heart. But I couldn't. I had trusted him and he had left, he had hurt me so deeply.

I couldn't tell him that this lie I'd just told him was the most hurtful thing the meanness inside me could think of.

"Go, Jaden," I said. "Go."

He walked from the room. He walked out of the apartment. I could hear doors slam. I could hear him walking away.

A few minutes later, watching from the window, shaking as I'd been shaking for days, I saw Jaden's form bike away from the building. I stood and I waited, and I waited for him to come back. Those twenty-five minutes felt like the longest I'd ever lived through. I began to bargain in my head. If he made it back, I would apologize. I would tell him the truth. I would tell him that I loved him. About the lights that came on inside me when he's around. I would be real, I would throw away the nails act, I would collapse in his arms and let him hold me.

But when he came back into my view, I could tell right away there was something wrong. He was leaning forward, pushing his bike with all his strength, racing away from . . . something. When the cob roller on a bike came into view behind him I wasn't surprised. Jaden was beating him, though. He was going to win. He was the fastest biker, he always had been. My heart was beating so fast I thought I would faint. Jaden was so close, he would be fine, everything would be okay. It had to be.

Then the cob roller ditched his bike and aimed his gun. Jaden fell to the ground. Then I dropped to the floor, screaming. I didn't stop screaming. I felt like I would never stop.

PART FOURTEEN

EVANN—MAY

1 My dad's apartment buildings were not his number one asset, but he had a lot of them, and they made him a lot of money. They didn't buy my *chou* little apartment in the East Village, and they didn't buy my art, but my dad often said before Bernice that they were my nest egg. That anything I needed in the future when he wasn't around would come from them. I guess he didn't know how right he was.

At first, when I was a kid, my dad had owned places in old neighborhoods, the ones he told me not to go to. *He* never even went there, just had other people who took care of them. He didn't have to deal with any complaints, which he said was good because the people who lived there were the people who tried to get free rent any way they could.

Then time went on, I grew up, and the city got better, like I said before. My dad turned a lot of his crummy old buildings into really nice ones. The people who lived there were the sort of people he *wanted* to rent to, not *had* to rent to.

Bernice came, and my dad lost a lot, that was for sure. So it was his duty, and my duty I guess, too, to salvage anything we could.

One day, I was sitting on the couch watching the OLED screen, and Tina came rushing into the room. She was in her workout clothes. She works out about a billion hours a day, I swear.

"Evann," she said. "Turn on the news. Turn it on right now."

I turned on my wristscreen and went to the New York local news. I saw a building there, but at first it didn't make much difference to me.

"What am I even supposed to be seeing?" I said.

"That's your father's building," she said. "One of them."

"Oh," I said. The camera was focused in on a group of people gathered around the door. "What are they all doing there?"

"They're *living* in it," she said. "Can you believe that? With no heat, or hot water, or anything; they've been living there like animals all this time. They must have destroyed everything in the place by now. I feel sorry for your father's renters."

"*Still?*" I asked. It seemed like ages since the storm. Little pockets of revitalization had popped up, but not this far out in Brooklyn, not yet. I assumed those parts of the city were ghost towns, all abandoned except for what was destroyed. But here these people were.

"There's more, Evann," Tina said. "Wait until the news camera pulls out."

I waited. Finally, there was a wide shot of the building. I drew in my breath. There was this amazing painting up on the wall of the building. As soon as I saw it, I thought of my Basquiat that had been destroyed when those people took over my co-op. I saw all the things in it that hallmarked greatness—true, real, *magnifique* brilliance. I had to have it. But there was no question about that. It was already mine.

"Tina!" I shouted, grabbing her. "We have to preserve that painting! We have to have it removed and preserved!"

"How would we do that?" she asked.

I couldn't contain myself. "Are you stupid?" She flinched and I felt sorry, but only for a moment. "There are two ways to preserve street art. Either we use a gel to have it transferred onto a canvas, or we remove the wall. The gel is okay, but the real beauty of the original should be kept intact, with the original canvas. So we have to remove the wall. Haven't you ever heard of that?"

"Well, no," she said, still looking hurt. Stupid, I swear.

"Tina, I have to call Daddy now. I have to talk to him. We have to make plans. We need to hire people, and get moving before it gets destroyed."

2   It was hot out, but the wind was whipping around two days later when Daddy and I stood in front of the building with Mayor Bradley and his bodyguards and the line of riot police and the helicopters. We didn't have to be there. I certainly didn't have to have Pollock there, but there he was, in the bag on my shoulder. The police could have taken care of it all. But we all wanted to be. Mayor Bradley was sucking up to my dad, as usual, my dad wanted to look out for me, and I wanted to see the painting up close. It was even more glorious than it had looked when I first laid eyes on it. There was a jagged, reckless beauty to the dark parts and was offset by the smooth lines and peace of the light ones. The artist was clearly a master. I wanted to cry standing there. I didn't of course. I had to look nice. I was dressed in a nice black

button-down dress because it was a somber thing, kicking all these people out, but I also had to look *fabuleux* in case any of the news cameras got a glimpse of me. The cops were talking through a bullhorn, but it didn't seem anyone was listening. Every now and again we saw heads peek up above window-sills, so we knew they were still in there. We didn't know how many. We didn't know if they'd put up a fight.

The front door was barricaded with all sorts of scraps of wood and metal. Apartment doors, chairs, couches, anything you could think of was pushed up against the entrance. The police would have to fight to get in. I thought about those people in there. It would be better for them to leave. Living like that must have been hell. We were doing them a favor, really. My father had already donated a bunch of money to the shelters they would be going to in New Jersey. We were doing the best we could, really.

Finally, after a lot of talk from the police with nothing happening, Mayor Bradley grabbed the bullhorn.

"We've asked you nicely, we've offered you a place to go," he said. "Now I am warning you. These premises do not belong to you. The owner wants to take possession of them. You are being given fair warning that, tomorrow morning, we will vacate the premises by force if necessary. I strongly suggest that you take your things and exit the building by choice."

PART FIFTEEN

JESSE—MAY

1 *By force*, he said. We all hunched beneath the window of Ale's room, listening. One by one, guns started coming out of waistbands. I damn near shit myself. We were getting to the end of this thing.

Night was falling, and we knew that whatever happened in the morning, a lot of us might not make it out alive. That was a real motherfucker, you know. Just proof that this world doesn't want people who are doing good, it doesn't want people who can rely on each other, it doesn't want anything without a dollar behind it, or, better yet, a trillion.

I looked behind me to the bed. Ale's rash had gone away, and his fever had broken. It might have been something viral, not bacterial. We didn't know. The kid still wasn't okay, though, listless and puking. We had to get him out of there.

Makayla was a little better than she had been in the hours immediately after Jaden was killed. *After Jaden was killed.* It all seemed like a dream. Jaden had been one of the best of us, certainly better than me, better than Makayla. And his body had been dragged off so the news crews wouldn't see it, taken to some morgue. He was gone. Nothing was bringing him back.

I thought Makayla had gone clearly out of her mind when it happened. We found her screaming. After a few hours, she came back from wherever she had gone inside her head, shaken as fuck. She was a wreck. She needed to leave the building, too.

All of us that were left stood in Ale's room until long things had settled down outside. The police never left, but they made themselves less of a presence. They lurked in the street like a group of wolves waiting for something to die.

After some time had passed, José, Sebastian, and I went back to our apartment. We were keyed the fuck up and there was no way any of us were going to sleep.

"There's going to be a firefight tomorrow," José said. He was clearly freaking out. Sebastian seemed calmer, but there was no denying that we were all losing our shit.

"Maybe we'll just fight them with the shields and batons tomorrow," Sebastian said.

It didn't calm any of us down. We'd all been in riots before. They were always bloody and brutal, and even when we got away, the things we saw in them didn't leave us for a long, long time.

"Maybe we should just leave," Sebastian said. "What do we have to win here?"

"I don't know if we can win," José said. "And I don't even know if we'll make it through the thing alive. But it seems important to stay and fight for all the good we've found here."

"But what's the point in fighting when we're just going to lose? What's the point in leading all these people to their death? Those cops are going to be shooting. They'll say we rioted, they'll say they had to use whatever measures they could to stop us. Especially once they find out we have guns. And what about the people who are out there just because they had no other choice? Like all those kids who joined the National Guard because they didn't want to work at the 24/7 and there weren't a lot of other options for them? Are we going to kill them?"

I shrugged. "I guess I feel bad for them. But only until they pick up their guns and start shooting. Then they're the enemy just like the rest of them."

"It can't be us versus them, Jesse. Then we're just like they are."

"But it is," I said, getting mad. "It always has been. We figured it out, we evolved past the shit they're still stuck in. They're the fucking philistines who promote all the shit we can't stand—the war machine and capitalism and sexism. You go up to those guys and find out how many of them make fun of mentally challenged people, or sexually assaulted someone who they pretended to be a friend of. You find out how many of them are *happy* to be holding those rifles, and how many of them *wish* they could go into other people's countries and blow their brains out in their own houses. And how many of them would ship you back across the borders they're dying to defend, and will if they catch you, if they even let you live."

Sebastian was pacing around the room, picking up things and tossing them back and forth between his hands. "I can't believe it's us vs. them like that," he said. "They don't know. They didn't have the chances we had to see things the way we do. Maybe some of them don't want to, and maybe other would if they had the chance. But I can guarantee you that most of them never got the chance."

I waved my hands. I didn't want to fight with him, not now. It was a discussion we'd had before and never saw the same side of. Sebastian had never, as long as I'd known him, lost his temper when anyone called him or his brother "illegals" or worse, or said anything shitty. He'd always talked to them, trying to make them see his side of things, and simply walking away when they didn't. José and I weren't like him in that way. We didn't have his patience.

"I just can't believe they're all bad," Sebastian said, refusing to turn away from the topic. "I can't see the world the way you do, Jesse, all black and white. I don't want to believe any of them out there wants us all dead any more than we want them dead. You don't want that, do you?"

I thought about it for a minute. In my darker moments, yeah, I would see the streets run with their blood. But is that what I really wanted, deep down? No. Not even if it had seemed my entire life that they wanted that for me. Not even if that's what they'd given to Jaden.

"I just want them to disappear," I said. "When they thought we had nothing left here, that's what they did. I want us to have a world without them."

"I just want them to understand," Sebastian said. "We're not going to get them to with shields and guns, that's for sure. I just don't know what to do."

"The system's all-pervasive, Bash," José said. "They're in the middle of it. We found a way out. We were lucky. And it sucks that they might die in it. I want them to break through, but I'm not a pacifist. So we'll fight them and they'll probably win. But it'll be a fight that people remember, and it'll be us standing up for what we helped build and organize and know is right. That's worth fighting for."

We sat there talking like that into the night. The night got darker. All that there was for light was a sliver of a moon shining through the window. Somewhere far off, we heard an animal howl. At first, we paid it no mind, but as it got closer, we began to wonder about it.

"It sounds like a wild dog," I said. "Or a wolf."

"What would a wild dog or a wolf be doing here in Brooklyn?" José asked.

"What if . . ." Sebastian said, then trailed off.

"What if what?" I asked.

"What if all those animals from the zoo are still alive?"

None of us said anything. We listened to the howls come nearer, then move farther away, disappearing back into the night.

2 At four a.m., we knocked on Makayla's door.

"Come in," she said. Her hands trembled like Jello that hadn't set.

"Look," I said. "We need to talk. We've been up all night, and dawn is coming soon, and as soon as the light comes, the cops are coming in here. And we're probably all going to die if that happens. What if we leave? What if we find a new place, somewhere else? We shouldn't fight them."

"What?" Makayla said, livid. "These two have been leaving fucking formations and rallying people to fight for *weeks* and now you're backing out? What are people supposed to do?"

"I won't lead any shield formations," José said. The way his head hung down, I could tell he still wasn't convinced he shouldn't. But after a night of talking to his brother, he had made a decision.

"We aren't proving anything this way," Sebastian added.

"Fine, we find another sienty building and make it what

we made here. Who says they won't come and take that one from us, too? Where can we go that they don't own?"

"I don't know," I said. "But we're not fighting today. We're not leading that kid in the next room into death, or anybody else. This isn't some protest where they'll fire rubber bullet at us. They're going to kill us all and drag our bodies out of here if we don't leave."

"Fuck," Makayla said, pacing around the room. "Fuck. Fine. Fine. One of you go out there. Get everyone and head out. Take Ale first. But if they shoot when you go out there, don't look at me for help."

I thought about it for a minute. "I should go first and tell them we're coming. I'm the last white person in the building, and they might think I'm some kind of freak, but we all know that the chances are less that they're going to shoot me. I'll go. I'll take Ale. José, Sebastian, you round everybody up and follow me."

Ale felt lighter than I would have imagined him to in my arms. He was still sleeping, his dark eyelashes barely fluttering as I lifted him. I walked him out the door, down the hallway, down the stairs, and to the lobby. As we went down the stairs, something clattered out of the pocket of Ale's jeans and he woke to grasp for it. The phone he'd been holding onto since I'd known him. I slipped it back in his pocket and he curled back up to my chest, content.

Wind from helicopters was blowing my hair all around my head as I stepped out into the daybreak. The pink light was a motherfucker on my eyes after the darkness in the building. There they all were. Riot cops, sound cannons, National Guard. And there I was, some scrawny freak holding a sick little kid from Mexico.

"Please don't shoot!" I yelled. I knew I was begging them

for my life. There was nothing left to do. "We're coming out."

I stepped out farther. José and Sebastian and all the rest of them were right behind me. As I got closer to the troops, some of them slapped me on the back as if I was their friend returning from a long trip.

"You did the right thing," one of them said. He looked relieved. For a minute I thought of Sebastian's words, that it wasn't always us or them, that it couldn't be if anybody was going to get by.

I turned back to look at the building. Everyone was far away from it except for one person. It was Makayla. She was wearing a heavy winter coat that she didn't need, and looked more solid than she had in weeks. She was waving her hands, urging us to get back, back.

The next thing I knew, I was flying through the air and there was as loud bang and my ears were ringing. There were pieces of brick and people flying over my head. Completely disoriented, I looked around for Ale, José, and Sebastian. Sebastian had cupped his body over Ale's, protecting him. I reached out my hand, and it landed on a piece of brick. I grabbed it close to me and wouldn't let it go.

3 Two years later, I'm still holding that brick. It's in the middle of the room, on the only piece of furniture we have—a table that we dragged in off the street after making sure there were no bedbugs in it.

After the building went down, they took us across the river to New Jersey for medical treatment. We were all in the hospital for days. As soon as I could get out of bed, I went and found Ale and stayed by him until they dragged me back to my room. He got better. He's a tough little kid, I'll tell you that.

José and Sebastian took Ale and went to a shelter for a while, and I made my way to Lux's house. As I stood outside her family's door with my ripped-up, smelly clothes and my tons of eye make-up and my skirt and mustache, I almost turned and walked away without ever knocking. But I knocked. Her mother answered. She said her son didn't live there anymore. I spit right in her fucking face, *her son*, but I was never so happy in my life. *Live there.* Lux was alive, somewhere.

It took weeks of asking around, weeks of crashing at the punk houses and weeks of searching. But then one day I walked into a party and there she was passed the fuck out drunk on the floor. I shook her and woke her up and she puked on me and that was just about the second-happiest moment of my life.

With Lux in tow, I went back and found Sebastian and José and Ale. The five of us traveled a bit, more inland, until we found this shitty apartment in just outside of Allentown. We sold wristscreens and other shit Lux had dumpstered, like always, and came up with enough money to get it. We knew it wouldn't be long before we got forced out of there, with all the people moving inland. But for the moment, it was ours.

It was a seedy place where nobody asked for much of anything besides our rent in cash every month. Nobody asked who the kid was, or who his legal guardians were, or anything like that. We made sure everything we dumpstered didn't have bedbugs because we knew no one would ever fumigate the house to get rid of them. That was the kind of place it was.

We watched on the news as the anonymous artist's work got removed from the places it was left. After that last painting, the one that had gone up on our building, he didn't paint anymore. No one ever knew who he was, where he had gone, if he'd been killed by police or a gang or what. We kept seeing other stories about New York, too. Ones where buildings like ours popped up all over the city, little pockets of resistance. They got cracked down on one by one. But they kept springing up. But then, slowly, the people who owned the city came back. City officials started building walls that were supposedly levies, but we all know walls keep out more than rising oceans.

The twins kept doing the work they'd always been doing, volunteering at the local activist space, working with undocumented immigrants, the homeless. They took Ale along with them a lot. We figured he should learn about the world the way we saw it. We want him to see through all the shit that some people never get a chance to see through.

At school, Ale's always the one with the questions that the teachers can't answer. Sometimes he asks us them, too. The other night, Lux came in from dumpstering a rich neighborhood with her usual stuff, and some perfectly good, fancy cupcakes in a box that someone had thrown away. I woke Ale up to give him one. As he was eating it, frosting all over his face, he said to me, "Makayla was a hero, wasn't she?"

I stopped. We hadn't talked about Makayla that much. Ale had been attached to her like woah and he cried and cried when he found out she was never coming back. I still felt guilty for giving her those zines, books I knew had info on how to build bombs out of household shit. But how could we have known?

"Wasn't she?" he asked.

I thought about it for a while. Makayla had done a lot of great things, that was for sure. She'd saved a lot of people's lives, and she had empowered them to help themselves. I couldn't put my finger on her final moments. In some ways, it was the ultimate act of resistance, all she could do besides give in. When she died, she took out two people from the building, three riot cops, and injured countless others. We'd been real with Ale about what she had done. But here he was, asking his hard questions.

"Makayla was a hero," I said, "in a way. I just wish she had found a way to be without leaving you like she did."

"But I have you and José and Sebastian," Ale said. "You won't leave, right?"

He loved us, and we loved him. Sometimes you have to lie to people you love when you don't know the answer.

"None of us are going anywhere," I said.

I lie in bed as long as I can, thinking these warm thoughts under a cheap, thin blanket. But then I wake up out of my daydreams to the sound of the guards yelling that it's morning.

4 Makayla did what she did, but Makayla died. The rest of us paid for it. The daydreams will never erase what really happened.

I woke up handcuffed to the hospital bed. There were cops all around me. Those guys are generally not such big fans of bombs.

The minute I was out of the hospital, I was put in a prison cell. They gave me a lawyer and shit, but he didn't care, nobody cared except to make us out as some demons who killed all these innocent people. José and Sebastian were deported. My trial was short and biased. Anarchist, bomb, murder. Goodbye, Jesse. See you in fifty years. Have fun with all the other women in the women's prison they're sticking you in.

I tried to find out from my lawyer what happened to Ale, but all he could find out was that Ale got put in the system. I tried to find out what had happened to José and Sebastian, but I never did. And Lux? I was never sure if she died that night or not.

I have this other fantasy I write down sometimes, too. In it, it's visiting hours. And someone walks into my cell and tells me I have a visitor even though I haven't had one yet. And I get out there. And it's Lux. And she's happy. She's so pretty and happy and all the things that drove her crazy about herself are different, and she found a good place to live, and how could she have helped but hear what happened to me, and she would've been here sooner, but ... but ...

I never figure out why. I rip up the paper and throw it away.

As I'm sitting here writing, one of the guards comes into the library.

"Hey, Jesse, you got a visitor," she says.

And she laughs. And I laugh. There's no one there. And there's nothing else left to do.

ALE

The lighting in the gallery had a crisp, but not overbearing, quality. Alejandro paused before walking through the door and took one last look at his reflection in the glass door. He straightened his tie and brushed nonexistent lint off of his dark suit. These sorts of events always made him nervous, made him remember the small boy in raggedy clothes that he hadn't been in many, many years. He wondered if anyone could still see that boy but him.

Reaching his hand in his pocket and touching the ancient cell phone he carried there, he walked through the glass door. The room was full of beautiful people, all dressed as well as him, all talking around glasses of champagne and laughing short, clipped, polite laughs. Against the white walls were familiar images, many of them reaching up to the vaulted ceiling, and a few that were small but bright. Some of the images were still on the brick that they had been painted on, but others had been removed and transferred into canvases. Alejandro had more than a nodding acquaintance with these works of art.

Across the room, he heard a laugh louder and more confident than the rest. He smiled and spotted her—a woman in her forties with long, sun-bleached hair, a trim body, and a black eye patch over one eye. The last bit was an affectation. A bionic had been fitted shortly after the explosion, after the shock had abated, after she had befriended Alejandro in the hospital, after she had convinced her father to take the homeless boy with no family into their home. But in the time between the explosion and the surgery, Evann had decided that the patch gave her a look of distinguishment and singularity, and had since never left her home without it. Wheeling around the gallery was her ancient dog, Pollock. His back legs has been lost at the same time Evann's eye had, but his modifications were more functional: wheels that spun behind his still-working front paws.

There she was, holding court, talking about the individual works, their relation to what had been happening in the city when they were painted. Her knowledge on the topic was encyclopedic. There had been little codified information to be found, of course, with New York in such a shambles in those days. Evann, after things had settled down after the explosion, had traveled all over the city, and to many other places, tracking down people who had lived in those streets, speaking to them, recording them, hearing their stories. Alejandro hadn't know her before, but he suspected there had been something like ennui radiating through her life. After she left the hospital, after she and her father took Alejandro in, there had been nothing like that. Her life had had purpose. She wanted to become, and eventually succeeded in becoming, the biggest collector of and expert on the artist that had sprung up in New York City in those months after Superstorm Bernice.

Evann and an older woman fell deep into conversation, separating from the crowd around her and the light talk it inspired. The woman was in her seventies or eighties, an age that, in the current conditions, spoke of the wealth needed to withstand all that had come. Alejandro couldn't judge her. After he'd moved in with Evann and her family, he had had all the luxury he'd ever dreamed of having. He had been bought new clothes and electronics, had servants, been doted upon, spoiled. He'd been sent to prep school inland, then college, then medical school. The tall, well-groomed, perfectly coifed man that he caught the reflection of in the glass doors was a product of privilege, no doubt.

As was this older woman dripping ostentatiously with jewelry. Her glasses hung on a jeweled cord that was pure affectation—no one of her background would have anything less than perfect eyesight, even at her age. She probably only wore those glasses for the excess of the cord, for the chance to position diamonds at the outer edges of the cat-eye rim. Alejandro listened as she leaned in close to Evann and spoke.

"Dear, I am quite interested in The Artist's last piece," she said in a voice that creaked at the edges of words.

Evann smiled, though, well as Alejandro knew her, he could tell it was insincere even if no one else suspected.

"Of course none of them are for sale," Evann said. "The purpose of this show is to let others view the collection, not the sale of any of the pieces. And, of course, that piece is particularly dear to me."

She looked up briefly and met Alejandro's eyes. Memories passed between them, blurry images in his mind of that day he could hardly recall from sickness, but would never forget, either. Being cradled in Jesse's arms when the building exploded, the way it hurt his ears, bodies pressed on top of him for safety, the hospital, when they told him about Makayla.

"You were there, weren't you?"

"It's something I don't really speak of," Evann said. And for all her showmanship around The Artist, for all her expertise and knowledge, she never did. She and Alejandro had, a few times, spoken of that day. But never, ever like this. Never for others, and never for show or sale.

Alejandro's eyes looked up to the final piece now. It was huge, taking up most of the wall it stood against. The piece was scarred, destroyed entirely in many places. After the explosion, Evann and her father had hired art preservationists to pick through the wreckage of the building, drawing out what remained, slowly piecing it back together. He remembered the day that he and Evann had been called to see the finished product. It looked much as it did then, but that day, her larger hand had slipped over his smaller one, and they had both wept.

"How was anyone ever sure it was his last?" the woman asked. "With the chaos in the city then, couldn't more have gone up unnoticed?"

Evann smiled, and this time it was not her perfect, yet insincere version. Alejandro could tell the conversation was making her emotional, and he began quietly to move closer toward her.

"No, he never painted again, we're sure of that. I believe—everyone believes, who I've spoken to about the time—that when he saw what happened, when his reaction to the beauty of what had happened in that building became what it became . . . everyone believes that at that moment, he lost the hope that had propelled the art in the first place. It was certainly his last piece."

Alejandro stepped next to her then, and reached out to take one of her hands firmly in his. His other hand moved into the pocket of his coat, to touch the ancient phone he carried there.

"My brother, Alejandro," Evann said, by way of introduction. She kissed him lightly and with obvious happiness on his cheek.

"But the hope was there," Alejandro said, even though no one had asked him, even though he knew it wasn't exactly his place. "It existed. And that is why this art existed, and still exists."

"Are you a collector, too, dear?" the woman asked.

Alejandro smiled, not to be put off. "I'm a doctor."

The older woman smiled, her eyes crinkling behind her cat-eye glasses. "Perhaps a different kind of expert."

Evann bristled in her mannered way. "Alejandro gave up his private practice and travels to areas ravaged by the Neo Water Wars with Médecins Sans Frontières. He ... he has a special knowledge of the sort of situations that produced this art. He *is* an expert."

Her hand squeezed his. There was so much both of them couldn't say, would never be able to say in a situation like this. The small boy in raggedy clothes asserted himself in Alejandro's head once again as he smiled and excused himself.

He stepped out of the gallery and into the bathroom down the short hallway. He locked the door of the single-stall restroom, washed his hands, and looked in the mirror. No one could see the boy but him. No one could see the scars that still ran up and down his arms from self-injury, no one could see the scars from the blast. No one would ever see how much he had loved all of them, all of those people who were no more—Jaden, Makayla, Jesse, José, Sebastian. No one could see how that building had saved him and made him the person he was as much as any luxurious house inland or prep school.

Checking once more to make sure the door was locked, he removed the ancient phone from his pocket. He hardly kept it charged anymore, never used it for anything. It was virtually unusable now, anyway. But on nights like tonight, he plugged it into a power socket just to be sure it would be there if he needed it. Like he needed it now.

He turned on the phone and swiped the geometric shape that was the passkey. He opened the videos and pressed play. He saw a man waving to him in a dark room while he held the phone. It was his father, the man he had called Papi. He remembered him still, even though it had been many years. He was tall and smelled like pipe tobacco and gave wonderful hugs. Alejandro the adult watched as Ale the boy in raggedy clothes held the phone, and his papi rushed around the room, heading for the door. It was the night of Bernice.

Then, the video became blurry, and then it focused outside, out the window. On the video, he could see water coming up the street. He could see his papi struggling with a car door outside the window. Then he was gone. And he never came back. Alejandro the grown man, the respected man, turned the phone off as Ale the boy began to sob. The video was all he had left of his father, of his life before the storm. He put the phone back into his pocket and left the restroom.

He walked back into the sparkling gallery with the bright, joyful people out for their night of culture. He had never pictured himself here, and sometimes it felt odd. But here he was.

Alejandro stayed for another hour before leaving with the excuse that he had an early flight the next morning. It was back into the field, back out of his expensive suit and into his doctor's scrubs. Back to tending those sick with easily treatable diseases that they had little access to the cure for, back to the endless cycle of rehydrating those with no access to water who would show up back in the hospital in a week or less, on verge of death from dehydration again.

Outside the gallery, Alejandro hailed a cab and climbed in. He turned on his wristscreen and began to doodle pictures as the car ran through the night. Faces. Makayla, Jaden, Jesse, José, Sebastian. A word. Hope.

Alejandro the man had and had not become what Ale the boy in raggedy clothes had wanted. He was not a great artist like that man who had carried him up the ladder outside the building that Makayla had blown to pieces. He forgave her, he really did. And he forgave himself. And he understood why the artist had never painted again. Beauty was beauty, hope was hope, but there was then, and had been ever since, so very much more to be done.

The car rolled through the darkness. Alejandro looked up and out the window as they moved away from the part of town that held wealth and excess into the part where fires burned in garbage cans and people huddled on the streets. He thought back to a painting in the gallery, the brightly colored fruits and the word "hope" hanging beneath them. He wondered if the people he saw now, warming their hands over the fire, would ever see it.

Acknowledgments:

First, I'd like to thank Joselin Linder, Mary Adkins, Nicole Solomon, Joanne Solomon, Christine Clarke, Sam Ritchie, Kate Tellers, Jessica Manion, and everyone else who read through the many drafts of this novel, helping it become what it is. I was blessed, while living in New York, with the most dedicated, professional, and generous writers' group, and will always be in debt to them. Tuesday nights will never be the same without them.

Additional thanks go to Sanina Clark, one of the most wonderful, powerful, intelligent editors I have ever had the pleasure to work with; Allison Paller, who worked tirelessly on promotion of this book; Dan Simon for keeping Seven Stories Press rolling and investing himself in works of the radical imagination; Sarah, Rob, and Bella Baker, whose home I lived in while finishing the last draft of the novel; Allen Fisher, who hired me for a job on a mountaintop in the Catskills that allowed me to create my own writers' residency when attending a traditional one was completely out of the realm of possibility; Elka Park Club, where I spent my days off in their clubhouse with a Whiskey Sour and my computer; Adam Wishneusky, who bought me a new computer to write on when I spilled my Whiskey Sour on the old one.

Lastly, to everyone who has ever spotted me twenty bucks

for groceries when I needed it: you all are too many to mention, but your belief in me and my work has stopped me from giving up more times than you know. Nobody does anything alone, and often, when we decide to dedicate ourselves to art and sincerity, our friends are the ones who keep us afloat. Thank you thank you thank you, always and forever.